COLTER'S PATH

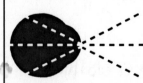

This Large Print Book carries the
Seal of Approval of N.A.V.H.

COLTER'S PATH

CAMERON JUDD

WHEELER PUBLISHING

A part of Gale, Cengage Learning

GALE
CENGAGE Learning·

Detroit • New York • San Francisco • New Haven, Conn • Waterville, Maine • London

GALE
CENGAGE Learning·

LIBRARY OF CONGRESS CATALOGING-IN-PUBLICATION DATA

Judd, Cameron.
  Colter's Path / By Cameron Judd. — Large Print edition.
    pages cm. — (Wheeler Publishing Large Print Western)
  ISBN 978-1-4104-6438-5 (softcover) — ISBN 1-4104-6438-5 (softcover)
  1. Large type books. I. Title.
PS3560.U337C65 2013
813'.54—dc23   2013030485

Published in 2013 by arrangement with NAL Signet, a member of Penguin Group (USA) LLC, a Penguin Random House Company

Printed in the United States of America
1 2 3 4 5   17 16 15 14 13

To Jedd Dotson and the rest of the
Class of '74, Putnam County Senior
High School, Cookeville, Tennessee

PROLOGUE

Knoxville, Tennessee
January 1849

Ottwell Plumb swabbed his broad tongue across a mouthful of gold teeth and said, "To get straight to the point, Mr. Colter, I am told you are the best. I am told that any band of travelers you pilot is as safe and assured of safe arrival as any such group in these times can be. And I am told you have made a successful journey to Oregon already, and one to California."

Jedd Colter listened, sipping on a mug of hot black coffee. He was a lean, weathered man of twenty-eight who stood an impressive six feet tall and was well featured, generally considered a fine figure of a man despite a tendency to go too long unshorn and unshaven. "I would say I have made *two* journeys to California, sir. It depends upon how you count it. The route I've followed has been the California-Oregon Trail.

7

Both my California journeys happened before the gold was found at Sutter's, just folks moving across to California to settle. My first journey was the long trot, the whole distance. The second band I piloted only the final half of the journey, replacing the original pilot who had died along the way. I got them pilgrims safely to their destination in his place."

"Well, here's to his memory, and your success in his stead," said Plumb, lifting his coffee in salute. Colter followed suit out of politeness, and marveled as a new smile provided another flash of Plumb's mouthful of gold. Plumb spoke again. "The fact that we share common North Carolinian roots, you and I and my partners the Sadler brothers, only enhances the logic of our collaboration on this grand venture. We have trodden the same hills and valleys, drunk of the same wellsprings, gloried in the same expansive Carolina skies. . . . It seems fitting that we should undertake together to be part of this nation's grandest new adventure!"

"Permit me to ask you something, sir," Colter said to the man he'd met only two hours earlier. "Is that California gold you've had them gilded choppers made from?"

Plumb smiled widely, displaying the

golden teeth to full measure. Then he squelched the smile and leaned a little closer to Colter. "Between you and me, Mr. Colter —"

"Call me Jedd."

"And call me Ottwell. Between you and me, Jedd, the gold in my mouth is not from California, though I allow people to believe it is. In my line of business, it pays to display some degree of, shall we say, flamboyance? Extravagance. Whatever draws the public eye. My combination of silver tongue and golden teeth brings attention to my plan. Showmanship, you see. Which is one more reason I have sought you out and hope to involve you in our work. Showmanship."

Jedd drew in a long breath. "I'm not sure how I fit into a scheme such as that one, sir. I'm obliged to say two things to you. First, I am one of the poorest examples of 'showmanship' you could have picked, if that's what you're after. I'm a man of the hills and mountains and plains. A rover and rambler. I shun human attention like a pox, and oftentimes, even human company. Second, I would advise you to find another way to advertise your venture, other than by way of your teeth. With the hunger for gold as high as it is in this nation just now, there are some who might find it more handy to

9

'mine' their gold directly out of your pie-hole than to pan it out of a stream."

"I can take care of myself sufficiently to avoid trouble," Plumb said, patting his chest in a way to let Jedd know there was a pistol hidden beneath his coat.

"I hope you can," Jedd said. He refocused the discussion. "What you're asking of me, Ottwell, is to work with your California Enterprising Company of . . . of . . ."

"The California Enterprise Company of East Tennessee," Plumb prompted.

"Right, right. You want me to work with your California Enterprise Company of East Tennessee as a scout, pilot, and trail adviser."

"Precisely so. Essentially the same work you have already done for others, but in this case we seek to specially promote your name and reputation as part of our company's attraction to the public.

"I believe your excellent reputation, and that of your history-making family, is something this venture can trade upon to increase the attractiveness of our effort to the general public. The more emigrants we can add to our band, you see, the better our profits . . . and your share of them. But, for you, it gets even better than that." Plumb took on a sly, between-you-and-me expression. "What you

10

haven't been told yet is that I . . . uh, *we* intend to pay you in a manner that will at least double your usual gain in such ventures, and do so in an ongoing way."

"How so?"

"In addition to the onetime fee that is your standard, and the additional percentage paid based upon the size of the group, we propose to pay you ten percent of profits made from the mining of gold by my partners in this venture, Wilberforce and Witherspoon Sadler. It is they who will be involved in the actual work in the diggings. For every hundred dollars in gold they obtain, ten dollars of it will go to you. This arrangement will stand as long as the Sadlers involve themselves in the mining of gold, either directly by their own hand or by those whom they hire."

"And I don't have to work the diggings myself for this income?"

"You needn't lift a pan unless you so desire."

"And if I did choose to pan for gold on my own? And found color? Would I then be obliged to share the same percentage back with you and the Sadlers?"

Plumb grinned and chuckled. "You are a man with the instincts of commerce, sir. It always pays to look around the next corner of every bargain, to make sure no hidden wolves are there, waiting to bite."

"Well? What is the answer?"

Plumb fidgeted and frowned. "I am in a situation in which it is difficult to speak for . . . I'm not sure I should . . ." He pursed his lips and crunched his eyebrows downward. "No. No. I'll *not* hesitate to speak on their account. Your involvement is crucial to our success. The answer is no, without equivocation. You would not be obliged to share any percentage of what gold you might discover on any *independent* claim of your own."

Jedd did not miss the extra emphasis Plumb placed on the key word. "Independent of you and the Sadlers, you mean?"

"Precisely. Should you labor on a claim held by the California Enterprise partnership, naturally the profits would be divided among all relevant parties. It seems only fair, wouldn't you say?"

"It does. Are you certain the Sadlers will go along with the provision regarding my rights to full possession of gold I independently obtain on claims other than theirs?" It was largely a hypothetical conversation; Jedd possessed little ambition for prospecting. If he struck color it would likely be by mere happy accident.

Plumb was growing more firm in his declarations the more he talked. "Do not worry about the Sadlers. *I* am the founder of this venture, and they will do what I say. Particularly if they know the agreements you and I make are crucial to our ability to secure you as our pilot."

Jedd had his doubts. The reputation of the Sadlers in this town, particularly the elder Sadler, was that of men who did not well abide being told what to do and perceived themselves as self-sufficient, not prone to require the advice or aid of others.

"I'm astonished, sir. What is there about me that would be of such value to you? There are a lot of California pilots available who would serve you well. I'm not trying to undermine my own opportunity by speaking to you this way, but since I insist that those I work for be fully open and honest with me, I consider that I owe equal frankness in return. And I'm frankly surprised by your focus on me."

Plumb squeezed his eyes and lips closed so that his face looked oddly pinched, and nodded profoundly. "An excellent notion and habit, sir, this speaking freely and honestly. Excellent indeed."

"Good. Now please answer the question."

Plumb squirmed as if struck with a hid-

13

den itch. "Yes, sir, yes." He paused and cleared his throat. "You are correct that there are other pilots to be had. But I have already touched upon the primary reason I have come to you: I invest my trust in good reputation. And in associating myself with those who possess it. Those who have earned a good name deserve to benefit from it. And you have earned such. Even before you, the Colter family was associated with the expanding American frontier for generations. Merely to hear it calls forth images of wild and unsettled mountains in the early days of the frontier, and of courage and leadership. Therefore I find it desirable to associate such a noted name with my new venture. Are you following me?"

"I follow. That's not to say I've made a decision about what you offer." In fact, Colter had decided, the moment he learned of the proposed recompense. He was in no position to turn away from high-paying work. After all, his ever-present financial strictures had already cost him the chance to marry the only woman he had loved — a woman of this very town, in fact. She had been ready to accept him, he believed. What she could not abide was his lack of resources.

He was a poor man, no question of it.

Always in need of money and work. Still, it went against his grain to appear overeager, so he did not jump too swiftly to voice agreement to Plumb's offer.

"I think you would find yourself in a happy position as we make our journey," said Plumb. "The commander of the venture, as we have titled him, is General Gordon Lloyd, no longer officially in a military role but still stalwart. The true, day-to-day leaders will be the Sadlers, however, General Lloyd being largely a symbolic figure. You would serve as a practical adviser to the Sadlers, keeping things on the path, as it were."

"What would be your own role as we proceed?"

"Oh, I will not make the journey myself, not immediately. I am a dreamer, a planner, a visionary . . . not an overland adventurer. And I possess little interest in working directly as a prospector. It is my belief that, over time, more will profit indirectly from the rush for gold than those who profit directly. The patient man shall prevail over all others. Travel, shelter, food, medical, legal, and spiritual counsel . . . all these things will be in demand by those who reach the far West. Those who provide those services will stand to benefit wonderfully."

"I'm prone to agree with you, sir," Colter said. "I myself find the possession of gold to be a pleasing prospect, yet I have little inclination to search the earth for it or spend my days squatted by a stream with a pan in my hand."

"Are you agreeing to my proposal?"

Jedd paused a few moments. "I admit to some hesitation born of the fact that you yourself are not making the journey. It causes me to question your own faith in the venture."

Plumb performed that strange screwing up of his countenance again, eyes narrowed to slits and puffed outward above and below his very black lashes. "I believe *deeply* in this venture. I intend for there to be many journeys of this sort across this growing land we have been given to live upon. But I know my personal limits and my place, Jedd. You are a man of trail and mountain and plains. I am a man of town and city. The forest and range in which I hunt is that of business and commerce. I shall travel with you in spirit and thought and even prayer . . . but I would be nothing but a burden should I try to make the journey myself."

Jedd nodded.

"Will you accept my offer, then? Shake

16

my hand in seal of the bargain?"

Jedd thought a few moments more, battling an innate hesitation to obligate himself to a venture he could not fully control, then thrust out his hand and said, "Looks like I'm going back to California."

Plumb's face beamed so brightly Jedd thought the man was about to burst into tears of joy.

That evening, as Ottwell Plumb made his way alone back to his hotel, he was pulled into an alleyway by three strangers, beaten unconscious, and robbed of his pistol, an antique watch, and his golden teeth. Most of the teeth were false and so were simply yanked out of his mouth by hand, but some were his natural teeth, gold-plated, and those were removed forcibly by fast use of some sort of large pincers or pliers.

Bleeding and pale, he regained consciousness on his own and found his feet after several efforts, then staggered on until he collapsed on a curb a quarter mile away. He was found and carried by helpful strangers to the office of a doctor who operated a private infirmary near the Holston River.

"I seen that fellow two days ago," one of the three helpful strangers said to his fellows after they abandoned him to the physician. "Had gold teeth in his mouth. Ain't no wonder such a thing happened to him, flashing gold teeth all around town."

"Just a fool," said another. "Just an unthinking fool."

"Will he live?" the third asked.

"I think so," said the first. "I don't think he was beat on all that bad. And like Jack just said, he's a fool. And fools generally survive most anything."

■ ■ ■ ■

PART ONE:
1849

■ ■ ■ ■

CHAPTER ONE

Jedd Colter strode up a particular Knoxville avenue and cursed himself inwardly for being there. A deep sense of dissatisfaction and restlessness, even outright unhappiness, pervaded his thoughts and showed in his demeanor. He walked alone, glowering into the gloom of the cooling evening.

Earlier he'd scolded himself for his feelings, knowing that by all logic he should be quite happy. Thanks to the peculiar Ottwell Plumb, he had before him a promising prospect that would occupy him for months . . . a good-paying piece of guide work that included at its conclusion a financial arrangement that probably would provide an ongoing income.

But why Plumb had presented such an extravagant offer, Jedd had no good idea. The reasons earlier given did not strike him as persuasive or complete. He was beginning to wonder if Plumb was legitimate.

Since the discovery of gold at Sutter's in California, many confidence men and scoundrels were seeking ways to profit, rightly or otherwise, from a growing national lust for California gold.

Jedd's thoughts, however, were not entirely on matters related to gold, piloting work, and Ottwell Plumb. For Jedd, the town of Knoxville would forever be primarily associated with one matter, one person, that being a young woman named Emma McSwain.

"Bah!" Jedd grunted under his breath. The better part of wisdom told him to turn into the first available alleyway and leave this avenue and the associations it held . . . but thoughts of Emma had brought him to this street and thoughts of Emma drove him on. He passed one alley, one coach driveway, one empty lot, then another and another, and did not divert his course.

And there it was . . . her house. The house wherein he had courted her, declared his love for her, caressed her, kissed her, succumbed to her charms . . . and where he had asked and was reluctantly given by her father the right to seek her hand in marriage. In that same house he had proposed to her that she become his bride, and she had agreed without any evident hesitation.

But then, after she had pondered his humbleness of resources, she had revoked her pledge and left him standing alone and hopeless. Standing almost upon the spot he stood now, in fact. He had looked up at her excellent dwelling that sad evening, a house quite fine for its time and place, heard the latching and locking of its doors, and known that what he had dreamed of was not to be. He was spurned, shut out, and locked out. And this despite the fact that Emma's father, a respected college president, supporter of community cultural growth, and investor in assorted businesses, had given his approval to their union. Zebulon McSwain had said that he favored Jedd for his daughter because of his evident good character and the notable heritage of his family, and the fact that McSwain believed Jedd had a good future ahead of him. He was poor now, but better times would come.

Emma, though, had ultimately been swayed away from matrimony because of Jedd's inability to provide for her the kind of life she sought not just in the future but immediately.

She had ended their engagement with tears of sorrow on her face. But not sorrow enough to send her back to his arms. His had been the fate of abandonment and a door that seemed forever closed to him.

"So why am I here now?" he asked himself on this cool 1849 evening. "Am I trying to inflict torture on myself?"

"That's what I was going to ask you," said a voice that, though instantly recognizable to Jedd, startled him anyway. He pivoted and faced Treemont Dalton, a man he had known since childhood and who had been his friend and traveling partner on many a journey for many years, including the same cross-country journeys that had caused Ottwell Plumb to seek out Jedd's services. Treemont had come with Jedd to Knoxville. Seeing Treemont now, Jedd was reminded that the pair of them had agreed to meet earlier at a particular tavern and share a tankard or two. Jedd, overwhelmed by the job he'd accepted with Plumb and distracted by his sentimental, sorrowful remembrances of Emma, had simply forgotten.

"Tree, if you'd startled me any worse, I might have knifed the entrails out of you."

"Jedd, I'd have had you twisted into a sailor's hitch and gutted like a slaughtered calf before you got your blade free of its sheath, and you know it."

"You got a big imagination, Tree. How'd you come to find me here?"

Tree sighed deeply and shook his head.

24

"Jedd, when you didn't show up at the tavern, I thunk to myself, where else would Jedd Colter be but here? The way I got it figured, you came all the way back to Tennessee in the hope you'd find Emma and discover her husband died in a fearsome whisker-shaving accident or something, and that she's been waiting for you to come rescue her from a life of living with Daddy as an old maid widow forever after."

Jedd had to chuckle. Tree was a man who could say things to him that would not be tolerated from any other. "Tree, it wasn't because of Emma that I came here. I'd gotten that letter, you'll recall. The one that was waiting for me in Independence, then a copy of the same in St. Joseph, and a third one in St. Louis?"

"From that fellow Plumb, or whatever his name is?"

"That's right. . . . Ottwell Plumb. Told me he'd be in Knoxville for a spell, meeting with his business partners, and that I should try to look him up if I was going to be back in these parts."

"Yeah, I'd forgot about them letters."

"Well, I didn't forget, and I found him. And I've got us a job. Got myself one, anyway, and I'll make sure you're brought in, too, even if I have to hire you out of my own pocket. I don't aim to do California pilot work without you coming with me."

"And you don't make enough money at it to hire me out of your own pocket, either. Is that what he wants? You to pilot a group to California for him?"

"It is. But this time with a prospect for more than the usual pay."

"Tell me about it."

Jedd and Treemont walked and talked, leaving behind the street upon which Emma had lived and not noticing the movement of an upper-floor curtain as they departed, as if someone had been watching. Jedd related to Treemont the proposition Plumb had presented. Tree was suitably impressed. Inevitably Jedd began to talk of Plumb's oddities, especially the gilded teeth. Upon hearing of the latter, Tree halted abruptly and looked oddly at Jedd Colter.

"Golden teeth, you say?"

"Yep. Quite a sight to see."

Treemont lifted a finger as if to tell Jedd to pause, and dug into his pocket. He pulled his hand out closed into a fist and held it out toward Jedd.

"Take it," he said, quite solemn.

"Take what?"

"Just give me your palm."

Tree dropped something small from his

fist into Jedd's hand. Jedd looked at it as best he could in the thickening evening gloom. "What is this?"

Tree pulled him by the sleeve to the vicinity of a lighted window facing the street. Jedd held up what Treemont had given him and saw it was a tooth. The root was its natural color, and crusted in dry blood, but what would have been the visible portion of the tooth was coated in gold.

"Where'd you get this?" Jedd asked his friend.

"Found it in an alleyway."

Jedd sighed. "I warned him this would happen," he said. "It ain't a wise move to make your own mouth a gold mine for any scoundrel who is willing to shoot you or knock you in the skull. I got to wonder if Plumb is dead."

Tree shook his head. "Not 'cording to a fellow who seen the whole thing and told me about it. This fellow said that Plumb was still alive when they hauled him off to a doctor somewhere. Bleeding and toothless, but alive."

"Maybe I've still got an employer and a piloting job, then."

"Jedd, I won't lie. I don't believe you coming back to Knoxville had to do only with this Plumb fellow and his letter. I happen to know you got a letter from somebody else, too."

"You reading my letters on the sneak, Tree?"

"Only when you go to sleep with one of them in your hand and the wind blows it over to the camping fire. I rescued that particular letter from getting burned up, and yes, I did see it. Enough to know who wrote it."

"Did you read it?"

"Not after I seen it was from her. I figured it was none of my business. But I won't deny I was tempted. You getting a letter from a married woman you used to have your heart set on — I figure it would have made for interesting reading. But I didn't read it."

"Now you expect me to tell you what she said to me," Jedd said.

"I wouldn't fuss about it. But it ain't my business, and I ain't asking."

"I don't mind saying. Kind of wanted to talk about it with somebody, anyway."

"I'm your somebody."

"You usually are." Jedd paused and exhaled slowly. "I think she'd have me back, Tree. From what she wrote, I think she would take me back if that husband of hers wasn't in the way."

"She's still married, Jedd. Ain't she? Still Mrs. Emma Candlewick? Or Wickhamton? Or whatever it is?"

"Wickham. Her cur of a husband is named Stanley Wickham. Far as I know she's still his wife. I know she was when she wrote the letter."

"She turned you away 'cause you had no money, if I rightly recollect. You still got no money. Why would she take you now if she wouldn't then? 'Specially since she's already got a husband and would have to go through the shame of a divorce to do it?" Treemont paused and looked more serious all at once. "You wouldn't break up a family, would you, Jedd?"

"Her husband hasn't been good to her, Tree. She told me about it in her letter. He's turned his back on her, treated her like rubbish. She's certain he ain't been faithful."

"Well, he's a fool, then. Any man who would pull away from an angel of a woman like Emma ain't got the sense of a garden slug."

CHAPTER TWO

"I was born a freeman, sir," said the black man who was fitting a boot to Jedd's right foot. Jedd was seated on a three-legged stool in a very humble little shop at the end of a dirt street in a disheveled part of town. "Born in the state of North Carolina, over near the coast, but I been in Knoxville for half my life now. I learned shoemaking from my uncle, who used to have a place just yonder across the street. He'd been a slave, but got hisself freed after he saved his master's family from a house fire." He looked over his shoulder and pointed at what looked to Jedd like an ancient barn. "Warn't much of a place, no question, but he worked hard at his trade and there warn't a finer shoe made than what was made by Otis Slott."

"That was your uncle's name? Otis?"

"Yes, sir. And me, I'm Ollie. Ollie Slott. My pap was Archie. Otis's brother."

Jedd wriggled his toes in the boot Ollie had just slipped onto his right foot, nodded, and said, "Ollie, I believe Otis apprenticed you well. That feels just right."

"Thank you, sir, but don't you go judging them till you've walked about in them a little. You can't rightly judge a fit until you've took some steps." With that Ollie slipped the remaining boot onto Jedd's left foot, feeling about Jedd's ankle with expert evaluative fingers as he did so.

Jedd stood and walked out into the empty street and back again. He wiggled his right foot again and the sound of a popping joint was heard.

"I heard the arch bone of your foot pop, sir," Ollie said. "Mine does that just the same way." He stuck out his foot, twisted it side to side, and popped it loudly. "I got to do that now and then, Mr. Colter, or at night that leg and foot will cramp up on me. You never saw a feller come out of his blankets as fast as me when I get hit with one of them cramps."

Jedd said, "A man's feet can distress him bad. That's one reason I need a fine-fitting boot like this one."

"Do you mind, sir, if I . . ." Ollie waved Jedd back toward the stool.

Jedd sat and with expert fingers Ollie

31

pressed about on the leather and evaluated the fit of the boots he had made. "What's the verdict, Judge Ollie?" Jedd asked.

"Feels like a good fit to this judge," Ollie said. "But it's the jury of twelve who have to render the final verdict in the case."

" 'Jury of twelve'?"

"Ten toes and two feet. Yours."

Jedd rose with a grin and took another little stroll into the street and back, then up and down the rough boardwalk a few paces. "Verdict's in," he said. "Fine fit. Finest-fitting piece of boot-wear I've ever had on these twin dogs of mine." He strode over and thrust his hand out to Ollie, who seemed taken aback by the gesture. Many of Ollie's white customers seemed to try hard to avoid even brushing against him. He stared at Jedd's extended fingers a moment before he glanced about quickly and accepted the handshake. Ollie noticed that Jedd, unlike many white men he dealt with, also did not wipe his palm against his clothing after touching Ollie's hand.

"Them boots should serve you well, sir, when you make your journey back to California," Ollie said.

"How do you know about that?" Jedd asked.

"Well, it only figures you'd go back, if

what I'm hearing is true."

"What are you hearing?"

"Oh, you know how folks will talk, sir, when someone has come into wealth."

Jedd pondered that a moment and could only conclude that word was beginning to spread that he had been hired to pilot a new band of travelers to California, and would be well compensated for it. Perhaps the story was being exaggerated; he didn't consider the deal he had made with Plumb to rise to the level of actual wealth, though perhaps it might seem so to an impoverished craftsman such as Ollie Slott.

Jedd reached into his pocket and felt the golden tooth there — Tree had left it with him — and wondered if his agreement with Plumb even existed anymore. Having his teeth pulled right out of his head could have soured Plumb on the whole matter of sponsoring a venture to the gold fields. Prior to visiting Ollie this day to pick up the new boots for which he had been fitted a few days before, Jedd had tried to discover the details of the attack and of Plumb's current condition, but so far had had no luck in gaining new information.

Jedd showed Ollie the gilded tooth. "Know anything about this?" he asked.

Ollie gaped at the tooth after he realized

just what he was seeing. In that momentary silence, Jedd noticed a sound coming from somewhere across the street . . . a muffled thumping noise, repetitive and varying in speed and intensity.

"Mr. Colter, sir, I seen a man with just such gold teeth as that here on the street a day or two back. Kind of a dandy dresser, with a strut in his walk. Don't believe I know his name. . . ."

"Plumb. Ottwell Plumb. He's the man who's hired me to become a pilot for a journey to California he's helping sponsor and get organized."

"I ain't heard about that, sir."

Jedd wondered, then, to what Ollie had been referring when he made the reference about wealth.

More muffled thudding came from across the street. It seemed to be coming from the old building where Ollie's uncle had once made footwear.

Jedd flipped the tooth to Ollie. "Any idea how Plumb came to lose that tooth, Ollie?"

Ollie caught the tooth reflexively. He looked at it intently. "Looks to me like it was pulled with pliers or tongs or some such."

"I think so. And I figure that while that was happening, them doing it were interrupted and took off running and dropped this one."

Ollie nodded in a distracted way. "Yes, sir. I think it happened in an alleyway somewhere up near the custom house."

"So you know about it?"

"I . . . I heard some talk."

"What did you hear?"

"I heard that some men seen this fellow flashing his gold Waterloos and decided they wanted them. So they followed him until they could get him into an alley. Knocked him out and went to gold mining."

"What kind of men?"

"White men, I was told."

"Any notion where Plumb is now?"

"No, sir. He was took to a doctor, I know, but I don't know if he stayed there or moved on. You said he'd hired you to work for him?"

"To pilot a group to California."

Ollie seemed puzzled. "I'd have figured a man in your situation wouldn't be needful of hiring out for such a task as that, sir. Seems like you'd not want the bother of it, considering the way things stand with you now."

"What do you mean, Ollie? The way things stand for me now is the way they stand for most everybody: a man's got to work for his living."

"Not if he's come into money, he don't. A man with enough money don't have to work at all unless he wants to."

"Just what have you been hearing about me? I get the feeling you think that I —"

There was a sudden crashing, splintering noise from across the street, followed by two loud thumps, as if heavy objects had been thrown to the ground from some height. Mixed with the thuds was the much fainter sound of masculine grunting. Ollie sprang up, worry in his expression, and without another word darted across to the barnlike building from which the sound had come. He grabbed at the door and yanked, but it was barred on the inside. Jedd could hear the rattle of the locking bar all the way across the street. But he didn't stay across the street long: a half moment later he followed Ollie across the avenue. "Stand back. . . . I'll see how these stout new boots you made me do for kicking in doors."

His offer went unneeded. Ollie had already pulled back, put his shoulder forward, and lunged full body into the door before Jedd even finished speaking. The door jolted, the bar on the inside jumped out of its holders, and all at once the door was barred no more. Ollie was inside in an instant. Jedd followed, and once in, paused for a few moments to take in and make sense of what he saw.

CHAPTER THREE

Jedd found Ollie kneeling beside another, bigger man with the same richly dark skin, gently waving hair, and full jawline. The man wore heavy workman's trousers, but no shirt or shoes. He lay on the dirty floor beside what looked like a giant cylindrical leather sack, well stuffed, and around him were great splinters and shards of wood, and most of a heavy, broken beam.

Jedd looked up and saw that the man and the leather cylinder had fallen down to ground level because of the breakage of a beam and the collapse of part of the floor of a loft above them. Though he had little time and a scant level of light in which to figure out what had happened, it appeared to Jedd that the leather cylinder had by its weight fractured a beam from which it had been hanging, then fallen to and through the loft floor and dragged the man down after it through the gaping hole.

Jedd took another look at the shirtless man and figured it out.

The fellow wore rounded, puffed gloves of leather on his hands, seemingly some sort of protective wear, resembling overstuffed mittens. Clearly he had been pounding at the leather sack when it had all given way and he had made his journey through the loft floor to the ground level below.

A fighter. He had to be a fighter who had been practicing and building his skills by punching at the hanging leather bag.

Jedd knelt beside the man and Ollie. Ollie said, "This is my brother, Rollins. Goes by Rollie. Rollie, this here is Jedd Colter. The one I been making the boots for. He's wearing them now. . . . See?"

Rollie rubbed one of the puffed gloves against his temple and blinked severely several times. "Can't see much anything, Ollie. I hit my head coming down and everything got blurred."

Ollie told Jedd what Jedd had already surmised. "Rollie fights for money; folks bet on him. Mostly fights slaves of white folks who train them for such sport, but Rollie is like me, a freeborn black man."

Rollie was squinting now, getting his eyes slowly back into focus after his disconcerting fall. "I've seen you before, Mr. Colter,"

Rollie said. "Back before you went off to Californy and struck it rich."

Jedd laughed at what seemed a joke. Rollie and Ollie appeared confused by the laughter, their heads cocking and brows quirking.

Jedd was puzzled. "Do you believe I really struck it rich in California? Where did that notion come from?"

Ollie gave a small shrug and shared an uncomfortable-looking glance with his brother. "It's general knowledge in Knoxville, sir. Well . . . general belief, anyway. Story is that you made a big strike, got a big pouch full of gold, then defended it 'gainst a whole gang of highwaymen and left three of them dead as iron and the other five running like rabbits with a pack of hounds on their tails."

"Well, it's wrong belief," Jedd said. "I've not so much as hefted a pan in California and sure ain't faced down a gang of highwaymen."

Looks of astonishment. "But everybody talks about how rich Jedd Colter got in Californy . . . everybody!"

"Honest truth, Ollie. I've guided settlers to California. But I've not prospected a lick."

"Well, the notion that you did prospect is

40

a strong one. I've heard men in this town talking up that they aim to go to the gold fields and become 'the next Jedd Colter.' I don't know who started the story, but it's spread all over."

"I have no idea how such a tale got started. And if I had such a rich claim, why would I leave it and come all the way back here?"

Neither of them replied.

"Lawd!" exclaimed Rollie suddenly, sitting up and scooting himself around a bit on his rump, until he seemingly found an acceptably comfortable position. "Falling through a loft floor with a heavy fighter bag ain't something I would put forth as a good notion for nobody."

"Hurting, huh?" Jedd asked.

"I've felt better."

"You're lucky you didn't break your neck," Jedd said. "And what's a fighter bag?"

Rollie thumped lightly at the big leather cylinder-shaped sack lying on the floor beside him. "Just my name for this thing Ollie made up for me to do my fight practice with. I always just call it a fighter bag. 'Cause it feels a lot like striking another fighter when you hit it. Just a lot harder than flesh is. That's why I wear them puffed gloves."

"I made the gloves, too," Ollie said with

41

unabashed pride. "I figure that, with them, Rollie could hit the bag harder without putting a risk to his fingers. A fighter can't abide broke fingers. Can't fight bare-fisted with broke or stove-up fingers. Rollie fights bare-fisted, but he practices with them gloves on."

Rollie held up his right hand and turned it, displaying the glove. "Works good, this glove does." He paused and grinned. "Me, I got all the muscle and meanness in the Slott family. Ollie got the brains, and the skill at doing fine and delicate work with his hands. Me, I use my hands for busting flesh and bone whilst keeping others from doing the same back to me. Not much that's 'fine and delicate' about that."

"Which one of you had the notion of hanging your 'fighter bag' up in the loft rather than down here below it?"

"That was me," Ollie admitted.

Jedd grinned and winked at Rollie. "That calls into question what you said about Ollie having the family brains. Old building like this, it's no surprise that beam gave way. Wood weakens with age, and that's a heavy bag."

"I know, I know," Ollie said, rising to his feet and pacing about edgily in a tight circle. "I just figured Rollie needed to be able to do his practicing without folks watching him through the windows. He don't like being watched."

"That's true," Rollie said. "I don't mind folks watching me fight. Kind of like it, in fact. I don't like being watched whilst I'm doing my muscle work, though."

Ollie said, "I reckon I should have looked closer at that beam we hung it from, Rollie."

"What's did is did. It fell, I fell, and that's the end of it. Nobody hurt and the bag didn't bust."

"It must have took a lot of leather to make that bag, Ollie," Jedd observed.

"Lawd, yes. . . . No telling how many boots and shoes I could have made from that leather. But a man helps out his brother, you know."

"Of course."

"We look out for each other. And for our mammy. She's still living here in town. Pap, God rest him, he's been gone and buried seven year now."

"I'm sorry. About your pap, I mean. It's good you take care of your mother."

"I'd go to Californy if not for Mammy," said Rollie. "I figure I might be one of the lucky ones and hit pay dirt, and if not, I could always fight there just like I do here.

43

There'll be entertainment wanted by them miners, and I've took note that nothing entertains white folk like watching one black fellow pound another."

Jedd didn't know what to say to that, so he said nothing.

"I've thought about going to the gold fields my own self," Ollie threw in. "But same as Rollie, I'd not want to leave Mammy . . . and besides, I figure there's going to be a lot of changing going on in Californy, and it might not pay any but a white man to go there till it all settles out as to how Negro folk are going to fit into the picture, you know."

Jedd couldn't argue. The white American majority had a propensity for keeping the best of everything for themselves. He knew little of politics and legislative wranglings, but the moment he had learned that gold was found in California, Jedd had felt certain that the course of events would wind its way around to the prospect of California statehood, and in the America of the 1840s, any discussion of statehood had to include the questions surrounding slavery.

"I understand your thinking," Jedd said. "There's not a very happy history in this nation for a man of color to look back upon if he's seeking evidence to give him hope of good things for his future."

"There are them who say all that truck will come round to war one of these days," said Ollie.

"I've heard the same," Jedd replied.

"I hope it don't go that far," said Rollie. "I wish they'd just make all the slaves free-men and move on from there."

"Nothing's likely to happen that easy, Rollie," said Jedd.

Ollie changed the subject. "When will you commence your new journey?" he asked Jedd.

"Plumb ain't said. Got to get off soon enough to miss the early snows, that much I can tell you. They time it too late for that, and they'll lose Jedd Colter as pilot."

"Ollie, I need you to help me hang my bag back up," Rollie said. "Not nowhere in a loft this time, either. I don't aim.to fall through no more floors."

"Hang it down here, and you'll have folk watching you through the window," Ollie replied.

"I'll hang a cloth over the windows. Should have done that before."

Jedd lent a hand, and soon the tall leather bag was hanging on the ground-floor level. Rollie put his gloves back on and began to punch at it, and Jedd was impressed with the amount of power the man's thick arms could generate.

"I hear . . . ," Rollie said between punches, ". . . that you fight . . . too, Mr. Jedd."

Jedd nodded. "Got into it by accident. . . . Had some trouble with a big fellow in a tavern in Carolina, and it came to blows. I dropped him and a fight-for-pay man happened to see it. Had a talk with me and made me a good offer if I'd fight for him. I was needing work at the time and took the bargain." Jedd held up his right hand and displayed a slightly crooked ring finger. "There's the price I've paid for it. Broke that finger on a man's jaw. I swear his jawbone was hard as granite. Never did heal back up like it should, and that finger's been crooked ever since. Hurts before it rains, too."

"Did that put you off fighting?"

"Only for a little while. Went back to it after I healed up again. I needed the money. I still fight every now and then. I got no good place to train myself like you have here, though."

Rollie noticed Jedd's eyes were on the gloves he wore. He held one of them up. "Want to give these a try?" he asked.

"I doubt they'd fit me," Jedd said. "Being made for your hands and all."

"If you want, you can try."

They fit. In moments Jedd was pounding away at the newly rehung bag with all his vigor. His blows didn't thump as loudly against the leather as Rollie's did, but came faster, like lightning. Rollie was awed by Jedd's speed and said so.

A mounting pain in the bent finger he'd already displayed cut short Jedd's work with Rollie's fighter bag and padded gloves. He thanked Rollie for the use of his equipment and passed the gloves back to the bigger man. Minutes later, as Jedd took his leave and walked away in his fine new footwear, he could hear the hard smack of Rollie's gloves against the leather bag even after he'd left the building and closed the door behind him.

CHAPTER FOUR

Later, walking to his hotel, Jedd passed an alleyway between two buildings fronted by a tall boardwalk that passed the alley opening. Jedd paused on the boardwalk to look into the window of a dry goods store that had not existed when last he was in Knoxville, and wondered who owned the place. As he peered through the dusty and rippled glass, he heard a muffled cough . . . from below his feet, oddly enough. Surprised, he looked down between his boots through a gap between the slats of the boardwalk and saw movement. Then another cough and a sneeze, and from beneath the boardwalk and into the nearby alley emerged a very grimy, heavily bearded man with tangled hair that hung like sodden Spanish moss on both sides of his head. It was like watching an ancient ogre clambering out of a forest cave. The man had no hat, but his hair was so thick and matted he appeared to be wearing a helmet.

"Hello, Robert," Jedd said to the man, who reeked of flesh too infrequently washed and liquor too frequently imbibed. "Been a lot of years since I seen you."

The man, who had been looking blankly at one of the alley walls, turned clumsily toward Jedd, squinted, and mumbled, then brightened a little in comprehension. "Jedd Colter? Is that you?"

"It's me, Robert. How are you?"

"Drunk. Like always. Drunk and poor." Robert Bertram's voice was so slurred Jedd could barely make out what he said.

"Well, I'm sorry for it," Jedd said. "I was hoping things might have taken a better turn for you from the old days."

"Ain't no better turns for Bob Bertram. Never have been." He paused, thick brows moving along with the laborious efforts of a besotted mind. "But I heard that ain't been the case for you, Jedd Colter."

"What did you hear? That I made myself rich in California?"

Bertram beamed, showing teeth like gray rocks overgrown with lichen. "Yes, sir, just that. Just that very thing! Proud of you, sir! Proud you done so good!"

Jedd shook his head. "Thank you for that, but what you heard is wrong. I've not even looked for gold in California, much less found it."

Bertram didn't lose his grin, just put on a slier version of it. "Don't you josh me, Jedd Colter! It's just me, old Bob! You got secrets, you can trust me to keep 'em. But you got to know that *that* secret is one that's done got out."

"Believe what you want, Bob. But the fact is I've been a poor man all my days, and nothing about that has changed. I wish it had. But it hasn't."

Bertram's look became regretful. "Jedd, I hope that ain't true. 'Cause I need help. I'm nigh starved to death, and I was hoping you might be able to lend me a little so I could get some food. I lost my work, y'see? Old man Pullam had me cleaning out his barn lot for him, shoveling the stables clean and such, but he died and his son wouldn't keep me on. I'm in a bad way, Jedd. Money gone, no way to make more. I don't want to turn thief, but I may have to." He suddenly coughed again, and sneezed profoundly and wetly. "And I'm coming down sick, too. I'm a sad and poor man, Jedd. I need help mighty bad. Mighty bad."

"You're drunk, Bob. You had money for drinking."

Bertram's already-red eyes reddened

further and grew moist. His slurred voice quavered with rising emotion. "I know, Jedd. I know. But that was the last of my money, and I needed that bottle. God, how I needed it! It's my medicine in times like these. . . . Without it I couldn't get through. I'd put a gun to my head, swear I would. Bang and dead. Bang." Then he sneezed again.

From beneath the boardwalk a second man emerged into the alley, surprising Jedd. The newcomer was a lean, black-haired fellow, as coarsely dressed as Bertram, but younger. His hat, relatively new, made him appear neater and cleaner than Bertram, though his face was just as grimy and his hair nearly as matted, but closer cropped. Jedd knew this man, too: Ben Scarlett, another Knoxville drunkard and street vagrant, but one who seemed to Jedd to possess more depth than most of his ilk.

Ben Scarlett pulled a tattered rag from the waistband of his dirty trousers and shoved it at Bertram. "Blow your nozzle into that, Bob, 'stead of flinging snot everywhere," he said. "That rag's fresh. Warshed it not two weeks back and ain't used it much since."

"You're a good friend, Ben Scarlett," Bertram said. "Only truly good friend I got." He blew his nose loudly and sloppily into the rag, then handed it back toward Scarlett. "You keep it now, Bob," the latter said, and Bertram pocketed the fouled cloth.

"Got any of the kill-devil about you, Bob?" Scarlett asked.

"Dry as powder, Ben. Dry as powder."

"Same here," Scarlett replied. He turned a mournful face toward Jedd. "Bob, you reckon a rich man like Mr. Colter here might take pity on two broke old dusty-dry drinking men?"

Bertram sniffled and pulled out the rag again to wipe his nose, then took a look to see what he'd delivered up. What he saw made him wince, and he threw the rag into a nearby empty rain barrel. "That's the sorrow, Ben. Jedd says he ain't rich at all. Says he's broke."

Scarlett looked at Jedd as if he were a wonder of the world. "Broke? Ain't what I'm hearing. I hear Jedd Colter got a whole creekful of California gold!"

"Ain't true, Ben. Wish it was," Jedd said.

Scarlett sighed. "Not much a poor man can do to help a poorer one, is there?"

"Not much. Sorry."

"Why are you back in Knoxville, Mr. Colter?"

"Call me Jedd. I'm back because a man

wanted to meet me here to hire me to pilot a California venture."

"You going to do it?"

"I am. Why don't you come with me, Ben? You, too, Bob. Put the liquor aside, get yourself free of it, and come to California where you have a chance to make something of yourself."

Ben was at a loss for words for a moment. "Costs too much money," he said. "How much is it to do it?"

"That'll be up to the men running the venture, Mr. Plumb and the Sadler brothers."

"Sadler brothers!" Bob Bertram exclaimed bitterly, and spat on the ground. "That puts me out right there. Them two got it in for me, especially Wilberforce Sadler. They'd sell me to the Injuns or feed me to the wolves along the way, just for meanness. Uh-uh. I'll be staying right here. 'Specially if the Sadlers are leaving town and going west."

Ben explained quietly, "The Sadlers had Bob here locked up when he stole a carpenter hammer from that store they got. He's had no use for them since."

"Warn't my fault," Bertram said. "I was drunk, and I needed a hammer. I was just looking at it, trying to figure if it was what I needed, and if I could afford it. I warn't stealing it. Just walked out with it in my hand, not really thinking about what I was doing."

Ben turned his face slightly to hide it from Bertram, and silently mouthed to Jedd: "He stole it." Jedd nodded slightly.

"What about you, Ben?" Jedd asked. "If you could come up with the money to pay your way, would you consider becoming an argonaut?"

"Argo-what?"

"Argo-*naut.* It's what they call them who are going to California to look for gold. I don't know why they call them that."

"I ain't fit to make the journey, Mr. Jedd, even if I could afford it. I don't much like traveling, and this old back and these sorry knees of mine couldn't handle squatting by a stream all day. I'd not be able to stand up again after a day or two. No, sir, it's Knoxville for me, for good."

"Ben, your 'old back' and 'sorry knees' manage to hold up when you spend nights curled up under boardwalks or sleeping in woodsheds. Hell, I heard once you spent a night curled up sound asleep in the bottom of a big, dried-out rain barrel. You could do better than you think in the gold fields."

"Got no money to make the journey, nohow," Ben said. "Nor any good way to get it."

Jedd found himself almost ready to tell Scarlett he would front him enough money for the journey and Ben could pay him back when he struck color in the gold fields. He caught the impulsive words just in time. As kind a gesture as it would be to help out the man, Ben Scarlett was not a good risk, and Jedd was himself too poor at the moment to validly make the offer.

"Gentlemen, it has been good to see you," Jedd said, touching the brim of his hat and turning to go. "I wish and commend the best to both of you. Now, you two stay put a minute. . . . I'll be back very shortly."

Jedd didn't know if Bertram's talk of being hungry was valid or simply a ruse to get drinking money. Even so, he went to a café around the corner and came out with a half loaf of bread and a little packet of cold fried sausages left unsold from that morning's breakfast offerings. He presented the food to the two vagrants, instructing them to divide it, but Ben Scarlett declared he had eaten aplenty that day and gave the entire lot over to Bertram. A valiant act, Jedd thought.

The way Bertram fell to the sausages made Jedd confident that his talk of hunger had been no falsehood, and the way Ben Scarlett intensely watched him eat made Jedd figure Ben's claim of being already well fed was based more on a generous spirit than on the truth.

Jedd walked away from the alley entrance, thinking of his own need for a meal and hoping he had enough left of his meager resources to buy himself one. He did. Enough for two, in fact.

It was hard to be poor. He'd had his fill of it. Figuring Ben Scarlett knew far greater poverty than he, he circled around again after a few minutes of walking, and found, as he had hoped, Ben walking alone, Bertram having finished his rough meal and crawled back under his boardwalk. Jedd buttonholed Ben and took him with him to the same café he had visited before, and bought himself and Scarlett a meal.

"Ben, this rumor about me having found gold in California . . . where do you figure it came from?"

Ben gave a quizzical shrug at the question, which had been asked over coffee and apple pie that could have been fresher, but which to a man such as Scarlett were like the victuals of paradise. "Rumors are like wind somebody breaks in church. . . . Unless you hear it with your own ears when first it emerges, ain't nobody who'll own up to it after the fact."

"You do have your own way with words, Ben. That I've got to say."

"Why, thank you, sir. Thank you indeed. And I'm a right good singer, too, if you don't mind me bragging on myself a little. I inherited a good singing voice from my great-uncle Earl."

"What do you know? And I didn't even realize you could inherit things from a great-uncle."

"Live and learn, Mr. Jedd. Live and learn."

CHAPTER FIVE

There was no written message, just a meagerly built black boy waiting in the lobby of the hotel to which Jedd had returned after finishing his meal with Ben Scarlett. The boy advanced toward Jedd as soon as he entered.

"Mr. Colter, sir."

"Hello, young gentleman."

"I've come to let you know you've been asked for, sir," the boy said. "My name's Lankford; most call me Lank."

"I'm Jedd Colter, Lank. But I believe you must already know that."

"Yes, sir. You've been asked for, Mr. Colter, sir. At Seventeen Addington Street, sir."

Jedd held silent a moment. He knew that address well. It had been *her* address, before her marriage to the deplorable Stanley Wickham. The same address before which he had lingered so recently with Treemont Dalton.

Her former address . . . or might it not be "former" any longer? Emma's letter that Treemont had saved from the campfire had hinted that her marriage was quite troubled and possibly moving toward a premature end. If that perhaps had happened, she might be back home in this very town. Back living with her father, Zebulon McSwain, president of Bledsoe College, the oldest institution of higher learning in Knoxville and indeed the entire state.

Might Emma herself have sent this invitation Lank had just presented to him? He ached to know, but Lank declined to answer the question. "I was told just to give you the address, no names."

"When, then?"

"Tomorrow evening, sir," Lank said. "Seven of the evening. That's when you'll be 'spected to be there. There will be supper in it for you, sir. A good one. My mama Jane is the cook. Mutton. Good, tender mutton."

"I'll look forward to it," Jedd said. "Do I need to send a written reply home with you? And if I do, should I make it out to a mister or a missus?"

The lad would not be tricked. He grinned up at Jedd and said, "No note needed, sir.

59

All I got to do is just tell what your answer is."

"My answer is yes. I'll be there," Jedd said. "Do I need to wear any fancy duds? I hope not, 'cause I got none."

"Just come as you is, sir. As you is. That's all that'll be expected. Have a fine evening, sir."

The boy scampered out the door, leaving Jedd smiling and puzzling over what might await him, and why, when he visited at Addington Street the next evening.

It took Jedd a long time to fall asleep that night, his mind filled with thoughts of Emma and speculations about the upcoming visit to her old home. At last his mind grew weary of racing in circles of speculation, and he drifted into sleep scolding himself for letting his imagination run off with him. He'd had his chance to win Emma, and she'd rejected him. She'd married another, and done was done.

Yet even as he fell asleep, countering thoughts pecked like hens at his mind: *She sent you that letter. She told you of how her husband had disappointed her, of his strayings and his coldness and untoward ways. She hinted at a possible parting of ways with him and perhaps a return to her home. And*

you know in the honesty of your mind that it is
your hope you can regain what you lost . . .
no, what you never had, but wished for and
might have had. He buried his head in his
pillow and rolled onto his left side, his
favored position for slumber.

Then he saw himself sitting on a cross-
topped church steeple, playing a fiddle with
his thighs rested on the horizontal bar of
the cross, legs straddled on either side of
the upright. Aware that there was no such
church nearby he could have climbed, and
that he had never held, much less played, a
fiddle in all his days, Jedd knew he was
dreaming and surrendered himself to slumber.

He awakened still thinking of the coming
evening appointment on Addington Street,
pondering how he would fill the hours of
the day until that time came. He began with
breakfast, purchased at the same café he
had visited the evening before with Ben
Scarlett. He'd expended almost every cent
he possessed already and was able only to
afford two day-old biscuits and a scrap of
salty ham, but these he accepted and washed
down with water.

His straits were dire ones, no doubt, and
he knew where he had to go if he hoped to
better them. Otherwise he would be forced

to flee his hotel with his lodging uncompen-
sated, and this he, as an honest man, was
unwilling to do. He had no horse left to sell.
He and Tree had already sold their mounts
to help fund their journey to Tennessee.

So he made his way across town to the
paper mill where the Sadler brothers kept
their offices, overseeing their empire. It was
a small empire by the standards of larger
eastern cities, but substantial for the area in
which it existed. Sadler holdings included
mills, stores, land sales, and publishing
interests. Jedd straightened his clothing,
fingered his shaggy hair into submission,
and wished he'd bothered to shave so as to
be more presentable to men of business.
Then he went inside, easily talked his way
past a shabbily dressed, very mild-
mannered, and sparely built secretarial clerk
with the astonishing name of Ferkus Varney,
and walked into the sanctum of the Sadlers,
a world alien to such a man as Jedd Colter.

Though the building in which it existed
was functional and plain on its exterior, the
second-floor suite where the Sadlers made
their offices was elegantly appointed. Jedd
immediately felt out of place when he
walked into the carpeted hallway and looked
at the big paintings decorating it. Most were
copies or stylistic imitations of classical

work, but rumor around Knoxville had it that some were rare masterworks of tremendous value. Jedd didn't know and it didn't matter. His concept of art was that which nature created . . . mountains, trees, rivers, thunderstorms. He found it difficult to see why folks found it necessary to put paint on canvas to make a false mountain that was no more than image, when by simply stepping out their door they could see the real thing.

Certainly he couldn't see much sense in investing wealth in collections of pictures and statues and the like, when there was land to be had. A man who had land had the most real and tangible thing there was, beautiful in a way a painting or drawing could do no more than crudely mimic.

But as Jedd looked around him, he was forced to remind himself that the Sadlers were men of power, influence, and wealth, while he was a restless wanderer so poor it nearly bankrupted him to buy a supper for a town drunk. So, who were the smart ones here after all? It was a question he didn't like to face, or to answer honestly.

"It's yonder, through that door," said Varney behind him, startling him. He wheeled and faced the spruce little man with a look so intense and fearsome that

Varney faltered backward, stumbling and falling to his rump.

"I'm . . . sorry," Jedd said, extending his hand downward to help the fallen man up. Behind him, just then, a door opened and three figures emerged. Jedd pulled Varney to his feet and looked at the newcomers, none of whom he immediately recognized. He figured, though, that two of them were the Sadler brothers, Witherspoon and Wilberforce, men Jedd had never met but had heard described. Witherspoon was short and rotund, head round as a billiard ball; Wilberforce was tall and looming and thin, his skin nearly a Mediterranean olive whereas his brother's was as ruddy as an Irish farmer's. Jedd turned a glance to the third man present; then the glance became a fixed and astonished stare, for this man he did know, though he was so changed Jedd had not immediately recognized him.

The violent loss of his teeth had changed not only Ottwell Plumb's appearance — his mouth was now crumpled and small, his chin sitting higher into his face than before, his whole countenance seemingly in a state of collapse — but also his demeanor. The pain of what he had endured lingered in the dimmed light of his eyes, the wrenched cast of his brows, the pinched corners of his puckered mouth.

"Mr. Varney, are you all right?" Jedd asked the timid clerk he'd just gotten back to his feet. Varney brushed himself off and gave nervous assurances of his welfare, his embarrassment thorough and obvious.

"Very sorry," Varney said. "Very sorry indeed."

"I regret having startled you," Jedd said.

"My own fault, sir. My own."

"Let's hush this nonsense and have ourselves a bit of something worth drinking," said Witherspoon Sadler.

"A little early to be doing that, don't you think, Withers?" said his brother, Wilberforce.

"I was thinking of coffee," Witherspoon said, glancing at Jedd. "My brother ever misinterprets anything I say."

Varney hurried into the office suite and off to a small kitchen area where a stove was kept burning for such times as this. He busied himself efficiently as Jedd turned to face Ottwell Plumb.

"I'm sorry for what happened to you, Ottwell," he said, and Plumb smiled, a very different smile than the last he had given to Jedd, when there were still gilded teeth in his mouth.

"You warned me, Jedd," he said. "You told

65

me there might be those ready to do me such harm for my golden teeth, and I'm hanged if you weren't right. I was struck down and subjected to, well, some fiercely unwanted dentistry not more than an hour after we parted, you and I. It was surely the greatest pain I have ever suffered in all my days so far, and if providence is cooperative, a level of pain I will never experience again."

"Enough talk of that unfortunate matter," said Wilberforce Sadler, pushing himself in front of Jedd and putting out his long-fingered, thin hand. Jedd shook the hand of a soft-palmed businessman unaccustomed to manual labor. "Ottwell tells me many good things of you, Jedd," Wilberforce went on. "It is acceptable to you to be called Jedd, I presume?" A small, fast smile. "Or is my presuming merely presumptuous?" He chuckled at what he clearly thought had been clever wordplay.

"Jedd is my name, and Jedd I am pleased to be called, sir."

"And you may call me Wilberforce. Or merely Wilber, as my brother, Withers, is wont to do."

Wont to do. Jedd squelched a grimace. Wilberforce Sadler obviously was one who invested too much effort in trying to sound and appear sophisticated. Such pretentiousness might pass unnoticed in Philadelphia or Boston or New York, but Knoxville was still far too much a frontier town for such airs to fit comfortably.

"It is fortunate that you have come by today," Wilberforce told Jedd. "We had just been discussing the fact that we needed to have a general talk about our upcoming venture. Though not all the relevant parties are present, there are enough of us here to have a worthwhile discussion."

The meeting occurred in a carpeted conference room that stood between the offices of the two Sadler brothers. Hanging on the patterned wall were large landscapes in oil, similar in style to the paintings in the hallway.

Jedd selected a chair at the side of the long, rectangular table and had just gotten settled when Witherspoon Sadler raised a fuss and hustled him to the head of the table instead. It was evident, from the glowering expression on Wilberforce's watching face as this happened, that he had intended that head-of-the-table spot to be his own, but Witherspoon was determined and prevailed. Jedd kept his chair.

CHAPTER SIX

The Sadler brothers had just seated themselves when another party entered the room: a young man, sandy-haired and attempting with little success to cultivate a mustache, and possessing piercing blue eyes, one slightly darker than the other. He wore business attire of a cheap make, and carried in his hand a leather-bound notepad with a heavy pencil fitted into loops on the spine. The unevenly blue eyes were quick and in constant motion, and gave most of their attention to Wilberforce Sadler.

"We begin," proclaimed Wilberforce. "The purpose we may give to our fortuitous and unplanned gathering today is simple: a general and introductory discussion of our venture, and the role we will play in it. It is regrettable that General Lloyd could not come by today, but to our misfortune he has been afflicted by ill health upon his rising this morning, and will not join us."

"Trots," Witherspoon stage-whispered to Jedd, grinning. "He was afflicted this morning with the trots. He'd planned to visit us today, but instead is visiting his privy."

"Withers!" bellowed Wilberforce. "Dignity! Dignity!"

The fatter brother nodded, chastened. "Liquidity of the bowels, I should have put it," he said. "My brother is of delicate and perhaps puritanical sensibilities, Jedd."

Wilberforce sighed, rose from his chair, and yanked his brother up by the collar. Witherspoon came stumblingly to his feet, almost falling, but Wilberforce did not let him go. Witherspoon straightened and let Wilberforce turn him to face him. Witherspoon appeared about to speak, but his brother's hand fired up and slapped Witherspoon's fleshy cheek, hard. Witherspoon staggered back and against the table, gasping loudly in pain.

Jedd was stunned. Nothing in the rather silly words spoken before seemed to Jedd to have been adequate to have prompted Wilberforce's slapping of his brother. Jedd suspected at once that what was really playing out here transcended the matter immediately at hand. These two brothers had provoked and annoyed each other in a thousand ways for all the years of their lives,

69

probably, and likely this was not the first time such minor violence had occurred between them.

The young sandy-haired man with the mismatched eyes whipped open his notebook, slid the pencil from its sleeve, and began scribbling notes.

Witherspoon, his left cheek a stinging red, glared at his taller brother. "The day'll come, Wilber, when that kind of treatment from you won't be abided."

Wilberforce laughed. "If you don't like hard treatment from me, Withers, don't disport yourself in a manner that earns it. And if you plan to alter the way in which I interact with you, well, I'm standing right here. But you know you won't do anything about it, any more than you ever have. Because some were born to lead and others to follow. Or, perhaps, to sit on their fat posteriors and keep their mouths closed if they know what's good for them."

Jedd looked over at Ottwell Plumb, who was seated at the far end of the table from him. Plumb was watching the Sadlers with a listless, hollow gaze. Jedd was immediately seized with an urge to get up and leave the place and put behind the agreement he had made with Plumb. There was something strange, flawed, and maybe poisonous here.

70

But years of having been raised to honor agreements and promises overwhelmed Jedd's instincts and froze him to his chair. He slumped back, shunning the impulse to flee but wondering just what it would be to travel all the way across the nation in company with such contentious men as these.

And who was the young scribbler so fervently recording the altercation? How, and why, did he fit into the scenario?

Witherspoon had returned to his chair after the slapping incident, but seemed ready to get up again when Wilberforce put his hand gently on his brother's shoulder and urged him to stay put. "You all right, Withers?" he asked, voice much softer, almost kindly. "That was a fierce blow, harder than intended. Are you all right?"

Witherspoon Sadler's shoulders began to heave and shake and his eyes moistened. Jedd had to look away, unable to watch a grown man weep so submissively and pathetically after such childish misuse by his own brother.

The scribbling continued on the notepad. Wilberforce turned his glare toward the young man. "Crozier, why are you writing? And what?"

The young man looked up, pencil stopping for a moment. "I'm doing what you hired me to do, Mr. Sadler," he said. "I'm recording the details of the enterprise."

Wilberforce shook his head. "No, Crozier. You were hired to record the details of the *journey* across the country and the successes we will experience in California's diggings, and report the same, with my clearance and approval, to the *Knoxville Standard.* This meeting is in *advance* of the enterprise, not part of it. Nothing that has happened here today merits notation or reporting. You were fetched here merely because of the fortuitous visit of Mr. Colter and the opportunity it affords for us to begin our planning."

"I must take notes of everything," Crozier said. "I decline to put myself in a position of lacking sufficient information, or having nothing to correct a failing of memory, because I was negligent in my note-taking."

Wilberforce leaned over the table toward Crozier. "You work under my hire, and my approval is required for what you write. Thus those notes are mine, not yours, and I instruct you to give them to me."

"These are private notes, not public documents," the young man countered in a shaky voice. "And I will not . . ."

Wilberforce seemed suddenly to loom up several inches taller, a vulture of a man with an intimidating glare that burned down at the young wordsmith. Crozier swallowed hard, and deeply, and managed to hide the trembling of his hands.

Wilberforce pondered the reporter for a few tense and silent moments, then slowly drew in a deep breath. "Do not seek to undermine my authority, Crozier. Such behavior simply will not be tolerated."

Jedd had realized who the young scribbler of notes was. He'd read an edition or two of the *Knoxville Standard,* and seen the name of reporter Crozier Bellingham bylined there. And somewhere along the way he had picked up an awareness that Crozier's employing newspaper planned to have him chronicle the travels of a selected band of Knoxville-based gold seekers, start to finish. Apparently the band of travelers selected for this coverage was to be the very one Jedd was to pilot. This was no surprise given that the Sadlers owned the *Standard.*

Jedd glanced over at Ottwell Plumb and again noted the drained, listless aspect of the man who, upon their first meeting, had seemed almost absurdly enthusiastic and vigorous. Jedd could account for the change only by reference to the brutal attack Plumb had suffered. It was downright sad to see the previously lively man sitting there lethargically, with his crumpled mouth. No gilded smile now. No smile at all.

Jedd turned his attention to studying one of the paintings on the wall while Crozier Bellingham and Wilberforce Sadler continued their tense and, to Jedd, somewhat cryptic exchange. Jedd had no intention of lingering in this place if the meeting didn't take on some substance quickly. He wasn't sure what Bellingham's role in the venture was — official chronicler, he supposed — but that was not his concern. He wanted to learn the details of the broader plan and precisely what would be expected of him.

At length Bellingham and Sadler seemingly finished what they had to say to each other, and the discussion turned to the enterprise at large, and Wilberforce presented a question to Jedd: "Ottwell has told us you are an experienced pilot, sir. How many journeys have you made along the Santa Fe Trail?"

Jedd looked him unflinchingly in the eye. "None. My experience is farther north, sir, along the California-Oregon Trail."

Wilberforce was, for three long moments, unable to blink or to find his voice. Then he turned and stared fiercely at Plumb, whose toothless mouth squeezed into an even tighter pucker under the wilting glare.

"None, he said. *None!* You have lied to me, Ottwell! You have hired a pilot under false pretense. You told me that Colter here has led multiple bands of travelers along the Santa Fe Trail . . . and now I find he has no experience on that trail at all!"

"I . . . I told you no such thing, Wilberforce," Plumb said. "You misremember my words. I told you merely that Jedd has led multiple bands of travelers to California. Any further specifics you have supplied with your own imagination."

Witherspoon stood. "Wrong, Ottwell. I also remember what you told us. My brother is correct: you clearly credited Mr. Colter here with experience on the Santa Fe . . . and on that basis we gave you our blessing in hiring him."

Plumb was pale. "I . . . I don't think I said . . . uh . . ."

A snapping sound revealed the breaking of Bellingham's pencil lead. The young man swore softly and produced another pencil from an inner pocket.

Wilberforce glared at him. "Crozier, put down that pencil! I told you, this is nothing meriting a record. Just preliminary discussion."

"And I told you, I prefer to keep complete notes," Bellingham said. "It is not essential for me to report from every note I take, but thorough notes I do intend to have."

"You are a belligerent and obnoxious young man, and your place in the enterprise stands in an increasingly precarious status," Wilberforce all but hissed back.

"Please," said Witherspoon. "Please." He looked all around, an expression on his face clearly intended to be placating and pleading, but which seemed only to aggravate his brother, who fired a harsh glance at him and muttered softly, "Shut up, Withers. Just shut up."

"Gentlemen," said Jedd, intervening in the disintegrating situation, "if my services are no longer desired, I am willing to withdraw without a complaint. Perhaps the best option is to leave you men to come to your own agreements, then see if I am still part of your picture. One thing I do ask, though. I traveled a long distance to be here, doing so at the invitation of Ottwell Plumb. If I am to be put out, it would seem fair to expect some degree of compensation for the time and expense already expended in order for me to be here."

Ottwell Plumb was on his feet, hands waving and head shaking. "No! No! No! I will *not* stand for this! Hear me, partners: Jedd Colter is *essential* to our success. I invited him on terms I had every authority to present, and if I misspoke to you regarding which route he has previously followed to California, it was accidental. You have my apologies for any misstatement I may have made and for any other misunderstanding to which I may have contributed. But I insist that we not drive Jedd away. I absolutely and firmly *insist!*"

Jedd eyed the door and pictured himself bolting through it, leaving this group and their venture behind. But he didn't. He'd agreed to let Plumb hire him. Even if the whole enterprise was looking increasingly off-putting and unpromising, he wouldn't just walk away.

He settled in his seat and did his best to exhibit a face of unworried dispassion as the three partners in the California Enterprise Company bickered and snarled at one another, and Crozier Bellingham listened and scribbled feverishly with his pencil.

Jedd looked again at one of the paintings on the wall, a depiction of a deep and shadowed mountain range stretching to a far horizon, and wished he were part of it, lost in that great solitude of hills and forests, far away from jabbering voices and the scratch of pencil on paper.

CHAPTER SEVEN

By the time the meeting was through, Jedd knew little more than he had known before about his new employers and what was ahead for him as their hired pilot. Mostly he saw that the men were prone to disharmony and possessed of conflicting personalities. Wilberforce was the natural dominant leader, and used his impressive height and voice to intimidate both subordinates and peers. And though his brother, Witherspoon, was, officially, his equal in the company, it was obvious that a subordinate was what he actually was. Clearly the short, rotund fellow with his smooth, florid face and shifting eyes was under the thumb of his brother. Equally clear was that both brothers were accustomed to that arrangement and at some level comfortable with it.

What was less clear was how Ottwell Plumb fit into the scheme of things. Not to mention the retired U.S. Army general, Gordon Lloyd, who was not even present for this meeting despite his title of "commander" of the venture. Plumb had told Jedd earlier that Lloyd would be a mostly "symbolic" leader, and now that he knew the dominating style of Wilberforce Sadler, Jedd suspected Lloyd would not be a leader at all, in any meaningful sense. Wilberforce would be the man to whom Jedd would report, and who would call the shots along the way.

Jedd had ambivalent feelings about that, Wilberforce being less easy to like than his milder brother, but at least Wilberforce seemed to have an instinct for recognizing and appreciating good advice. He quizzed Jedd extensively about details of how and when they should start the journey, what problems they would likely encounter, how long they could anticipate being on the trail, and what they would find when they reached their destination. Jedd gave the best answers he could, though privately he pondered that his recommendations would be more authoritative if the trail they were planning to follow was not new to him.

It was no surprise, though, that the company planned to travel the Santa Fe Trail. That path, a more southern route than the California-Oregon Trail, was already becoming established as the most likely choice for overland travelers from this region of the country. Even if Jedd had not traversed that particular way himself, he was the only experienced trailsman and as such would be of great value to the emigrants.

The Sadlers apparently thought so as well, because as the gathering broke up, the brothers presented Jedd a modest but very welcome advance against his future earnings. He left with the thought that perhaps the odd siblings were not such bad sorts after all.

Jedd was still well ahead of the time he would be expected on Addington Street. He issued an invitation to Crozier Bellingham to join him in a nearby tavern, and the young man readily accepted. Jedd was provided with an opportunity to gain the perspective of another person on the exploit both of them had become part of.

"There is much difference of opinion in this town regarding the Sadlers," Bellingham said after a few minutes of drinking began to mellow him. "No one disputes their success in business, but there are many who find them difficult to abide."

"I can see how such could be the case," Jedd said.

"Indeed. Indeed." The youthful Bellingham, Jedd noted, spoke with the tone and mannerisms of an older man. "Wilberforce offends many by his condescension and forcefulness. Witherspoon is seen as soft and weak and timid, though on occasion he will rise to counter his brother." Bellingham looked around them, pulled in closer, and spoke at a confidential level. "And the fact that he has never married, nor even been seen in public in the company of a woman, has led to . . . talk. You understand what I am trying to say."

"Or trying not to say, maybe."

"Exactly. Precisely."

"Is it true, you think?"

"I don't think so. I've seen him come in the newspaper office too many times and make a point of speaking flirtatiously with Mrs. Spangler."

"Who is she?"

"A woman who helps with the printing. Very good at it. Learned it from her husband, who operated the press until he died two years ago."

"Witherspoon has his sights on this widow, then?"

"He is at least interested in her. But he's a very shy man. He has to have the pretext of business reasons before he'll talk to her. So he's forever coming in asking to read over the Sadler advertisements, and he always finds something to change in them, just so he can go over it with her. Takes him forever to do it, too. And sometimes they never get around to talking about what needs changing."

Jedd chuckled. "I'm glad he's got something in his life to make him happy. I get the feeling his brother doesn't contribute much toward that end."

"They get on well enough most of the time. As long as Witherspoon remembers his place."

"I guess we'll all be learning our own places, and Wilberforce's, when we hit the trail." Jedd took a long swallow. "And just what is *your* place, Crozier? You working for the newspaper or for the Sadlers?"

"Both. And also for myself. I'll be sending back reports of progress to the newspaper so folks back home can keep up. But the paper is paying the Sadlers, not me, for what I send, and they pass on part of it to me. Too small a part, in my point of view. And on top of that, the fact that my pay comes directly through them makes me their employee, and puts me, and what I write, under their control."

"Doesn't sound like a particularly comfortable situation," Jedd said.

"It's not," said Bellingham. He leaned forward slightly and spoke more softly after shifting his eyes side to side to make sure there were no obvious eavesdroppers about. "What they don't know is, it's not my *only* situation."

"You lose me now." Jedd pondered for a few moments, then ventured, "Are you planning to look for some gold of your own once you're in the diggings?"

Bellingham leaned even closer, shaking his head. "My gold comes through pen, not pan. I'm going to write more than happy little stories for the newspaper, stories that the Sadlers control." He paused and then his volume became even lower. "On my own, I'm writing a book. The definitive account of the whole gold-in-California phenomenon. The good of it, the successes of it, and also the other side. The failures and disappointments. This nation has the right to know the truth."

Jedd said, "I think I follow you now. The popular notion is that you can walk along the bank of a creek and pick up gold nuggets like a child finding pretty pebbles. A lot of people are casting off everything they've had, and everything they've done, to go become gold gatherers."

"Yes. And the newspapers feed the fire.

California this, California that. The future is all in California, gleaming in the streams and hiding in the gravel of the creek banks. Nothing else can compare, and no one can achieve the same kind of wealth by any other means. So they would have us all believe."

"And I take it you don't?"

Bellingham leaned back in his chair, scratching at his chin. "Shall we just say that a good newspaperman comes equipped with a healthy dose of skepticism?"

"Upon what do you base this skepticism?"

"On the mere fact that Americans have been settling in California for years now, and to my knowledge most have not become fabulously wealthy by sending their children down to the creek behind the barn to fetch back bucketfuls of gold. And this, it seems, is what many gold-struck easterners of the present moment seem to think they will do once they reach the far coast."

"There are those who carry their expectations to the extreme, I'll grant you," Jedd said. "But keep in mind that the earlier travelers to California have gone in search of land and a new life for themselves, not specifically for gold. Maybe once there are enough there to search every stream and river and gully, we'll find the dreams are all going to come true."

Bellingham gave a smirking little smile. "If you keep talking that way, the Sadlers are going to love you indeed, Jedd Colter," he said.

"Well, I'll hope they do. I like to stay in good favor with those I work for."

"It is my intention to work ultimately for *myself,* even when I'm officially working for them," Bellingham said. "I'll write the Sadler's promotional little newspaper reports for them and help them spread the story of how they are serving as the agents of good fortune for every man who pays them to do so. Folks back home will read my stories and worship the Sadlers from afar, as they intend. Meanwhile, I'll write my own book, the true and full account, and see it published. And if all goes as I suspect it will, the Sadlers and all the other promotion-before-truth California pushers will have to sing out of the other sides of their mouths. The truth will be out and the American public will no longer be fooled."

"That may be a hard book to sell, Crozier."

"How so?"

"Because people would rather coddle their dreams than see them shattered."

"I'm not in the dream business. I'm in the

truth business."

"As long as it serves your purposes, it seems."

"Meaning?"

"Meaning you just finished saying you're going to go ahead and do your newspaper reports in the way the Sadlers want them done. And we both know that will mean promotionalism. In short, you're willing to use the resources and opportunities provided to you by the Sadlers to gain what you need to take the wind out of their sails farther along. That's why you were so feverish in taking notes down in our little meeting today, right? You wanted to make sure you didn't miss anything that you could use later on to make the Sadlers look dishonest, or silly, or bad, or harsh."

"You misspeak, Jedd Colter," Bellingham said. "I do not dislike the Sadlers. Wilberforce, yes. Witherspoon I'm actually rather fond of."

"But you are willing to discredit him nevertheless."

"I want to write a book that will establish my credentials in the field I wish to pursue. In order to do that I must make my own journey to California. The Sadlers and their odd little friend Plumb are providing me with that opportunity in exchange for something they need: reports back to the people from whom they hope to find future California emigrants. I am helping them and they are helping me. There is nothing wrong or untoward about it."

"But you seem eager to have your book destroy the popular conception of California opportunity."

Bellingham shook his head. "My goal is not to assassinate popular conceptions as an end in itself. What I seek is simply to present the facts, whatever they may be, regardless of whether they resonate with popular notions. I do admit to strong doubts that California gold will prove to be a way to instant wealth for most who seek it."

"Good enough, then." Jedd took another sip. "Me, all I want to do is get another group of travelers safe to California, collect my pay, and then do it again as long as the work is in demand." He was thinking, but did not say, that success in prospecting on the part of the Sadlers might make it unnecessary for him to pilot another emigrant band again. Assuming the deal Plumb had made with him held up.

"Here's to us both and our own California dreams, then," Bellingham said. Glasses clinked softly, and they drank.

CHAPTER EIGHT

Standing at the doorway of the McSwain house on Addington Street, Jedd had a strong impulse to bolt. Simply being where he was made him manifestly uncomfortable. When last he'd stood at this same door, Emma had been with him. She was gone now, of course, married to another. . . .

Or was she? Jedd still did not know exactly what awaited him here, or why he had been invited. Might everything have changed? Might she be inside this house, awaiting him, a woman newly unattached?

A distinguished, well-dressed servant opened the door and greeted Jedd formally, all but sweeping him inside and instantly taking charge. Jedd cast glances all around, refamiliarizing himself with the house where once he had spent many happy hours in times past. He searched every corner, every shadow, every random reflection he could find around the room, but was disappointed.

He did not find Emma.

"Mr. McSwain is ready to receive you now, sir."

Jedd was led into the sprawling dining room.

"Jedd," said Zebulon McSwain.

"Good evening to you, Mr. McSwain," Jedd said to the slender, expensively dressed man already seated at the head of the long table. McSwain looked younger than his years, little changed physically from the last time Jedd had seen him, though his previously dark brown hair was sprinkled with more gray.

His face was different though, somehow. Not physically different, but presenting a demeanor that didn't fit Jedd's recollections of the man. He struck Jedd as worried, burdened. Though McSwain was smiling, the smile seemed artificial. He stared at Jedd as though he had something to say but couldn't quite find the words.

Within minutes Jedd was seated at the far end of the table from his host, wondering what was the point of such distance between them, assuming conversation was intended. Just the way things were done among the uppity, it seemed.

Delicious smells enticed Jedd as servers appeared and began doling out food. Jedd was disappointed to see that there was no third setting in place at the table. Obviously neither Emma nor anyone else would be joining them for this dinner.

McSwain read his thoughts, apparently. "She is not here, Jedd. Perhaps it would have been more thoughtful of me to let you know from the outset that I, and only I, issued this invitation to you. But frankly I was afraid you would be less likely to come if you knew Emma would not be with us."

"It would have been a delight to see her, sir, no denying it. But she is a married woman now and I respect the sacredness of that institution. It would have been inappropriate for me to have set my sights too firmly on seeing her. She belongs to someone else."

Instantly McSwain's expression became openly sorrowful. "Yes," he said. "Someone else. Not you who would have been the love of her life, nor me, her father. Another, far less worthy, has her."

A pall descended over the conversation for the next several minutes. An excellent dinner was served, but Jedd found little enjoyment in it. . . . He was conscious of his unsophisticated, common clothing as compared to McSwain's fine business suit, and of his own rustic table manners, which he tried to correct by clumsily imitating Mc-Swain's elegant dining style. It was not easy to do for a man who had been raised in a rough-and-ready household where many meals were eaten from wooden trenchers or the most basic of crockery.

The meal ended quickly, both men eager to move past it. Jedd still did not know why he had been called to this place.

Over brandy and cigars a few minutes later in a well-furnished parlor, McSwain drew in and exhaled a long, deep breath, then looked Jedd squarely in the face.

"It should have been you."

"Beg pardon, sir?"

"Don't call me 'sir,' Jedd. Call me by name. I was very nearly your father-in-law, after all. That is what I'm referring to when I say it should have been you. Emma should have married you instead of the lout she chose."

"I . . . I don't know what to say to that, Mr. McSwain . . . Zeb. I've got to say, though, that I'm inclined to agree. It was a bad time for me when she cut me loose. I've forgiven her, but still I wish, like you just said, that it had been me she chose."

"Yes indeed." McSwain paused. "And I daresay she almost certainly holds the same view now."

That, Jedd thought, was an intriguing comment. He asked a very direct question. "Is she not happy in her marital situation?"

"Stanley Wickham is a difficult man. Harsh. Perhaps cruel. I am certain he has been unfaithful to her. He has struck her sometimes, I suspect. . . . There were bruises on her arms the last time I saw her. She tried to hide them, but then, when Stanley was not aware, she made sure I saw them. She didn't say how she had received them, but it wasn't necessary for her to do so. Her look, the way she indicated him with a flick of her eyes in the direction he had gone . . . I knew who had injured her."

The thought of Emma suffering at the hands of a man so unworthy of her enraged Jedd to the point that he rose from his chair and paced about the room, struggling for something to say and not finding it.

"He is a hard man, Jedd. Not one any father would want to see his daughter marry. I wish that in some way I could have made her see the truth about him before she chose him. But I couldn't see it clearly enough myself." McSwain glowered. "It should have been you she chose. It should have been *you*!"

Jedd remained unresponsive, thinking to himself that this was surely one of the strangest, most strained conversations he'd ever been faced with.

"She chose Stanley Wickham over me because he has money, Zeb. Me, I'm a poor man. Poor all my life."

McSwain studied Jedd with a frown. "Poor in the financier's sense of the word, yes. You are rich, however, in capability. In potential. And in character. And *that* is the kind of wealth that Emma's husband — God, how I hate even to acknowledge that 'husband' is what he is — it is that kind of wealth that he lacks. Had Emma married you, she would have had something so much better than she got. . . . And eventually, I believe — perhaps very soon — you will possess wealth of the monetary variety as well."

"Zebulon, I don't understand why you brought me here tonight to tell me this. Is this leading to something? Is there something you want from me?"

McSwain drank again before he answered. "There is, Jedd. I have heard you are about to lead an emigrant band to California. Is this true?"

"I am to pilot such a group. . . . Leadership, in the full sense of the word, would be in the hands of others."

"General Lloyd, you mean."

93

"And the Sadler brothers."

McSwain smiled quickly and wanly. "I know the Sadlers well. They are . . . *interesting.* Interesting men."

"I don't yet know them well, but I suspect that 'interesting' is as accurate a description as you could speak."

"Mm-hmm."

"So, why does our emigrant band interest you?"

McSwain's expression became excessively earnest. "I want to be part of it."

Jedd gaped a couple of moments, then very nearly stammered as he said, "You . . . *you* are thinking of prospecting for gold?"

"Is the notion so absurd?"

"It's just that . . . well, don't you have a lot of things that hold you here in Knoxville? The presidency of Bledsoe College, for example?"

Suddenly McSwain was unable to hold Jedd's gaze. "Jedd . . . Jedd, things . . . change."

He told Jedd the story. Though he had served for several years as seventh head of the college founded in 1786 by clergyman and educator Eben Bledsoe, a dramatic change had occurred. Bledsoe College as an independent entity was soon to be no more. It was being absorbed by another Knoxville college formed about a decade later than Bledsoe's academy, East Tennessee University, formerly known as East Tennessee College and before that as Blount College.

"And since Bledsoe is being made part of the other school, there is no place for a president of Bledsoe College," Jedd surmised aloud.

"Exactly. My position ceases to exist."

"But surely there would be a place for you somewhere in the combined institution."

McSwain leaned back in his seat, steepled his fingers, and studied the ceiling. "There is no more political an institution in existence than an institution of learning, Jedd. I wish I could say that I have made it as far as I have in the academic life without making enemies. But it would not be true. There are those out there who would gladly see harm done to me, even see me destroyed. I am in a most precarious situation at present."

Jedd had expected to hear nothing like this. Was McSwain telling him that there were those who would harm or kill another person over something so trivial as the affairs of an academic institution? Surely not.

McSwain looked at him more intently. "I called you here tonight, Jedd, first to let you know of my high regard for you, my belief in your character and your future, and my wish that Emma had made a better choice regarding you in her affairs of the heart. Second, to tell you I wish to become part of your emigrant band to California. I must get away from this town and this situation I am in. And my best prospect lies in going to the place where new lives and situations are to be forged. The place of new beginnings. The land of promise."

Jedd said, "California is no land of promise. Just of *opportunity.* There's a difference. I think most who run to California expecting instant wealth will find that wealth will come only after a long period of very hard work. Or maybe not at all. For example, there are stories around town saying I made some kind of major gold strike in California already, then defended my gold against a bunch of thieves. You'd think I've been picking my teeth with gold toothpicks and skipping gold nuggets across the river, the way some have talked around here."

"Whatever the case, I must go. If not to California, then some other place where I can lose myself and not be found."

Jedd pondered the man who at one time might have become his father-in-law. "Let me ask you straight out: Are you in actual danger, Zeb?"

McSwain's face seemed to sag and age before Jedd's eyes. Before he could answer the question, though, a noise outside, a muffled thumping, caught both his attention and Jedd's. McSwain hurriedly moved, hiding behind a door and peering out around it like a scared child shielding himself from imagined phantoms in his bedroom.

The sound had come from the area of a rear window. Jedd rose and headed toward it, asking, "Are you expecting other callers than me tonight, Zeb?"

"None at all." McSwain pointed toward the door through which their dinner had been carried, then hooked his finger leftward. Jedd, understanding, nodded and slipped out the door, then turned left, and moments later exited the house and found himself behind it.

He saw the source of the noise they had heard: a man was trying hard to slip away from the back of the house and make for a storage shed in the back lot. Jedd moved fast and had the fellow held by coat collar and arm in half a moment.

"Ben Scarlett," Jedd said. "What the devil are you doing out here?"

CHAPTER NINE

"Jedd!" Ben Scarlett exclaimed as he realized who held him. Jedd felt the drunk relax a little in relief. "You nigh scared me to death!"

"Well, you making noise out here scared Mr. McSwain just as bad!"

"I was just looking for something, Jedd. Didn't mean no harm."

"Looking for something? Something to steal, you mean?"

Ben was the image of offended righteousness. "I ain't a thief, Jedd. I'm a drunk, but I ain't a thief."

"Then how do you explain this?"

"Jedd, at houses where there's money, there's food, too. Some of it gets thrown out the back door for the dogs and cats and varmints." Ben paused, studying the look on Jedd's face. "Sometimes the varmints that need it most are the two-legged kind. You might look down on me for it, but there's been times aplenty when I've been glad to fight with a dog for a throwed-out pork chop with a couple of bites of meat left on it. It goes with the life I live."

"I don't pass judgment," said Jedd. "In my own life I've taken meat from the remnants of a critter that fell victim to wolves and coyotes and such, and washed it down with muddy puddle water. Out in the wilderness, I've flapped my arms to run the buzzards off from something a lot of folks would turn away from, but which to me was going to be that night's stew meat. I'd throw it in a cookpot with roots and wild turnips and such I'd foraged out for myself in the woods. So like I said, I don't pass judgment."

"Well, I like that. A man like me gets where he expects to be judged most all the time."

"If you're going to be nosing about behind people's houses, Ben, I wouldn't worry about getting judged. I'd worry about getting shot."

Ben was unable to find a good retort, which seemed to annoy him. "Is that right? Well, maybe you'd best be worrying about what might happen to you if you come busting out and surprise folks like that while they're minding their own business and just looking for a scrap or two."

"Lord, Ben, are you threatening me?"

"No. Just saying that you're lucky that it was me you found out here, and not the gent who was poking around here and then run off when I showed up. He didn't look none too friendly, and he had a gun in his hand."

"There was somebody out here with a gun when you showed up?"

"That's what I said."

Jedd looked around into the darkness, thinking about the conversation that Ben's noisemaking had interrupted, wondering just what it was Zeb McSwain had done to get himself into such a state of danger.

A trace of juices from the fine piece of mutton that had been set before Ben Scarlett only five minutes earlier remained on his plate, so with a glance at his watching tablemates that let them know he was about to violate propriety, he swabbed a finger through the juice and thrust it into his mouth. He had violated propriety already by wolfing down the mutton like a starved pack dog, holding it in his hands like fried chicken.

"You were a hungry man, Mr. Scarlett," said Zeb McSwain, who had invited the vagrant in for some of the best food of his life once he learned that Scarlett had been foraging for old kitchen scraps outside his house.

"Mighty nice of you to feed me, sir," said Ben. " 'Specially since I wasn't supposed to be out there."

"Ben, I'll never let any man go hungry at my back door. But forget about that. Who was this fellow you saw out there with a gun?"

"Never seen him before, sir. And he didn't linger for no introductions. Nor did he say a word. He cut out and busted clean through that hedge you got back there."

"Did you get a good look at him?"

"Good enough. Tall fellow, hair the color of dark sand, big hands, strong. Notched ear."

"What ear?"

"Notched. His right ear. Piece cut out of it, like he'd come out on the worst end of a knife fight sometime past."

"I'm glad he didn't hurt you, Ben."

"I doubt it was me he was here to hurt."

McSwain frowned. "Indeed, my friend. Indeed."

Jedd sat silent, taking this in and wondering who would have cause to threaten McSwain, and why.

"Mr. McSwain, is it true what they are saying?" Ben asked.

"What are they saying? And who are 'they'?"

"Just folks round town, that's all. They're saying you won't be heading up Bledsoe College no more."

"There's not going to be a Bledsoe College anymore, not as an entity to itself," McSwain replied. "So they won't need a president for it."

Ben lowered his head and looked like a man with something to say and reluctance to say it. "I heard it a little different than that, sir."

McSwain frowned. "Don't put stock in rumors, Ben, no matter what they are."

"Good advice, sir. I had trouble believing it, anyway. I can't figure anybody wanting to sack a good leader."

McSwain shot a glance at Jedd to see if he had comprehended what Ben had just said. He had. And McSwain was troubled to know that a mere town drunk would be aware of the acrimonious and forced nature of his departure from the institution with which he had been long associated.

McSwain addressed Jedd. "I told you, Jedd, that I have made enemies. Apparently some of those enemies have made certain that my personal affairs are made public. Mr. Scarlett is correct. Even if Bledsoe College was not being absorbed by the other college, my position of leadership was gone. Accusations were made to give grounds for pushing me out of the presidency. Those accusations have been not only harmful to my reputation, but actually dangerous to me as an individual. We have seen an example of that tonight, with this armed fellow whom Mr. Scarlett so fortunately frightened away." McSwain looked at Ben. "I owe you a debt of gratitude, sir."

Ben shrugged and flickered out a grin. "Just looking for something I could eat, that's all. Happened to be in the right place at the right time to run off a notch-eared troublemaker."

Jedd asked McSwain: "Are you saying that whatever trouble or rumors or charges or whatever it was are vicious enough that somebody would want to see you hurt?"

"Or dead," said McSwain, nodding. "You can see, Jedd, why I find the prospect of traveling with your emigrant band to California to be such an appealing one."

"I can." Jedd was overwhelmed with a desire to ask just what McSwain's alleged transgressions had been, but politeness restrained him, and McSwain volunteered nothing.

"Do not believe everything you hear on the street, Ben," McSwain said. "And I ask you . . . keep it to yourself that I am leaving Knoxville."

"I'll do that, sir. Going to join your daughter, are you?"

Jedd was again surprised. "Emma is in California?"

"She is," McSwain said. "In a new, fast-growing mining town called Bowater Gulch."

"With *him.*"

"Yes. With him."

"I received letters from Emma, Zebulon. They were the biggest part of the reason I came back here. Those letters came from Knoxville, not California." He paused. "Do you know anything about those letters, Zeb?"

McSwain flicked his eyes at Ben Scarlett for half a second. The man didn't want to speak with an extra set of ears listening in. Ben picked up that message, rose, thanked McSwain again for the unexpected meal, and departed. Jedd watched him go, then stared at McSwain, waiting.

"I doubted a plea from me would be enough to draw you back here all the way from Missouri," he said. "I had those letters written by a local woman who could be trusted to keep quiet, and who possesses the ability to copy very closely the handwriting of others. She imitated Emma's hand quite well, using an old letter Emma had sent me as a guide. I told her what words to write. I am sorry for the deception, but it was crucial that I speak to you."

Jedd thought of the things the letters had said, things that had given him hope that, somehow, there might yet be a future for him and Emma. Anger rippled through him at the realization it was all false. Had he been a man of lesser self-control, he might have risen and allowed his fists to convey his feelings to McSwain.

"I can't see what was 'crucial' in involving me," Jedd replied. "You can join the Sadlers' California venture without any help from me. All that is required is to inform the Sadlers' secretarial clerk, Mr. Varney, pay the fee, and be prepared to leave at the designated time and date. I'm just the pilot, the guide. I neither recruit nor sign up individual travelers. You didn't need me back here at all."

"There is more to it all than you yet know," replied McSwain. "Now is not the time to explain it, while your feelings are stirred up against me. I do most sincerely apologize for having drawn you here with a false letter."

"Tell me why you did it. *Now.* Not later. Now!"

"Well, I will tell you part of it. Wilberforce Sadler chairs the trustee board of Bledsoe College. The same board that declared itself desirous of losing my service as president. I could hardly expect him to welcome me into his band of California travelers unless I have the support and influence of someone he has cause to listen to."

"And the rest of the reason?"

"Later, Jedd . . . later. Not just yet."

Jedd rose and without another word left the room, then the house. He strode down Addington Street with Zebulon McSwain watching him through a window. Jedd felt a fool. Deceived by forged letters! How could he have been so gullible? And what could have motivated Emma's father to such a depth of deception?

There was more here than Jedd was able to figure out. It was surprising, confusing, and most of all, infuriating.

A black-and-white cat walked into Jedd's path and darted quickly across. He stopped and watched the cat vanish into a hedgerow beside the road. "Cicero?" Jedd called softly. He'd just realized that something had been missing at McSwain's house, something that had always been there before. It was Mc-Swain's beloved old black-and-white tom-cat, Cicero, which Jedd had seldom seen anywhere except on Zeb McSwain's lap. Emma had never liked the cat because it made her eyes water and nose run to be near it for long, and Jedd had been amused many times when she'd made half-serious accusations to her father, claiming he cared more about the cat than about her. Mc-Swain, naturally, had always refused to respond to such comments.

Cicero had not been there tonight. That must have been Cicero who just ran across in front of him. But no. This cat had possessed a completely black head, whereas Cicero had a white face with one black ear and one white one. Quite distinctive. Maybe this newer cat was one of Cicero's feral offspring.

His mind left the subject of cats and drifted back to McSwain himself, and the unrevealed trouble that had beset him and taken his career. It was overwhelmingly puzzling.

Jedd walked for twenty minutes, expending pent-up energy, and then a realization came that he knew someone who might be able to add some clarity to the mystery of

McSwain's situation and peculiar behavior.

He was well away from Addington Street when he stopped suddenly, listening hard to the sounds of the town. One in particular caught his ear, distant and strange. He puzzled over it, then walked on until it had faded into nothing.

In his big house, Zebulon McSwain had heard the same sound, and was now seated in the darkest corner of his bedroom, into which he had locked himself so securely even his servants could not enter. He kept an ear turned toward the window, listening for what he had heard to be heard again. But he heard it no more, and was grateful for the silence.

Home for Crozier Bellingham was a little block of rented rooms in an upstairs corner of a cheap boarding house. Humble as it was, it was cozy and secure, and he enjoyed being there at the end of a long day. With the strained meeting with the Sadler brothers and the human oddity named Ottwell Plumb now some hours behind him, Bellingham was glad to stretch out on his narrow bed, hands behind his head, and stare at the ceiling while awaiting the coming of sleep.

He was blinking on the edge of slumber

when a pounding at his door jolted back his awareness. He sat up fast, then jumped out of bed. "Who's there?"

"Crozier? Is that you? Jedd Colter here!"

Bellingham went to the door and opened it. "Come on in, Jedd."

"Need to ask you about something," Jedd said. "It has to do with Zebulon McSwain."

Bellingham ran his fingers through his hair and nodded Jedd toward a chair. When Jedd was seated, Bellingham asked, "So, what do you want to know?"

When Jedd had asked his question, Crozier Bellingham paced about the room as he answered. "Jedd, the truth is, I don't know the precise problems that McSwain had with his college board. I don't think anyone knows except for the people directly involved."

Jedd shook his head. "There have to be rumors, at least. McSwain is a notable man in this city, and when something happens to a notable man, people talk."

"Why do you care, Jedd, if I may ask?"

"Because he's told me he wants to go with us to California. And he's in trouble of some sort. . . . Someone's after him. There was a man with a gun sneaking around outside his house tonight. He ran when he was seen."

Crozier was intrigued. "Interesting. And surprising. The kind of men who serve on college trustee boards don't tend to skulk around houses with guns."

Jedd replied, "But some of those men might hire another person to do such a thing. So you don't have any notion at all of what put him and his higher-ups at odds?"

Bellingham sat down and leaned toward Jedd, an earnest and secretive look on his face. He answered almost as if there were hidden, listening ears all around, "Jedd, the rumor I have heard, and it is purely a rumor from my standpoint, is that there was a theft."

"McSwain stole something?"

"So say the whispers on the street, for what they are worth. Which perhaps is nothing."

Jedd thought hard for a few moments. "It would have to be something of value to the college. Maybe . . ."

"College funds?" said Bellingham. "That's what I suspect. He stole college funds. Probably after he found out that the trustees were about to let Bledsoe College be absorbed by another institution, and the president's job was inevitably about to dis-

110

appear. McSwain saw the end of his career rushing at him and grabbed what he could while he still had access to it. That's my guess."

"And now the trustees, or somebody on the board of trustees, want to get back what he took? And are willing even to threaten his life for it?"

"Maybe so," said Bellingham. "Maybe so."

Jedd mulled it over. "So that would give McSwain a reason to put as much distance as he can between himself and his old life. And then fate throws in its hand. Along comes gold being found in California, giving him a pretext for leaving that few are likely to question, since so many others are uprooting and making the same move." Jedd paused, thinking again, and continued more quietly. "And for him there's a whole other reason to go. His daughter, already in California, with a man not worthy of her. He can go to her, maybe have a chance to make her situation better than it is."

"You're losing me now," Bellingham said. "I don't know about any of that."

"Never mind it," Jedd said. "It's just me speculating about things."

Bellingham went to a nearby table and picked up a leather-bound book that looked like a small ledger. He opened it and Jedd saw pages of neatly written words. Bellingham flipped through to the first blank page, sat down, and with a pen and small bottle of ink, began writing.

"That's not the same book you wrote your notes in today," Jedd observed.

"No. That was my notepad, where I record things in their rawest and barest form, just notes and facts and general broad observations. What I'm writing in now is my personal journal, where I put it all together in a way that makes sense, at least to me. This is what will eventually become the book I write about the California enterprise. An outline of the key elements and themes and story of my book, if you will. *My* book, *my* work . . . not those self-serving newspaper reports the Sadler brothers are looking for."

"Are you going to write something about Zebulon McSwain in your book?"

"I'm going to write about whoever and whatever proves to be the most interesting, all of which will make itself evident as we go along. But writing about McSwain in the direct sense, or any other actual living individual, for that matter . . . no. Because what I will write will be a novel. I shall be the Charles Dickens of the gold fields. I am determined to do so. You're the first person to whom I've revealed that. I hope you don't think I'm just a foolish dreamer."

"You'll write a made-up story, you're saying?"

"Only in a sense. It will be a made-up story that follows actual reality. Our journey to California, and the people and situations and events that will constitute it, those will be the ore from which I mine my novel. Names and so on will be changed. And some details will certainly be changed as required to carry the story through."

"Why not just write it straight, using the actual folks involved?"

Bellingham, though previously weary, was becoming enlivened and animated by Jedd's questions. This was his subject, the kind of thing he'd thought through and could readily articulate, so he was glad to talk about it. "There are advantages to a writer in telling certain stories in the form of fiction," he said in a professorial tone. "Fictionalization frees the writer to hone and refine his story, making small adjustments and deviations that allow the tale to be told in the most entertaining manner rather than as a slavishly fact-bound narrative. It lessens his concern over an accidental libel or slander of an actual person. And most of all . . ." Here Bellingham paused, drew in a deep breath, and delivered an obviously practiced line. ". . . it frees the author from the narration of mere *facts* and allows him to instead present *truth*. For though truth does not contradict facts, it does *transcend* them."

Jedd wasn't accustomed to such heady concepts — his conversations were more likely to run to how best to set a fish trap or read deer sign — but he nodded politely. Bellingham looked pleased with himself for his profundity and gave a tight little smile.

Jedd grinned back, but thought of Ottwell Plumb and of the bickering Sadlers and their delicate little personal secretary, Ferkus Varney, who, Jedd had ascertained in the earlier meeting, would accompany his bosses across the country. *I'm going to be surrounded by strange little noddy fools all the way to California,* Jedd thought.

After a series of further meetings, arguments, and displays of personal eccentricities, the process of advertising the upcoming venture of the California Enterprise Company of East Tennessee, signing up eligible participants, collecting participation fees, and finalizing the many background arrangements necessary for the effort at last were addressed. By the time the enterprise was ready to commence, letters of recommendation from men of prominence had been obtained, lines of credit secured, and a small band of scouts and armed, quasi-military defenders hired and put under Jedd Colter's authority. Knoxville's finest restaurant had been relieved of its best chef, an Irish-born culinary craftsman named Hewitt O'Keefe, and O'Keefe was engaged at an overly high price, to serve as company cook. His profusely described plans for fancy dishes that would make ordinary trail fare "look like porcine swill by comparison," as he put it, gave Jedd yet one more aspect of the enterprise about which to feel doubtful. He'd spent enough time on road and trail to know that preparation of the kind of foods O'Keefe planned was impractical to the point of being impossible. But Jedd kept his mouth shut, unwilling to create a new potential point of conflict with the Sadlers.

Jedd had qualms as well about a plan for the journey that Wilberforce Sadler insisted be emphasized in all advertising: an anticipated short three-month cross-country overland passage. He intended to pledge that those who threw in with the California Enterprise Company of East Tennessee could look forward to a fast start on gathering California wealth and an early, triumphant return home, with pockets bulging with nuggets and leaking glittering dust.

What gave Jedd the most pause about the pledge of a fast journey was General Gordon Lloyd, who proved to be the slowest-moving, slowest-talking man Jedd had ever encountered. The old military man slurred and dragged his way through the first planning meeting he attended, a meeting he allowed to begin only after leading the longest, most deliberately spoken prayer in human history. Every syllable was dragged out to the fullest possible extent. And the first item of business brought up after the extended "amen" was a provision, demanded by the general, that no travel would occur on Sundays, that day being set aside for rest, prayer, worship, and reading of the Bible.

Jedd had nothing against rest, prayer, worship, or Bible reading, but clearly the chance for fast progress was being lessened dramatically . . . and there was no guessing what other ways to slow things down the somnolent General Lloyd might come up with along the way.

It was likely to be a long spring and summer, Jedd thought as he listened to General Lloyd's droning voice. And a long, long trail.

■ ■ ■ ■

Part Two:
The Narrowing of
the Funnel

■ ■ ■ ■

CHAPTER TEN

Crozier Bellingham had not intended to become a wagon driver, but a broken ankle suffered by the original driver hired by the Sadlers to man one of the two wagons they were taking for themselves left a vacancy they had difficulty filling on short notice. The job might have gone to Ferkus Varney, but he was a delicate and weak man, possessing little promise for such work, and was thus passed over. When Witherspoon offered the young journalist the chance to learn on the job the skill of being a teamster, Bellingham heard himself agreeing.

Part of the attraction was that the Sadlers had commissioned the construction of two completely new, high-quality wagons, created by the finest wagon maker in the eastern end of the state. The sturdy, blue-painted vehicles were striking to see, smooth in motion, rugged in construction, yet as finely finished, jointed, and crafted as an excellent piece of furniture. The chance to drive such a well-built conveyance would in itself hold appeal to any young man. What sold Bellingham most on the job, however, was the opportunity for extra pay, the guarantee the work provided of being always able to ride rather than walk, and the excellent view his perch provided. From the driver's seat he could observe and etch into his mind in great detail the movements, sounds, feelings, and perspectives of a cross-country wagon train. And given that Witherspoon Sadler would usually be riding at his side, he would no doubt hear many details of the inner workings of the expedition that would provide wonderful grist for his writings. His novel, of which not a word was yet written, was becoming grander by the day in the vision of its hopeful creator. Who could say? Maybe the story would be written from the point of view of a California-bound teamster Bellingham could base upon himself.

The train moved out of Knoxville, westward, on May 26, 1849, eighteen wagons and fifty human beings strong. The first leg of the long journey would be into and through Kentucky, to the city of Louisville. Aware of his inexperience, Bellingham dreaded the rough country through which they would have to travel, but was sure the practice would be valuable training for the endless miles facing them once they reached Independence and the start of the transcontinental part of their journey.

Bellingham sat straight-spined on his driver's perch as the California Enterprise Company of East Tennessee rolled out of Knoxville with a large crowd of admiring citizens waving from the sides of the streets, pleased to see two and a half score of their friends and neighbors actually beginning such an epic adventure. It brought to the city a sense of being part of something vast and national in scope, a movement that at that moment was probably being reflected in a score of other departures from other cities and towns all across the nation.

Wilberforce Sadler took advantage of the parade atmosphere to wave broadly at the crowd from the driver's perch of the lead wagon, one festooned with flags both decorative and patriotic. The name of the California Enterprise Company of East Tennessee was painted on both sides of the canvas wagon cover. Little shims of whittled pine had been placed strategically, and temporarily, on the wagon wheels to create a drumroll noise, adding drama to the movement of the head wagon in the long, street-filling wagon train.

In the middle of the train the wagons gave way to a large block of riders, livestock, and pedestrians leading packhorses. Jedd Colter was among the horsemen and wore clothing that had been insisted upon by the Sadlers: a Crockett-styled buckskin outfit intended to remind those who saw it that Jedd came from a noted frontier family of the region, known for woodcraft and significant contributions to the frontier heritage of the region. Jedd, who never liked to strut himself before others, wore the getup over his own protest and kept his eyes fixed mostly straight ahead, declining to return the waves and greetings sent his way from onlookers. He did wave at Robert Bertram, who had hollered at him from an alley and raised in greeting a crockery liquor jug from which he was swigging. Jedd figured it was stolen. If the opportunity had existed, he'd have gladly passed on his costume-like garb to the old drunkard, who would probably wear it with pride.

The entire group consisted of forty-five males and five females, two of the latter being wives, the other three daughters. Over half the argonauts were single young men. A few of the older men were leaving wives and families behind, the plan being for those families to either join their patrons later or just remain home to await the gold-laden return of their men in a few months. In a couple of cases, arrangements were already in place to bring the family to California later by a ship voyage around Cape Horn and north from there to the California coast.

No such arrangements were needed in Witherspoon Sadler's case, there being no wife and family. The man had never married, though those who knew him well could testify that this was not due to any lack of interest. The unfortunate fellow had gone through several failed attempts at romance, trying hard to find a wife suitable to a prominent man of business, some woman with sufficient intelligence, dignity, beauty, and gravity to compete with Wilberforce's wife, Grace. So far, though, the rotund, unimpressive Withers had failed to find his true love.

As someone with his ear and eye turned to life in this town, Bellingham was aware of Witherspoon Sadler's long and unproductive quest for a spouse. And the man's actions made clear to all his wish that he were a more appealing prospect for the ladies. Despite being a well-off man financially, Witherspoon faced challenges in being seen as an eligible bachelor, chief among them his unappealing physique and piping voice. Even so the man tried hard, and usually ineptly, to cut a dashing figure for the feminine eyes of Knoxville when opportunity arose. That trait of behavior, Bellingham figured, accounted for why Witherspoon left Knoxville riding not on his wagon seat, as would be expected, but instead astride a fine horse from which he could wave in grandiose fashion to the ladies on the boardwalks. And he wore a buckskin outfit just like Jedd Colter's . . . perhaps unmindful that he cut a very different kind of figure than did Jedd, who was as lean and muscled as Witherspoon was portly. On Witherspoon, the effect of the buckskin garb approached comedy. The broad smiles he received from the women as he rode along derived not from admiration but amusement.

The long train of wagons, packhorses, riders, and pedestrians maintained its parade-like quality for some miles out of Knoxville for the sake of the rural folk who watched from their fields and yards and porches. At length, though, the structure loosened. Jedd left the party long enough to hide in a grove of trees and change back to his usual garb, clothing that a true woodsman would actually wear in field and woods rather than what an actor portraying a woodsman might wear on a New York stage. He abandoned the unwanted garments behind a sycamore.

Witherspoon did not change out of his buckskins, being persuaded that they rendered him a fine figure of rugged masculinity, but he did trade saddle for wagon seat in hopes that the wagon would be kinder to his hemorrhoid-afflicted posterior. And thus Crozier Bellingham found himself, as earlier anticipated, with a seatmate. Witherspoon was in a mood to talk.

"There is something fine indeed about bidding goodbye to the past and taking to a new way," he said. "Do you not agree, Crozier? I'm sure you do, sure you do. That, to me, is one of the most luring things about this entire, burgeoning rush for California gold: in California all will be fresh and new. Old acquaintances, old contacts, old friends, and old enemies, these will be erased as if they never were. This is a vast land on which we live, Crozier, vast enough that even the thousands who will cross it will be as mice crossing a plain, moving in the same direction and aiming at the same destination, yet spread so widely that they will be largely unaware of one another. The odds of encounter with one's past are remote. It's a simple matter of logic."

"I'm sure you're right," Crozier replied, making mental note of the conversation for later addition to his journal.

"He is not right."

Crozier, startled by the unexpected voice, turned his head and saw that Jedd Colter had ridden up beside them and had overheard all that Witherspoon had said.

"What do you mean, I'm not right?" Witherspoon called over. "How could it be otherwise than what I said? It is such a huge, broad land out there before us!"

"That's true. I know that far better than most, sir, having crossed that land more than once."

Witherspoon winced a little at the subtle but clear pointing out of the fact that he held no particular qualification to make comment on the subject at hand, while Jedd did. Jedd let the moment hold, then pass, and went on.

"What you said makes sense on its surface, I'll grant you that, Witherspoon," he said. "But where it breaks down is that you're forgetting that, big and broad as this land of ours is, them who cross it don't traverse it like water down a sloped roof, spreading out everywhere. It's more like water going into a funnel, and funnels start out wide but narrow down. Take us here, for example.

We're heading up to Louisville, and from there we'll be making our way over to Independence, from whence we'll commence the main part of our journey. But we won't be the only ones. Every day there's folks who come in to Independence and St. Joe and other places like that, from all over our side of the nation. From the top of Maine to the coast of the gulf down south. They're the water from the broad part of the funnel, and Independence and the other launch points for the westbound trails are like the narrow part of the funnel. The part where everything comes together and for a little time is all at the same place and flowing out in the same direction. Not spread out and vast at all. Not there. And there's other places along the way where the funnel narrows again. Places like Fort Kearny and Fort Laramie up on the California-Oregon Trail. And Santa Fe on the trail we'll be following. The odds are right good, Witherspoon, that many of us in this company will encounter folks we've known before while we're crossing this big, vast country you were talking about. It's happened to me already. You got to remember that folks in this country have been heading far west for a goodly while now, heading to settle in Oregon or California, and sometimes stopping off before they get there. First time I traveled the California trail, I chanced upon no less than three folks I used to know all the way back in my North Carolina days. And two more from Knoxville. Folks who had decided to go to Oregon but had never gone that far, settling in just past Independence. The narrowing of the funnel, you see. Bringing folks together into one small area. Squeezing a thousand different paths together into one. And I've heard of the same thing happening to lots of others. And it'll happen all the more now that there's the lure of gold and even more folks going west."

Witherspoon looked oddly unhappy to be hearing this, and Bellingham noticed it and turned an inquiring gaze upon him. Witherspoon cast his eyes heavenward a moment, then sighed and said, "Well, I understand what you are saying, Jedd. And I confess that it makes sense and takes into account things I had failed to think of. But I do not relish hearing it. I've come to hope that passage to California might be like moving through a veil and leaving everything behind, all the old problems, all the old unsettled accounts. Letting the past be past in the fullest sense. A second chance for a man to make himself what he hasn't succeeded in making himself the first time through."

Jedd eyed Witherspoon and felt mild pity for the man. Clearly Withers was at some level unhappy with himself as he was, with his lonely life as it had been dealt to him so far. He'd hoped that this great adventure would make a clean break with the familiar life so a new and better one could begin.

Jedd knew better. It could not be that way, not fully. A man might cut down the weeds of his past and clear his grounds in anticipation of new growth, but the roots of old weeds always remained, even if unseen, and in time grew again. Past accounts could not be left unsettled. Eventually they came around again, demanding payment.

He almost said as much to Witherspoon, but didn't. The man looked too distressed already. Who could say? Maybe in Witherspoon's case, the past would indeed simply fall away, and California would bring him a kind of new birth and new, better life. Jedd hoped so. He couldn't help liking the man. Especially when he compared him to his brother.

At the absolute end of the train was a wagon driven by a prim man with a proper British look about him and a stack of poetry books beside him on his seat. His name was Nigel Straw, and his last experience of driving a wagon had occurred in his youth in Essex. He'd left wagon driving behind in favor of education and a career in higher education, most recently as a professor of language and literature at Bledsoe College, where he had been one of the few members of the faculty supportive of the presidency of Zebulon McSwain and unfavorably disposed to the idea of Bledsoe's being absorbed into another college. So, when McSwain had approached him with the notion of accompanying him to California, the impulsive Straw had not required more than ten minutes of thought before he made his decision. Still young, still willing to work hard, and lacking in academic snobbery despite his skill and effectiveness as an educator, Straw had no qualms about returning to his youthful work as a wagoner and moving on from there to a life of pan swirling and kneeling beside California waterways.

Near the edge of town the roadway was broken and rough and Straw, feeling he was falling too far behind the train, cracked his whip. The wagon jolted forward and caught up fast, and at the same time Straw heard a loud *thunk* behind him, something falling to the wagon bed back under the canvas cover.

He winced, knowing what it was.

"Are you all right back there?" he called softly over his shoulder. "I heard the bottle fall."

A man's face appeared through the cinched canvas opening behind Straw and peered up at him with bleary eyes. "I'm fine. Spilled some, though, damn it."

"Sorry about the bump, President Mc-Swain. Rain has washed ruts into the road back there."

"All is well, Nigel. All is well. But please don't call me 'president' anymore. It just salts the wound. Salts the wound." And Mc-Swain withdrew back into the shadowy wagon interior while Straw marveled at the decline of a man who had once been among the most distinguished in his town. At that moment he was glad McSwain had joined the Sadler trek to California. If ever any man needed a new start, it was Zebulon McSwain.

The dirt road smoothed and the wagon rolled easily and without much vibration. Back under the cover, McSwain finished the last of his liquor and threw the empty bottle off the back of the wagon, cursing at the town of Knoxville and the trustees of Bledsoe College as he did so. Hell with all of it, and all of them! He'd been rejected, pushed

131

away, stripped of his dignity and his status, and he would not forget or forgive it. He was still muttering curses as he lay down on a blanket among the gear and luggage stowed around him and fell asleep.

A mile outside town, a man emerged from a roadside thicket and deftly made his way to the back of the wagon bearing McSwain. He glanced around quickly and, undetected, climbed up and through the gap in the canvas and hid himself behind a wooden crate inside the wagon. There he listened to the snores of the former college president passed out on the wagon bed, and sang softly to himself a song about gold in California. The whispered music of his own voice pleased him.

Up on the driver's seat, Straw whistled loudly and drove the wagon along without any clue that he was carrying an extra passenger, having heard nothing of the man's stealthy intrusion or his faintly intoned song.

Though most of Knoxville had turned out to see the departure of the Sadler brothers' emigrant train, two residents of the town had been among those otherwise occupied. Ollie and Rollie Slott stood in a very humble cemetery, side by side at a freshly filled grave that bore a homemade wooden cross as a marker. On it was crudely chiseled:

MARTHA SLOTT
B 1783 D 1849
MUCH LOVED MOTHER
AND FOLLOWER OF CHRIST
ASLEEP IN THE LOVE
OF JESUS

Ollie Slott reached up and dabbed a tear from his cheek. Since the death of his and Rollie's mother two days before, and her burial only the prior day, Ollie had struggled to keep his emotions under control, mostly failing. Her illness had come fast and hard and the Slott brothers had found themselves bereaved so suddenly that it felt like the slap of a hand or the strike of a fist.

"I'm going, Ollie. And I want you to come with me," Rollie said.

"I think I'll stand here a mite longer," Ollie replied. "Seems like I can feel her here with me when I stand where she's buried."

"I ain't talking about going from this burying ground, brother. I'm talking about the big adventure half this country is part of. Hear what I'm saying? I'm going to California! With Mammy gone there's nothing to hold me here now but you, and even that wouldn't figure in it if you'd come with me. We can go there, work our trades just like we do here, me fighting, you making boots and so on, and we can look for gold, too. We've lingered here in this town way too long, all because of Mammy. She's gone now. We can go, too."

Ollie stared at the wooden grave marker and said nothing. "Talk to me, brother," Rollie urged. "Say you'll go with me. I don't want to make such a big journey with no friend at my side."

"The Sadler group was to leave today," Ollie said. "Too late to be part of that. And too costly for poor men like us, anyway."

"There'll be others going. Or we can make up our own group. Get us a wagon and aim it west, and keep rolling till we see the golden glitter."

"You make it sound easy, Rollie. Wouldn't be so. Not really."

"It ain't easy watching the days of your life slip on past with nothing better to show for it, neither."

Ollie opened his mouth to reply but seemed to deflate before he could speak. His eyes played once more over the new grave of his mother, and tears welled anew.

Rollie stayed beside him a few minutes more, then patted his shoulder and trudged out of the little graveyard. A few minutes

later, Ollie followed, alone, tears still streaming in silence down his dark face.

CHAPTER ELEVEN

It did not take long for Crozier Bellingham to see that most of what he would have to record in his notes and journal, and to report back to the newspaper in Knoxville, would be mundane, at least at the start. Wagons rolled, packhorses plodded, dogs trotted beside wagons or slept on the drivers' platforms at the feet of the wagoners. Typical Tennessee countryside lay all around, changing little as they traveled, so that any sense of progress was minimized. Witherspoon Sadler sometimes rode his horse, but more often accompanied Bellingham on the driver's perch, and twice took over driving duties, clumsily. Bellingham found Witherspoon an odd man, to say the least, but friendly and generally cheerful, though he could descend into a dark humor at unexpected moments. Even so, Bellingham liked his company.

Bellingham sent his first report back to

the *Knoxville Standard* early in the journey, posting it from the village of Jamestown in Fentress County, Tennessee. The short piece was thoroughly gone over by both Sadlers, though there was nothing in it to generate any offense or problems. Witherspoon made no changes except the addition of a reference to General Lloyd as "somnolent in manner," an observation that was undeniably accurate but instantly stricken from the report by Wilberforce. Wilberforce struck several other items as well, unnecessarily, and Bellingham saw that the man intended to exercise near total control over what the public was told about the California Enterprise Company of East Tennessee. Bellingham wished to protest the changes, but discretion kept him silent. It was obvious to him that Wilberforce's editing had been done solely to drive home the point to Bellingham of who was in control here.

The newspaper reports didn't really matter much to Bellingham. Those reports ultimately were the Sadlers' concern; Bellingham was merely a hired craftsman helping bring them into being. What mattered to him were the notes and journal writing he was doing on his own steam, laying the foundation for his later novel of the gold fields. Over that piece of work, neither Wilberforce Sadler nor any other extraneous person would exercise control.

But Wilberforce would be present as a character in the novel, albeit in disguised form. An equally disguised Witherspoon would be there, too. Also in the novel would be some version of Jedd Colter, a man Bellingham found dashing and appealing, a figure easily and naturally useful in a work of fiction as a hero boldly venturing through a wild and dangerous world.

The Sadler train passed through Anderson and Morgan counties and on into Fentress County and Jamestown, where Bellingham posted his newspaper report and everything came to a halt for two full days when General Lloyd declared his wagon needed repair. He put it in the shop of a Jamestown wagon maker who did not appear particularly skilled. By the time Lloyd was satisfied that his wagon was fit for travel again, most of the emigrants were restless and quietly grumbling among themselves that Lloyd was perhaps too old and unenergetic for this venture. "Listless Lloyd," Bellingham scribbled in his notes after hearing someone use the phrase, and the concept for one more character in his novel came into being.

The holdover in Jamestown was not fully

unwelcome to all of the travelers. Several had friends and relatives in that area, and took advantage of the time to pay calls upon them. Three young Jamestown men scraped up the required fee, produced a wagon that passed inspection and was declared sufficiently rugged for the journey, and joined the Sadler group. Some questioned the wisdom of allowing the party to grow in such an unplanned way, fearing it would make the emigrant band overlarge and unwieldy, but Jedd Colter assured the travelers that this would probably not be the last time such accretions would occur, and that some degree of alternating growth and shrinkage should be expected and accepted. His words were persuasive and the new argonauts were welcomed.

The mood was not so receptive on the first night after the wagon train crossed into Kentucky. Jim Crabtree, a burly member of the guard delegation, came striding through the camp with two men held in his grip by their collars, and walked the pair to the wagon of Wilberforce Sadler. Wilberforce glared at the two men, one of them in particular receiving most of the hostility. Wilberforce walked up to that man, who was still firmly in Crabtree's grasp, and leaned into his face.

"And why are you here, McSwain?" he demanded. "What need do we have of a thief in this company?"

Zebulon McSwain did his best to look Wilberforce in the eye, but it was a faltering attempt. "I am a duly paid and approved member of this band," he said, his voice quavering.

Jedd Colter, listening and watching along with a high percentage of the rest of the group, wondered what Wilberforce had meant by the "thief" reference, and whether he should step in and in some way defend McSwain from the kind of manhandling Crabtree was giving him.

"Unhand me!" McSwain said to Crabtree. "There is no call for this treatment!"

Jedd stepped up to make the same demand, but Wilberforce spoke first. "Let him go, Jim. He's not going to run anywhere. Too cowardly to try it."

Crabtree simultaneously shoved McSwain away from him and let go of his collar. The man stumbled clownishly and barely kept upright. But he recovered quickly and stood up tall, putting a challenging look of offended dignity on his face.

Wilberforce looked at McSwain as if he were a worm. " 'Paid and approved,' you say. I don't buy it. Had your name come up before me, I would have rejected your application forthwith."

Witherspoon walked up behind his brother and cleared his throat, startling Wilberforce and making him turn. "His name didn't come up before you, Wilber," he said. "It came before *me*. And I saw no reason not to approve him. He paid his obligation upon application and showed every sign of being sincerely interested in the purpose of our enterprise. So I approved him."

"Of course he is 'sincerely interested' in what we're doing here," Wilberforce replied. "It provides him a chance to flee Knoxville in a way that has a veneer of acceptability. A thieving coward in flight can hide himself among those who are making the journey out of more respectable and proper motives."

"What did he steal?" Witherspoon asked. "I'm not aware of anyone among us claiming a loss of property or possessions."

Wilberforce looked around at the large group of watchers and listeners. "For the sake of dignity and the good name of a college upon which I have served proudly as a trustee, I will refrain from speaking the details in such a public arena," he said. "Suffice it to say I can be trusted when I declare that former President McSwain is a thief. And a particularly scoundrelous one at that. There is good reason why the word 'former' attaches to his title."

"Well, I know nothing of that," replied Witherspoon. "All I know is the man had long held a high reputation in our community, and that he wanted to join us and was able and ready to pay for the privilege."

"He would not be here had I known of it," Wilberforce said, and the look he gave to the humiliated former collegiate leader was withering. Jedd admired how well McSwain held up beneath it, and promised himself to get to the bottom of what this alleged thievery business was all about.

At that moment the other man in Crabtree's grasp managed to wriggle free and dance aside. With the attention focused on McSwain up to that point, Jedd had not even noticed that the second captive was none other than Ben Scarlett.

"I think I know you, sir," Wilberforce said to Ben. "I've seen your vile self drunk in the gutters more than once. Worthless piece of street rubbish! What's your name — Scarlett, I think?"

It was Ben's turn to put on as dignified a look as he could . . . a challenge given the raggedness of his attire and his typically unshorn and unshaven condition. He was not as tall as Wilberforce but somehow managed to make himself appear nearly so.

"My name is Benjamin Scarlett, sir, and I do not appreciate being called 'rubbish.' I am a man and a citizen of Knoxville, and I expect the respect proper to such a status."

"You're a damned town drunk," Wilberforce replied derisively. "One of too many of your ilk in our city. You are far from the kind of citizen California will need as it builds its future on the gold we all expect to find." Wilberforce turned to his brother. "Withers, are you going to tell me that this . . . this vagrant is also a 'paid and approved' member of our group?"

Witherspoon shook his head. "I know nothing of him and cannot account for his presence among us," he said.

"Sneaked into a wagon, I'll bet," a nearby man said. "I know Ben Scarlett. Nice enough gent when he's sober. But sober don't happen as often as it should."

Wilberforce stepped in front of Ben and looked down his long nose at him. "Is that what happened, sot?" he said. "You sneaked onto a wagon?"

Ben did his best to maintain the self-possessed look he'd managed to achieve, but clearly it was difficult. He stammered meaninglessly at his challenger; then his eyes began darting from side to side. Looking for escape.

"He's with me," said Jedd Colter, stepping up and placing himself at Ben's side. "I invited him to come, and I'm paying his fee."

Ben looked at Jedd with an expression of confusion, respect, and gratitude mixed together. Meanwhile Wilberforce stared Jedd stonily in the eye and said, "Are you speaking the truth, Jedd?"

Jedd cocked up one brow. "You wouldn't imply I'm a liar, would you, Wilberforce?"

Ben Scarlett, beginning to gather courage because of Jedd's support, bounced on the balls of his feet like a fighter ready for a scrap. "Yeah!" he shot at Wilberforce. "You calling my friend a liar?"

Wilberforce wrinkled his nose like a man smelling filth, and said, "You stink, sir. Like a heap of dung. Like a mountain of rotted potatoes. Like a worm-eaten corpse."

Ben's face reddened, but he saw the prudence of restraint and took a step back from the man. Jedd stepped up in Ben's place.

"There's no call to talk to him that way," Jedd said. "I'm going to ask you not to do it again."

Wilberforce lost a good deal of haughtiness when faced with Jedd's intense, blue-eyed gaze.

"I doubt I'll have cause to address him, or anything about him, again," Wilberforce said. "If you are this man's sponsor, Jedd, I'll accept him. But I know his habits and ways, and I'll expect you to keep him under your wing and out of trouble while he is among us."

"Ben will give you no trouble. Will you, Ben?"

"No, sir. No, sirree. Not a bit. You got the word of Ben Scarlett on that."

Wilberforce laughed. He looked around at the crowd. "Well! I'm satisfied! I've got the word of a man who pees his own pants regularly! A man who squats with dogs in a ditch to do his necessaries! A man who would give up his last bite of bacon for a swig of rum. A man who —"

"That's enough," Jedd said.

Wilberforce glared at Jedd but shut up and turned away.

Ben faced Jedd. "Thank you," he said. "But he was right. I did sneak onto a wagon. And I ain't paid no fee."

"Stay close to me and I'll see you're all right," Jedd said quietly. "And, Ben, while we're traveling, stay away from the liquor. Will you?"

"I'll try."

"Try hard, you hear me? Really hard."

"Are they going to try to make you pay my fee?"

"Don't worry over it. I encouraged you to come to California, you'll recollect. I'll do what needs doing."

"It's what you said to me that put the notion in my mind. You know, about California being a place where a man can maybe get a new start."

"I've had some further discussions along that line lately," Jedd said. "They've reminded me that there's another side of this thing that you can't overlook. You can get a new start in California — no question about it — but new starts don't go far if old problems are left festering. A man can travel across a whole nation, Ben, and his old ways and habits and problems can follow him sure and steady as a faithful old hound. He goes off and thinks he's left it behind. Then he wakes up one morning and the old hound's scratching at the door just like it used to . . . and before he knows it, his new life has turned back into the same old one he tried to get away from. Do you know what I'm saying, Ben?"

Ben Scarlett looked away, wistfully, and watched a buzzard circling off above the nearest wooded hilltop. "I think I do, Jedd. I think I do. You're telling me there's some things a man can't shuck off just by putting miles behind him. Like maybe . . . his drinking, if he does too much of it. Like I do."

The travelers were not far along when the first significant rumblings of discontent over leadership emerged. It took the form of an unauthorized meeting among the men to talk over General Lloyd's heightening tendency toward lethargy and indecision.

The immediate issue was horses. From the outset, some of the group had complained that Lloyd's decision to use horses to pull the wagons was a bad one. Mules were the predominant preference, though some declared oxen would have proven best in the long run. Whatever the individual preferences, most seemed agreed that the general had been overly dictatorial in how the decision had been made. He had not even consulted the Sadlers, nor Jedd Colter, but had made his choice based on his "long experience in the military realm." Or so he told the restless and glowering crowd that challenged him.

"I want to hear what Colter thinks about it!" a man called out. "Ain't that one of the reasons he's here, to tell us what we need to know about such as this?"

General Lloyd lifted his chin and looked fleetingly like the dignified officer he once had been. "I don't object to hearing what Mr. Colter has to say."

Jedd found himself forced into the conversation. "General, a man can transport his hind end to California by way of any number of dragging beasts. Hell, he could string enough cats together to do the job, if he could manage it. That'd be something to see, wouldn't it? Wagon with a quarter mile of cats yoked up and pulling along together . . . man would think he'd gone lunatic, seeing something like that."

"What are you babbling about, son?" the general cut in. "What's this childish nonsense about cats? You're saying we should be pulling our wagons with cats?" A titter of laughter in the crowd made the general glance at the people and give a fast and uncharacteristic grin. He wasn't accustomed to making people laugh, and found he liked it.

Jedd said, "No, sir. What I'm saying is that no matter whether a man is pulling his wagon with horses or mules or cats or salamanders, when he reaches some of that mountain country in the West, he'll wish he had oxen. Other times, it may not matter so much." Jedd paused, deciding whether or not to continue. What the devil? "What *does* matter, though, is that all that early-on talk about this being the group that will make the California crossing faster than anybody else is going to wind up as nothing more than idle talk, the way we're going. Taking time out to argue over dray beasts only slows it more. Here's the fact: what we've got is horses. It's like marriage — for better or for worse, you end up having to go with what you picked. It's time to quit talking and keep moving. A little faster, if we can do it."

"I used to live in Kentucky," said one of the few women in the group. "There'll be no going faster for a long spell yet. The Kentucky country's too hilly. It will take us a long while just to move the wagons through the mountains without having them skid back down backward on the up-slopes or run out of control on the downslopes."

Jedd and the general shared a mutual shrug. "Oh well, then," Jedd said. "We press on as best we can." And General Lloyd nodded sadly.

Chapter Twelve

If anything said inspired the "commander" of the California Enterprise Company of East Tennessee to try to pick up the speed of the journey, the commander failed to show it. The train moved only a few more miles before General Lloyd called it to a halt again, declaring that his wagon and a couple of others required repair. Jedd anticipated that Wilberforce Sadler would rise in fury and maybe even oust the general from his leadership position. It didn't happen. Jedd began to wonder if maybe the old military man had a hold of some sort over the Sadlers . . . knew something incriminatory about them, maybe. Or was owed something by one or both of the brothers.

For whatever reason, the Sadlers glumly let the poky old man grind the venture to a halt while his wagon was disassembled and put back together again, slowly. Jedd heard Wilberforce ask his brother, "Reckon that wagon maker is Lloyd's twin brother? They move at the same speed." To which Witherspoon replied, "Move? You've actually seen the general *move?*"

Wilberforce laughed and cordially patted his brother's shoulder. It was a rare and astonishing event for all who saw it.

With nothing else that seemed more worth doing during the period of waiting, and with open country all around him, Jedd took Treemont with him and the pair hunted for a full day. Coming back into the camp that evening, bearing fresh meat, they saw something new: a man, not previously part of the group, seated before a canvas on an easel with a brush in his hand, painting an image of Wilberforce Sadler's wife, who was nicely dressed and seated primly on a chair somebody had dragged off a wagon.

"I'll be!" Jedd said. "You see that, Treemont? We got us a picture painter here."

"Well, it's something to do while everybody waits on the general, I guess," Tree replied.

"What? You think he'd want to paint your ugly face?"

"Hell no. But if he's going to paint pretty women, I'm glad to watch. The women, not him."

"Well, Wilberforce's wife is pretty enough, I'll grant you. But she's Wilberforce's wife. That's the end of that story."

The painter was named Dupont Gale and had wandered into the camp in the late morning, seeking a passage to California. He had little money and sought the right to cover his fee by labor, creating portraits of attractive women — attractive, at least, once he was finished enhancing their images in pigment. He also painted men who considered themselves important enough to be enshrined on canvas and were willing to pay to make that happen. Wilberforce Sadler was already signed up for a turn in the model's chair after his wife's turn was through.

Jedd, a classic frontiersman figure by any standard, drew Gale's artistic eye. Gale urged Jedd to sit for a portrait, but Jedd would have none of it. It went too strongly against his nature. Even so, over time he caught Gale sketching him on the sneak when he wasn't busy at his easel. Jedd soon began avoiding the man. He had visions of a picture of himself hanging in the hallway at the Sadlers' headquarters back in Knoxville, and didn't like the idea. At last the artist stopped asking, but spent more time observing and sketching Jedd when he wasn't looking.

It appeared he would create a portrait of Jedd Colter, with permission or not.

As time passed, it was clear that General Lloyd's propensity for dragging things out was not about to change. The man was incapable of making any decision without thinking it through at least three times. His slowness became a humorless joke among the members of the wagon train. It was evident that the passage of the California Enterprise Company of East Tennessee was likely not to be the fastest crossing on record, as intended, but the slowest.

They hadn't even yet reached the Mississippi.

Once through Jamestown in Tennessee, the train of wagons moved north into and through Kentucky, heading for Louisville. Jedd, a traveled man, knew better than some what they faced. Hills and hollows, mountains and streams of many sizes . . . the wagons seemed to crawl along, and often even the crawl slowed when, on the steeper inclines, it was necessary to use long poles to help hoist the wagons up and forward. Then it was usually necessary to use skid boxes beneath the wheels on the far side of the hills to keep the wagons from sliding, or pushing the horses into an unsafe and uncontrollable pace. Progress slowed substantially in such terrain, so much so that even General Lloyd complained.

"You get down and shove on this pole awhile, if you're not happy," said Treemont to the general at one point while trying to help urge a wagon up a steep incline with a lever pole.

Lloyd's face reddened at the challenge and he stammered a moment and said, "Insubordinate scoundrel!" before petulantly riding away from Treemont on his plodding horse.

"Good riddance," Tree muttered just loud enough for the old military man to hear.

Near the end of May, Crozier Bellingham wrote the following in his journal:

Louisville at last! We reached the city on the twenty-sixth and the general spirit among the emigrants is one of hope that finally, if we are fortunate, we are past our hardest obstacles until we cross the plains and reach the western mountains. If the rugged country of Kentucky was sufficient to slow us as much as it did (with the help, of course, of General Poke-along Lloyd), I shudder to think how long it will take us to

154

finish our journey.

The plains, I am sure, will be much easier to cross than what we have dealt with so far. Beyond the river the country will be flatter for a great distance. It is my hope we will be able to make up for some of the time we have lost, though I know my inexperience and thus wonder if I am merely hoping wishfully rather than realistically.

For reasons not readily obvious, General Lloyd seemed to gain some new energy and motivation for a few days. He made arrangements to move the expedition forward a little more rapidly. Most of the wagons were put, already loaded, aboard a riverboat for shipment to St. Louis. A delegation of men, including Treemont, Ferkus Varney, the artist Dupont Gale, and a few others, was sent along on the voyage and would later reunite with the others. Those others, with provisions refreshed, made the journey overland, Jedd leading.

Witherspoon Sadler rode at Jedd's side some of the time, mostly, Jedd noticed, when the widow Rachel McCall happened to be close by. She was one of the few women among the travelers, a late addition to the group, making the journey with her brother, Robert Dukane. She was an attractive woman with hair the color of a chestnut hull, and wore it long and flowing down across her shoulders. Despite being very feminine in voice, features, and build, she was physically strong and considered herself the equal of any of the men around her. In fact, the impression given was that she thought she was most likely on a plane well above most of the males . . . except perhaps Jedd Colter. Jedd caught her looking at him quite often, and she was not abashed when he caught her at it. He was as flattered as any man would be by such attention, though the truth was he thought her a somewhat odd woman, mostly because of her habit of wearing rugged trousers instead of dresses, and riding in a man's saddle, straddling her horse. It was considered scandalous by the other women. The men were openly intrigued by her.

Particularly Witherspoon Sadler. If the widow Rachel was anywhere within view, his eyes were on her. If she glanced his way he gave her a smile, and on a couple of particularly daring occasions, a wink. Rachel usually pretended not to notice. Her own attention was perpetually focused on Jedd Colter. It was obvious to any who cared to observe it that the main reason Rachel McCall insisted on riding on a horse rather than a wagon was that it made it easy for her to be near the horseman Jedd. Where Jedd rode, Rachel rode not far away.

Also not far away was, usually, Witherspoon. By keeping near Jedd he kept near Rachel McCall. The rotund fellow's obvious attraction to a woman far too beautiful for him was an ongoing point of humor among the other travelers. Witherspoon was oblivious of the fact that he was being laughed at on all sides. He'd made no declarations of his affections to her, nor had any meaningful conversations at all with Rachel, so as far as Witherspoon could see it, his feelings were fully hidden to all but himself. In reality he might as well have written them across his broad forehead.

Witherspoon was riding near Jedd when the overland portion of the group neared St. Louis. By now the group had traveled so far that they all felt seasoned as travelers. Having at last reached the Mississippi River country, there was a welcome sense of having passed an important milestone. The longest part of the journey remained ahead, but even so, they would soon be at Independence, the town generally perceived as the gateway point for overland passage to California.

"How does it go from here?" Witherspoon asked his brother and Jedd as they stood together looking across the band of travelers and the broad river beyond. "Men, freight, and dray horses by water to Independence, right?"

"That was the plan. It's changed," Wilberforce replied.

Jedd said, "The general?"

"Of course. He's heard stories of cholera, that the riverboats are rife with it."

Jedd frowned. "Is it true?"

Wilberforce shrugged. "He is afraid to take the chance and find out. Which, I must admit, makes a certain degree of sense, given that it is possible for us to reach Independence by land."

"Yes . . . but once again, we're hopelessly slowed. We're falling further behind every day, and it's already too late to make it up later. Our pledge of speed-of-crossing has already been kicked to the ground, and now the general is proceeding to stomp it flat. We may set a record as the *slowest* passage."

"I know, Jedd. I know. But here we are."

"I find myself astonished," wrote Crozier Bellingham a few days later in a June entry in his journal.

After days of delay owing to General Lloyd's fear of cholera on riverboats, it seems now it does not matter because he had decided we will not go to Independence at all. Cholera fears again. The general has heard the disease is in that town. No verification, only rumors. Even so, General Lloyd has changed our destination to St. Joseph.

Jedd Colter and the Sadlers are obviously frustrated but, showing the deference proper to leadership, are keeping their thoughts to themselves. I have been instructed by Wilberforce Sadler to present the change in plans in my newspaper reports as routine and unimportant. I am doing so, but like much else they seek to suppress, even yet the truth will find its way out through my pen when I begin the writing that they know nothing of, and which will be seen by many more eyes than my meager and localized little half-truth newspaper reports.

Days dragged on with General Lloyd insisting upon handling the arrangements for all alterations of plans. No one expected him to achieve any changes quickly, and he did not frustrate that anticipation. But even the most pessimistic about the general's lethargy were surprised when it was early August before the wagon train departed St. Joseph.

They were near Fort Leavenworth when General Lloyd, striding across the camp one evening with a jovial smile on his face and an atypical happy greeting for everyone he met, staggered suddenly to his right and fell, grunting as his head struck hard against a wagon wheel. He crumpled down like a body without bones as drool flooded out of his mouth and his head lolled to one side.

Several people saw him fall, but the first to approach his limp form was a man who had kept himself nearly invisible to most in the band of emigrants. Zebulon McSwain knelt at Lloyd's side and spoke softly to him, calling his name and feeling about on his flopping wrist.

"Is he dead?" asked a girl of about twelve, the youngest traveler in the group.

McSwain shook his head. "Not dead. He's got a pulse yet. But I'm thinking his heart has gone bad on him. Needs a doctor, no question about it." He looked at the little girl, started to ask a question, then paused and asked the question of a nearby man instead. "Is there a physician among us, sir?"

"Who are you?" the man asked. "I ain't seen you before, I don't think."

"I keep to myself. Stay in my wagon most of the time. Can you answer my question about a physician?"

The man knelt beside McSwain and studied the pallid face of General Lloyd, who was unconscious. "We do have a doctor. But he's not much good. Too much of this." He extended the thumb and little finger of his right hand and tilted the thumb toward his mouth in imitation of a tipped bottle.

"Well, if he's the best we have, we must fetch him," said McSwain. "I'm pessimistic regarding the chances of General Lloyd surviving a wagon ride into town and a search for a physician there."

The man rose and darted off into the camp. McSwain could only hope he was going to fetch the doctor he'd referenced.

"Do you know that man who just left?" McSwain asked the little girl, who still stood by, staring at the pathetic and unmoving General Lloyd.

"His name is Gibbons," she said. "Charlie Gibbons. He's my uncle. I'm Lorene Gibbons."

"Can I rely on him to bring that doctor back, miss? Because General Lloyd needs one."

"No," the girl said sorrowfully. "Never rely on Uncle Charlie. Likely he won't be back.

My papa says that Uncle Charlie is 'sorry stuff.' Even though he's his brother."

But Uncle Charlie did come back, minutes later, dragging along a middle-aged man who was trying to stuff a slender metal flask back into a pocket but failing because Uncle Charlie was repeatedly yanking him by that same arm. As the pair reached General Lloyd's side, the flask thumped to the ground, clattering on a stone. Charlie Gibbons scooped it up and pocketed it, telling the doctor he'd give it back to him later.

"This the patient?" the supposed physician asked.

"Yes, Doctor," said McSwain. "This is General Lloyd, the commander of our expedition. He has been stricken and has passed out."

"I ain't far from the same situation," the supposed doctor said. "He been drinking?"

"I don't think so, sir. I can tell that you have, though. Are you in any shape to evaluate this man?"

"I'm finer than a baby boy's chin whiskers," the doctor said as he lowered himself, with effort, to his knees, upon which he swayed a little as he scooted toward General Lloyd. "I already know what's wrong with him. He's passed out."

What a dolt, McSwain thought. "But why?"

"Probably his heart. He's old. His face and mouth ain't drooping, so I figure it probably ain't a stroke. You sure he ain't been tippling, though?"

"If he was I knew nothing of it. Not that I've been sitting around watching him. But he's a man of strong religion and not a drinker at all, or so I've heard."

"Well, all I can do for him right now is sit with him a bit and see how he does. We might have to take him into town for more help later if he appears to need it. Charlie, let me have my flask now, if you would."

"Can't do it, Doc. You need a clear head if you're going to keep a sharp enough eye on the general there."

"That's why I need my flask. To keep my head clear."

"Can't help you on that, Doctor. You're drunk enough already."

"Drunk? I ain't drunk."

Charlie said, "Yeah, and I got nary a hair on my hind end."

McSwain, a man with a strong sense of propriety, winced at Charlie Gibbons's crudity.

"I want my flask. It's a good one . . . real silver," said the doctor.

163

"Ain't got it, even if I wanted to give it to you. A fellow come by a minute ago and slipped it right out of my hand." In fact he'd given the flask to the man just to be rid of it, seeing the doctor had imbibed more than he should have already.

"You're lying!"

"I ain't."

A hundred feet away, seated on his haunches while watching a woman cooking stew in a kettle over one of the many cook fires burning around the camp, Ben Scarlett took a swig from his new flask and blessed his good luck. He'd been aching for a drink for hours, and considering a trip into the heart of town in search of a saloon, but this unexpected turn of fortune would make that unnecessary. There was enough liquor in the slender flask to do him. He drained off another swallow and said a quick prayer that this kind of luck would continue for him when finally he reached California and began looking for gold.

If ever they made it. It had seemed a very long trail so far from Knoxville, and by far the longest and hardest part of the journey hadn't even commenced.

For one man, though, the journey was finished. The next morning, Wilberforce Sadler stood on a cask before his assembled travelers and announced that General Gordon Lloyd, after a life of service to his nation and his fellow citizens, had quietly passed away in the night after suffering an apparent failure of the heart. He would be buried for the time being beside a nearby brook; his relatives would be sent word of his passing and the location of his grave so they could disinter his remains for burial in their family cemetery in Kentucky.

"We have lost a friend but can take comfort in the fact that he is now in heaven," Wilberforce intoned.

"Nah," said a man in the crowd. "No way he's there yet. He's somewhere dragging his feet. Somebody probably told him there was cholera there. Give him a few months, he might make it within view of the pearly gates."

FROM THE JOURNAL OF CROZIER BELLINGHAM
SEPTEMBER 8, 1849
The death of General Lloyd some days back brought grief to our band, despite his admittedly annoying slowness, because of the great respect in which he was held because of his military achievements. Yet it also brought hope that we would see a speeding of our progress. It is now clear

that we are hopelessly behind and will not likely make up much of our lost time.

I believe the one most disturbed by this is Wilberforce Sadler, being a man of great pride who was most vocal in the early stages in declaring our passage to be assured of record speed and the "advantages" of having General Lloyd at our head. He has spoken to me many times in recent days about how to present, in my reports, "clarifying reasons" for our obvious failure to achieve the speed of travel we claimed would mark our progress. I am making no argument with his ongoing censorship and distortion of my reports. They are for his own newspaper, after all, and the writing that I am truly interested in is work over which he can exercise no control: my novel of the gold fields. I have told only Jedd Colter and Zebulon Mc-Swain of my planned work of fiction.

Zebulon McSwain is a man of mystery and oddity. Seemingly disgraced, driven out of his distinguished and lauded position in Knoxville higher education . . . and apparently hiding from some threat, some danger, that he declines to explain. I wonder if the man has at some level lost his mind. He keeps himself almost entirely apart from his fellow travelers, hiding away most of the time in a wagon, to be hauled along therein like a piece of luggage, rather than taking a turn at driving, or sometimes opting to ride or walk, as most others do in order to make their activities diverse and more interesting. Strangest of all to me is that, at most times, he keeps clutched in his arms the stuffed remains of a cat, apparently a much-loved former pet that has now gone on to whatever glory awaits felines, if any. What causes such odd behavior in an educated and long-respected man? And what sin did he commit to cause his ignoble removal from the now-defunct Bledsoe College? I hope to learn answers to these questions over time, for the benefit of characterizations within my future novel of the "Gold Rush," as some have taken to calling our national phenomenon.

That is as good and accurate a descriptor, I suppose, as any other one might conceive. Though our slow-as-a-tortoise pace, thanks mostly to the late general, certainly does not cohere with the notion of a "rush." At the pace we are keeping, and sometimes losing, California may be no more than a myth of the ancients, like Plato's Atlantis, by the time we reach it.

It is late now, and I put away my pencil

to take to my blankets. We are at Council Grove — so far, so very far, still to go.

California, where are you? And why are the miles west of the Mississippi so long?

CHAPTER THIRTEEN

Repair problems with some of the wagons brought the familiar specter of delay to call upon the California Enterprise Company of East Tennessee again even without General Lloyd to cause it, leaving them essentially stranded and "thumb-twiddling," as Witherspoon Sadler enjoyed saying to all around him. He seemed to find great humor in the phrase, unoriginal as it was, and declared himself the "second-place best thumb twiddler" in the camp, giving the first-place title to Zeb McSwain, who contributed very little to the overall migration. McSwain, who remained so perpetually hidden that some in the party had yet to lay eyes on him, was perceived by most who did know him as a classic example of a starry-eyed academic, out of touch with the "real" world around him that grittier and earthy folk had to live in. He was a freeloader and a tagalong, and the fact that Wilberforce Sadler was open in his disdain for the man did nothing to help the way McSwain was perceived.

Jedd was troubled by McSwain on several levels. He was ever mindful of McSwain's support for him in the matter of the beloved-but-lost Emma, and pitied him for the loss of status he had suffered. But such was life. If McSwain had suffered loss, it was only because, in an earlier day, he had lived on the other side of the fence as a man who gained much through his life and work. McSwain, at least, had had something of value to lose. Some went through life never possessing anything worth having, like old Ben Scarlett, who seemed to be trying to be the first man to cross the nation in a state of endless intoxication.

By the time the wagon train truly got on the move again, a few things had changed besides the death of General Lloyd. With the support of the Sadler brothers, Jedd had begun obtaining mules to take the place of several dray horses, knowing that mules would endure better once the mountains were reached. The mountains seemed far away to most. The plains were endless, flat yet with a vague upward pitch that made the travelers feel they were moving up a shallow, eternal rampway leading to nowhere. It was a tricky adjustment for those accustomed to hillier terrain. Nothing to do but endure it and go on.

"Don't fret," Jedd counseled his charges. "Before we're done you'll wish it was all this easy."

As progress continued, some matters improved. Game became more available, and Jedd, Treemont, and a few other hunters kept busy supplying the camp with meat, wild turkeys for the most part, but later, buffalo and other bigger game. On evenings when the atmosphere in the camp was rich with the heady scent of sizzling buffalo steaks, spirits were high.

The process of meal delivery had changed. O'Keefe, the former restaurant chef, had decided that life as a camp cook was not for him, and had abandoned the enterprise, much to Wilberforce Sadler's disgust (Wilberforce ordered Bellingham to report O'Keefe's desertion in the sternest terms possible, so that his name would be sullied among those he knew back in Knoxville). Had he known of it, O'Keefe would hardly have cared. He was now the new head chef in one of the best eateries in St. Joseph. Without a single main cook, the travelers were divided into "mess groups" — groups who cooked and shared meals together, each group tending to its own needs and making sure supplies were sufficient. Ferkus Varney, because of his clerking talents and organizational skills, was given oversight and told to look for problems, conflicts, shortages, and the like, in the area of food supply, preparation, and sharing. Rachel McCall, who still admired Jedd Colter while Witherspoon Sadler hopelessly admired her, was assigned to help Varney in the food supply area. It was a sensible assignment, Rachel having joined Jedd's party of hunters who kept the camp in meat. Jedd had figured she had volunteered her services as a way of getting close to him, but she surprised him by proving to be the most able hunter, besides Jedd himself, in the group. She could outshoot Treemont on his finest day, and had been the first hunter from the wagon train to bring down a buffalo. And she proved a capable liaison between the hunters and the cooks of the camp.

Jedd was actually beginning to think he might be able to like the rugged Rachel after all. But liking her was a far cry from loving her. His love was still attached to another, the faraway, married, and out-of-reach Emma.

When Jedd discovered accidentally that three of his scouts and hunters were unable to read, a notion came to his mind that wound up being at least the partial salvation of Zeb McSwain. He talked to McSwain about it while the man sat in the back of his wagon, scratching his dead, stuffed cat behind the ears as he had done while it was still alive.

"Zeb, please, please . . . put that cat down and quit doing that. You're making folks here believe you're downright lunatic, acting like that with that blasted dead critter," Jedd told him.

McSwain looked sorrowful, sighed, and put the preserved animal aside. "I know. It's a habit, I guess, something to keep my hands busy, and to keep me in touch with better times from my past."

"It's a dead cat, Zeb, that's what it is. I know it's Cicero, and I know you cared a lot about that animal. But it remains a dead cat, and you can't pat and scratch on a dead cat without making folks think you've gone out of your head."

"Do you think I'm out of my head, Jedd?"

"Not really. But I got to admit that watching you with Cicero like that makes me . . . nervous, I guess. On edge. It ain't natural."

McSwain drew in a long, slow breath and resettled himself. He glanced over to where he had just placed the stuffed cat, but he did not reach for it. He gave Jedd a forced smile. "And what is this idea you wanted to talk to me about?"

"Well, Zeb, it's simple. I'd like you to consider setting up some classes to help some of the folk in this group learn to read. There's a goodly number who can't, and you'd be a prime fellow to teach them."

McSwain said nothing at first but stared out the back of the wagon, thinking hard.

After a while, Jedd asked, "What are you pondering so?"

"Just wondering if I'd be able to do it."

"You were a professor for years. Even while being president of that college, you were still teaching."

"Teaching adults who already had the basics of an education. It's very different, teaching something so basic as reading. You'd probably have better luck rounding up a former schoolmarm or schoolmaster out among the people there."

"Ain't got a former schoolmarm or school-master amongst us. Just a former professor and college president." Jedd paused, then added with a smile, "One who sits around scratching the ears of his dead cat in the back of an emigrant wagon."

McSwain looked unsettled, fidgeted, then shrugged and laughed. "When you put it that way, it makes me think that maybe there is indeed some way I could better spend my time."

"Think what you could do for somebody, teaching him to read. He could read all the great books. He could read his Bible. He could read a dictionary or 'cyclopeeder or whatever that word is, and keep on learning more and more. You could give that to folks, Zeb, and you could even do it while you were panning gold most of the time, if you've truly got the notion of that."

McSwain mulled a minute or so more, then glanced toward his luggage and moved as if to dig something out of it. Jedd sat up straighter. "If you're about to start cat-scratching again, time for me to go."

McSwain chuckled. "Sit tight. No cat this time." Then he reached behind a small trunk and pulled out a bottle. He held it up with a smile. "Wine. Good wine. I refused to leave for California without it. I'd like us to have a glass in honor of your brilliant idea."

"I'd be pleased. Does this mean you're thinking of . . ."

"It means I'm saying yes. I may prove to be the least effective reading teacher ever born, but I'll certainly give it my best try."

"Obliged to you. Touched, even."

From elsewhere in the bundles and boxes, McSwain produced a couple of mugs. Jedd worked on the cork in the wine bottle and managed to somehow get it out. They poured and drank, then repeated the process.

Jedd laughed, and McSwain asked him what had amused him.

"Oh," Jedd answered, "just imagining Ben Scarlett out there somewhere in the camp with his nostrils twitching, knowing that somebody's hid out somewhere, having some wine without him being there."

McSwain laughed, too. "Do you suppose Ben can read?"

"Believe it or not, he can. I've seen him do it. Stood and read a newspaper once that old storekeeper Baumgardner back in Knoxville had pinned up outside his store, so I know it wasn't just like a sign he'd memorized. He was reading."

McSwain sipped from his mug, hesitated, and looked solemn. "I despise asking this, but I just realized I don't really know if, if you . . ."

Jedd smiled. "Yes, I can read. And I ain't offended by the question, for there's plenty of good folks who can't. Treemont can just barely work his way through a printed sentence, if it's simple, and there's many others who can't do even that."

McSwain nodded and raised his mug. "To the rolling Zebulon McSwain Academy of Literacy."

"Hear, hear!" The men clicked their mugs together and drank. Just then someone stuck his head in the back of the wagon.

"What you gentlemen up to?" asked Ben Scarlett, nostrils moving as he caught the smell of wine.

"Come on in, Ben," McSwain said. "Let me see if I can find us a third cup."

Five days later, Jedd Colter awakened to the smell of frying bacon, sat up, and saw Crozier Bellingham kneeling over an iron skillet heated over a well-tended fire. The bacon was in the skillet, and given the way Bellingham was hovering in the smoke, Jedd figured he'd smell like bacon for days.

At the moment the smell of bacon was the finest scent Jedd could have asked for. He climbed out of his bedroll and made his way over to the young journalist-turned-cook. "Fine-smelling meat you got frying there, Crozier."

"I was counting on the smell of it waking you up," Bellingham said. "I wanted to be sure you had some of it."

"Well! What provokes this burst of concern

for my well-being?"

"I'm a good man, I guess."

"Crozier, you ain't a man at all. You're a child. A mere child."

"Bah!"

"Really, though, is there something you need from me?"

"I just wanted to tell you something. Something that happened to me and Ben Scarlett."

"Ben Scarlett? You running about with him now?"

"I could do worse. He's got a good soul in him."

"I know what you mean. So, what happened to you and Ben that I'd need to know about?"

"Remember what you said once about that funnel idea of yours? The 'narrowing of the funnel,' I think you said?"

"I remember. Why?"

"I'm beginning to think there's something to it."

"I know there is. I've seen it happen too many times . . . people running into one another out here on these western trails and in these western towns. These places where the funnel is narrow. Folks you'd never think would have a chance of running into each other by accident. Funnel them all into one direction, onto one or two routes, and it's going to happen, though. Can't help happening. Have you run across somebody you know?"

"Well, not exactly. We did run across somebody, Ben and I, while we were out fishing yesterday — remember that little creek? But we didn't know him and he didn't know us. He knew you."

"Me? Did he ask after me?"

"He did. He asked if we were part of the emigrant train that had come out of Knoxville. I didn't trust this fellow and was inclined not to answer him, but Ben Scarlett is so kind and trusting toward folks that he just said yes, we were. This fellow, kind of a big, ugly, turtle-mouthed gent with brown hair all curly like it should have been growing down inside his trousers, know what I mean, 'stead of on his head, he grinned big and said he'd heard that an old friend of his, Jedd Colter, was piloting our group. Well, like the first time, I didn't want to speak, but Ben bobbed his head up and down and said, 'Yep, Jedd Colter is with us, sure 'nough!' And it was like a cold wind blew across that man's face, though he tried to hide it behind a big grin."

"I'm feeling a bit of a cold wind myself," Jedd said. "It hit me the moment you described him. Did he say what his name was?"

Bellingham nodded. "You ever heard of a man named Jake Carney?"

Jedd said nothing, just sat unmoving, staring at the skillet of bacon that no longer held any appeal, and his silence said more than any words he might have spoken.

"I'm sorry, Jedd," Bellingham said. "We should have kept our mouths shut, not knowing who this man was or what he wanted with you. Though I do want to point out it was Ben, and not I, who gave it all away. But he didn't mean any harm. . . . Ben never does. And I still don't know who this Jake Carney is, or what he wants with you. But I could tell that, whatever it is, it isn't good."

Jedd looked woefully at Bellingham. The previously bright morning around and above him suddenly seemed darker, brooding, oppressive. "No, Crozier, it isn't good. But it didn't seem to matter much before. I didn't think I'd ever run across him again, or him me."

Bellingham smiled bitterly and said, "The narrowing of the funnel, eh?"

Jedd nodded. "The damned funnel."

A stranger with an odd, backwoods way of

talking showed up in camp that night, asking after his old friend Jedd Colter. Jedd was quietly snoring in his blankets at the time, near his dying fire at the edge of camp. The newcomer had ridden close by him without seeing who he was.

Witherspoon Sadler happened to be the man who approached the stranger. What had attracted Witherspoon was the man's hat, a common-variety flop hat that somehow had a cocky aspect to it that made Withers confident it would nicely set off his buckskin outfit, which he wore mostly when he knew he'd be close to Rachel McCall. He was quite sure she was impressed with the sight of him in his rustic garb — he'd seen her looking quickly away a few times when he'd glanced over at her, and had known she'd been eyeing him on the sneak. What he hadn't seen was the half-hidden smile of mirth on her face when she turned away from him.

Rachel didn't dislike Witherspoon; she considered him a kind and gentle man, different and better than many she had known who tried to impress her with their grit and ruggedness. Of course Witherspoon was, in his own mind, trying to appear gritty and rugged, too, but was unknowingly doing it so ineptly that she could only find it funny.

When she was a little girl, Rachel's only real toy had been a straw-stuffed, furred creature she childishly called Aminal, something her mother had stitched together for her from a couple of old beaver pelts. Exactly what species of beast Aminal was intended to represent had not been evident from its appearance, but to Rachel's mind it had been a fat, lovable woodchuck. Now Rachel was grown and Aminal was long gone, but when she took an amused glance at Witherspoon Sadler in his unflattering buckskin garb, it was as if her childhood companion had come back, full-sized and transformed into a man. In the privacy of her thoughts, Rachel thought of Witherspoon as Aminal, and prayed constantly that she would never slip up and call him by that name out loud.

"Good evening, sir," Witherspoon said to the man who had entered their camp. "I'm told you're asking after someone."

"I'm looking for Jedd Colter. I hear he's the guide and pilot for this group?"

"If he is, could I tell him who is calling?"

"An old friend. I'd rather surprise him than give him my name right off, though. He'll know me when he sees me."

Witherspoon was a trusting man by nature, but if his more worldly-wise brother had exerted any worthwhile influence upon him, it was in teaching him not to be so ready to assume the best regarding strangers. Witherspoon pondered that he didn't know this man or what he wanted with Jedd Colter, and his inclination was not to immediately bring the two of them together. Especially in that he knew Jedd was sleeping in anticipation of an upcoming predawn guard shift for the camp. It wouldn't be right to disturb his rest without at least knowing there was good reason. And that this stranger was not dangerous.

Witherspoon did not give an answer right away, and the stranger gave him an intimidating look . . . not hard to achieve with the timid Witherspoon.

"Tell you what," Witherspoon said. "Jedd is sleeping right now because he has to be up for guard duty late in the night, but we'll go sit nearby so we'll know when he wakes up."

"Guess that'll have to be good enough," the man said.

"What's your name, sir?" Witherspoon asked.

"I'm Rand Blalock, from North Carolina. I knew Jedd when he was a boy and I was sheriff in the county he was born in, there in the mountain end of the state."

"I'd guess he'll be glad to see you."

"He will. We go back a long way, Jedd and me."

CHAPTER FOURTEEN

Jedd dreamed, and in his mind he was back in North Carolina again, rifle in hand, knife in sheath, powder horn and "possibles" bag strapped across shoulder. At his side was his father, alive and strong and just as he had looked in Jedd's youth. They strode together across a familiar ridge, hunting deer.

In the dream they were not alone. With them was Rand Blalock, the local sheriff, longtime family friend, and frequent hunting companion of the Colters. As usual, Blalock was talking too much and walking too heavily and loudly, annoying his companions. When Jedd's father would ask him to be a little quieter, Blalock would take obvious offense and reduce his talk to a mumble that made him hard to understand yet still carried farther and more loudly than it should. He had one of those voices.

Then it seemed to Jedd he heard another

185

voice besides Blalock's, and it wasn't Treemont's. Yet it was familiar, but it didn't belong in a dream of North Carolina.

At length Jedd awakened and sat up. The first thing he noticed was that Sheriff Blalock really, and amazingly, was present, seated on the ground near the smoldering fire that was now reduced to red-glowing coals. And he saw the origin of that second voice: Witherspoon Sadler, seated in a rotund heap nearby Blalock.

Blalock looked much older than the version of himself Jedd had tracked along with through the Carolina woods. Jedd realized that he'd been dreaming about Blalock because he had been hearing the real man's voice through the veil of sleep. And he'd heard Witherspoon's voice likewise.

The oddity of the situation hit and he frowned at Blalock. What was he doing here? When had he showed up?

"Howdy, Jedd," Blalock said. "You're looking fine. Last I seen you, you was yet a boy."

Jedd lithely rose from his sleeping place and advanced to Blalock, hand outthrust. "And you're looking fine, too, Sheriff! Where'd you come from?"

"First off, I'm sheriff no longer and ain't been for a long time. And I came into your camp tonight because I'd heard you were part of this band of argonauts. I hoped I'd find you, and I have."

Jedd, shaking off drowsiness very quickly, grinned widely. "Glad you did! You heading to California to get your share of the gold along with nigh every other man in the nation?"

"Not me. Too old for such foolishness."

"Well, I sure hope California gold ain't foolishness, for that's where we're heading, and gold's what everybody's after."

"No foolishness in it for the young. But it's not an old man's venture. Only one thing could take me all the way to California, and it ain't gold."

Witherspoon rose, trying his best to spring up as easily and spryly as had Jedd. He staggered and wobbled and might have stepped right into the remnants of the fire had not Blalock grabbed his shoulder and pulled him back.

"Blast!" Witherspoon exclaimed, embarrassed. He looked around quickly and Jedd knew he was making sure Rachel McCall hadn't been close by to see him playing the stumblebum.

"Just relax, friend," said Blalock. "Nothing to be nervous about here. You'll find me an easy kind of man."

"You'll find me a clumsy one," Wither-spoon muttered.

"Sheriff, what brought you here if you're not going to California?" Jedd asked. He knew the "sheriff" designation was not now accurate, but he'd grown up knowing Blalock by his then title, and there would be no way to shake himself of it now.

"I'd come to Knoxville looking for you," Blalock replied. "That was how I learned you'd gone off with this here group. I followed even though I figured there was little point in it with the head start you folks had on me."

"Well, us folks have had a lot of delays, too," Jedd said. "We were under the leadership of General Gordon Lloyd, and he proved to be a very slow-moving, slow-acting fellow. He's passed on now, sorry to say. But it will probably help us go faster."

"I heard he'd died. Too bad, that."

"He was a good man. Just slow. But why were you looking for me in Knoxville? I been gone from there for several years. For that matter, why were you looking for me at all, anywhere?"

"I went to Knoxville because it was the last place I knew you to be. I didn't know you'd gone off west."

"Well, I went back when the whole matter

of piloting for the Sadler group came up. And I had a private reason to go back, too. But why did you need to find me?"

Blalock's face, which always had possessed a sorrowful look, in Jedd's judgment, because of Blalock's drooping eyes, looked even more sad than usual all at once. Blalock sighed loudly and slowly. "Jedd, I come bearing some sad news."

Jedd felt a cold dread crawl over him. "What is it, Sheriff?"

Blalock's eyes shifted quickly. "Jedd, is Treemont Dalton still running with you?"

"He is. He's part of this very same group."

Blalock winced. "I'm right glad he ain't right here with us at the moment, for there's bad news about his people."

Jedd swallowed. "Tell me."

"You remember Tree's cousin Carver?"

"Surely do. Why?"

"He's dead, Jedd. Murdered. Flat-out butchered. And not just him, his family, too. Wife, children, all of them."

"Good God! What happened?"

"It ain't fully known just what happened because there was no one who saw it. No one left alive, anyway."

"Who did it?"

"Seems to have been done by somebody who came through and stayed with the family a few days. Nobody in the area knew him, and nobody knows why he was there. He might have been kin of Carver's wife. His name was John Collier. Ever heard Treemont mention that name?"

Jedd thought it over and shook his head. "Not ringing any bells with me. Was Carver's wife a Collier before she married?"

"No. Beth was a Bradburn. But she could have been kin to some Colliers. Hell, they're both kin to my people, you know that? The Blalocks have ties to the Daltons and Bradburns both."

"Why would this Collier have to be kin to the family at all? Maybe it was just somebody they knew."

"Could be. But folks who talked to the current sheriff, Jim Campbell, said they had it in their heads from somewhere that this Collier visitor was kinfolk with the family on Beth's side. So somebody must have been told that along the way, by Beth or Carver or one of the children."

"Any notion at all why this Collier would have done this?"

"Not a bit. They were found outside the house, laid out in a line, all seven of them. Shot in the back of the head, every one of them. No blood in the house, so somehow he — or whoever did it — had gotten them all outside. Or maybe they were killed here and there and dragged to the same place and laid out in a line. Apart from being shot like they were, the corpses were left in decent condition. Except for Carver."

"What was different with him?"

"He was chopped up. No other way to describe it. Cut into pieces — arms and legs hacked off, feet cut off at the ankles, hands cut at the wrists, head severed — but then the pieces were all laid out in place, like he was whole. Strangest thing I ever saw. But the fact that Carver's remains were treated so much worse makes me figure that motive for it all might have had something to do with him more than the others."

"You saw it yourself, then."

"I did. I ain't been sheriff for a long time now, but I still held a deputy status up until a short while ago and happened to be in town when the boy who'd found them rode in and gave word. I went out with Sheriff Campbell to the house. It was hard on him, real hard. There was a time, you see, when he'd courted Beth Bradburn himself. Carver Dalton asked her for her hand first, though, and she said yes. Broke poor Jim Campbell's heart clean in two that she married somebody else. And he sobbed like a child when he saw Beth lying there dead with that flyblown hole in the back of her head. 'She should have married me,' he said to me. 'If she'd married me, she'd not have been here for this to happen to her.' That's what Jim Campell said. 'Should have married me.' "

"I know some of what he went through," Jedd said. "I was set to marry a gal name of Emma McSwain, daughter of the president of a college in Knoxville. She cut me loose, though. Didn't even have a marriage offer from anybody else when she did it, either. She decided I was too poor, too broke, to be a husband for her. She ended up marrying a man named Stanley Wickham, and from all I've heard, he's naught but a sorry bastard. Treats her hard and mean. Unfaithful, too. But he had a bit of money, so if money was what she wanted, I reckon she should be happy."

"She still in Knoxville?"

"No, sir. California. He took her there."

"Well . . . and now you're going there. Reckon you'll see her?"

"I reckon so."

"Well, Jedd, I got to tell you that this fellow who killed the Dalton family, the story is that he's gone to California, too. Or maybe just on his way. Whether by land or sea, I don't know. That's what led me to hunt you down. I wanted you to know what had happened before Treemont did — and I wanted to tell you that there's a damned good reward up for the capture or killing of this John Collier."

"I'm no manhunter, Sheriff Blalock."

"I know that. But I got a feeling a good friend of yours might decide that he's going to do some manhunting, once he knows what was done to his kin."

"You're talking about Treemont."

"Of course."

Jedd thought it over and saw that Blalock was right. Treemont was devoted to his kin, and he'd been particularly close to his cousin Carver Dalton. When he wasn't out hunting with Jedd, he was fishing or trapping with Carver. Tree had shared space at the table of Carver and Beth Dalton. He'd be devastated when he learned what had happened to them. And probably bent on vengeance. That would be Treemont's way.

Jedd looked seriously at Blalock. "I don't think Tree should be told right off that Collier might be in California. I'm afraid he might spend all his time, once he gets there, trying to hunt the man down and call him to account."

Blalock merely nodded.

Witherspoon had been sitting by listening quietly to all that was said. He made a strange "urp" noise in his throat and drew the attention of the other two. Witherspoon swallowed hard and said, "He was cut to pieces and then laid back together, like puzzle pieces?"

Blalock nodded. "That's a fact. But I failed to mention that his arms had been switched, and his legs laid back in place upside down, so that he was lying on his back but his feet were pointing downward. And his privates had been cut off and shoved into the hole in the back of his head. Horrible thing to see. Horrible."

Witherspoon tried to speak, but merely achieved making that strange noise in his throat again. He came to his feet much faster this time, not stumbling like before, and rushed off behind the nearest wagon, from whence the sound of his retching could be clearly heard.

"Not a man of strong stomach," Jedd said to Blalock.

"No. Evidently not. I can't much blame him, though. I nigh did the same thing when I first saw that family lined up dead."

The call of a familiar voice came across the camp, and Jedd looked up to see Treemont heading toward him and Blalock. Tree wore a big smile and bounced along cheerily. When he saw Blalock he froze and stared, then laughed aloud. "Sheriff? Is that you?"

Blalock stood and grinned back falteringly. "It's me, Treemont! How are you, boy?" Then, quietly side-speaking to Jedd, he whispered, "You'd best tell him, Jedd. He'll take it better from you than from a plain-spoke old son of a gun like me."

Jedd wasn't so sure, but there was no time to do anything but quickly nod. Treemont came up and wrapped his arms around Blalock and gave him a firm hug. Blalock looked at Jedd over Treemont's shoulder, the expression on his face that of a man ready to flee.

CHAPTER FIFTEEN

At the age of fifteen, Squire Hale Napier of Philadelphia already felt like a seasoned adult. His father had died three years earlier, and after that the boy had been frequently forced to serve as the functioning head of the family. His mother, though devoted to her brood and capable domestically, was intensely shy and easily overwhelmed by difficult situations. Squire, though, had his birth father's natural strength, self-possession, and mental dexterity.

It hadn't been easy for Squire to adjust to his mother's second marriage two years ago. Under the circumstances, he didn't mind the idea of his mother being the wife of someone other than his father, but he did wish she had married someone less like herself. Squire's stepfather, Joe Napier, was a good man, but he was even more timid than his wife. More timid than Ferkus

Varney or Witherspoon Sadler, neither of whom Squire or any of the Napiers had ever had occasion to meet or hear of.

The California-bound Napier family, though at the moment encamped immediately adjacent to the site occupied by the California Enterprise Company of East Tennessee, were part of an entirely different and smaller band of travelers, one that had come out of Pennsylvania. None of the Napiers had ever set foot on any terrain farther south than northern Kentucky, so the Sadler group was composed purely of strangers to them.

Squire was moving among the Tennesseans just now, however, having drifted over from the Pennsylvanian encampment with a distinct and secret purpose in mind. He drifted silently between the campfires and wagons, scanning the Sadler camp closely, searching.

Exactly what he was looking for he could not have said, but he would know when he saw it. Then, Lord willing, he'd be able to get his hands on it and take it to the one who needed it.

It wouldn't be so bad, would it, to steal something that would maybe bring comfort to an ailing little girl, a child so sick it appeared unlikely she would live to reach

California? Did not Squire's little sister at least have the right to die with some sort of cheering personal possession in her hands? Winnie loved dolls, tops, carved gadgets — any kind of plaything — had since she was very small, but all of hers had been lost or left behind when the move westward began. Squire was determined to find her a toy or two. Something to distract Winnie from her deteriorating physical condition. The little girl was in such a dejected mental state of late that she spent more time talking about her wish to be buried by a roadside, where there was life and movement and activity, than of any hope of recovering and enjoying life and movement and activity for herself.

Her family had higher hopes. The Napiers believed that, if they could reach California, the climate could bring health to their declining little one. That prospect was, to them, far more attractive than any gold could be.

If they could reach California . . . that was the key. But to do that, Squire believed, the girl would have to regain her determination to hang on and live. Anything she could have that would make life more pleasant for her would go far toward giving her that determination.

Squire moved through the camp, so quiet

and careful that hardly anyone noticed him. And he searched.

When rain came, those who usually slept beneath the sky found themselves scrambling for cover, inside the wagons or beneath them, beneath improvised tents, within any available natural shelter or random shed or abandoned structure that might chance to be handy.

This rain had come with little warning, and Ben Scarlett had been sufficiently in his cups to not notice it at all until he was half drenched. He then made a zigzagging, stumbling line for the wagon nearest him, which happened to be the one in which Zebulon McSwain spent most of his time hidden away. McSwain was not in his wagon at the moment, though, having taken a stroll into the nearby camp of the Pennsylvanians, and where he had fallen into conversation with a trio of strangers.

Caught by the storm away from his own camp, McSwain had accepted an invitation to wait out the weather in a roomy tent with his new friends. Because friends had been hard for him to claim in recent times, he was glad to be where he was. These people knew nothing of him, of Knoxville, or Bledsoe College and his ignoble ouster therefrom. In the company of these northern folk, he found a foretaste of what he hoped California would be for him . . . freshness, newness, a place and chance to start new without being surrounded by prejudgments and preconceptions regarding him. As he told the Pennsylvanians about himself, he lied freely, knowing they could not know the difference. He became a successful Knoxville merchant rather than a disgraced former collegiate leader. They nodded acceptingly, having no reason to disbelieve anything he told them.

One camp over, as Ben Scarlett was clambering with some difficulty into the back of McSwain's wagon, he was suddenly bumped backward as another person exited the same vehicle. Ben tilted back and fell to the ground, landing on his rump as the one who had collided with him took a jump across him and darted away, heels slinging mud. Pratfallen, Ben quirked his head and looked after the fleeing figure of Squire Hale Napier.

A boy. Just a youth, one Ben did not believe he'd seen before. The boy had something clutched in his arms that Ben did not clearly see and couldn't identify. He ran in the direction of the adjacent camp where Ben knew those northerners were.

"You could have took a moment of your time to help a poor old drunk get out of the rain, son," Ben muttered. Then he pulled himself to his feet and managed to climb back up and roll in beneath the sheltering wagon cover. He quietly called the name of McSwain but got no reply. Evidently McSwain was elsewhere.

Ben found a comfortable place and sat looking out the loosely cinched, horse-collar-shaped rear opening of the wagon cover, listening to the drops pelting above him, and, after a few minutes, swigging from his new flask, which was at the moment still half-filled. A little while later, he was leaned back against the side of the wagon, sleeping to the lulling music of the rain.

Treemont took it hard.

Jedd struggled for ten minutes, trying to find a way to work his way into the bad news Blalock had brought. There was no way to do it. All Jedd could do in the end was grasp Treemont by his shoulders, look in his eyes, and say, "Tree, listen to me: your cousin Carver has been murdered, and all his family, by a man name of John Collier." Tree had gaped at Jedd, then the tears came. They heightened as Jedd gave him more details, which he somewhat sanitized, because Jedd found the description of the mutilation so hard to inflict upon his friend.

"I have to find Collier and make him pay," Treemont said.

"You can't change the fact they're dead," Jedd said. "I want to see this Collier brought to justice, too. But nothing you can do with him or to him will do a thing for Carver and his family."

"It'll avenge them. And it'll sure as hell blazes make me feel better," replied Treemont. Jedd knew better than to argue with him.

Treemont then insisted that Blalock give him a more detailed description of the whole sordid matter than Jedd had presented, including the condition of the bodies and Blalock's assessment of how much suffering was or was not involved. Jedd suffered through the repeated account and wished Treemont would try to turn his thoughts to other matters for now. It wouldn't happen. Jedd knew Treemont too well to expect it would.

CHAPTER SIXTEEN

Zeb McSwain threw back his head and laughed heartily at a joke just told by one of his new Pennsylvanian friends. He'd not laughed so freely in the longest time, and it was like a cleansing in his soul. Hope for his future grew inside like a swelling light. It could be like this, the way it was now. He could start over and find a good life again.

Feeling invigorated, he stood and walked to the opening of the rain-pounded tent. There was little to see outside but campfires steaming in the rain that had extinguished them and other people peeping out of tents and wagons of their own. McSwain wondered if the rain would let up soon. If not, he was perfectly prepared to spend the night here in this neighboring emigrant camp, and return to his own camp and wagon in the morning. As long as no one bothered his most important possession hidden in his wagon, it wouldn't make any real difference where he slept tonight.

He wished then that he'd brought that item with him when he came over here. He could keep guard on it then and not have to worry and wonder. On the other hand, he'd probably have risked making these new acquaintances look askance at him as a strange fellow. Seeing a grown man clinging to a dead, stuffed cat like a treasure would probably have been off-putting to them, as it had to Jedd.

If only Jedd knew. Then he'd understand. But Jedd could not know. No one could.

Continuing to stare out into the rain, Mc-Swain thought back to his fine house in Knoxville, unoccupied now. He wondered if the man Ben Scarlett had caught nosing around the place with a gun in hand had returned there since. He smiled privately to think of the fellow's disappointment, finding his prey completely absent.

Would he pursue? McSwain allowed himself to doubt it. Surely there was not sufficient motivation for *that*!

Or was there? Anytime significant money was involved, one never knew just how far things might go.

Here in this tent on a rainy plains night, however, it was easy to feel safe. He would not be followed, not be found. Not be hurt.

Or worse.

McSwain turned his thoughts away from the past and its pursuing demons, and aimed them forward and westward. To California. What would he find there? What kind of life would he make for himself? Would he find himself someday back in the world of academia, or would he actually attain success in the gritty world of mining? Could such a denizen of classroom and library as he hope to find in himself the capability of pursuing such an earthy line of work?

Others were doing it. The conventional wisdom had it that almost no one was, in California, what they had been in their original haunts and old lives. Everything changed. The world was washed so clean that even personal histories were scoured away. McSwain found himself mouthing a biblical passage but with a secularized twist: "Old things are passed away; all things are become new."

What of Emma? Would he find his daughter easily? How would she receive him? Would he be welcome in her present world? Might she see him as an agent of needed and welcome change for herself? A catalyst to break away from the man she had had the bad judgment to marry and now knew for what he really was?

McSwain hoped she would. He had no regard whatsoever for Emma's husband, his own son-in-law. Stanley Wickham would lead Emma to ruin if she stayed with him long enough; of that McSwain was quite sure. It was something known by intuition rather than reason, and normally McSwain prided himself on being a reason-centered man. Even so he had no doubt he was right in his negative judgment of his daughter's husband.

He hoped she would break away from the wretch. If, upon reaching California and finding her, he could help her achieve that, McSwain was ready to do so. He'd kill the son of a bitch if he had to.

And with that thought, McSwain realized that he was already transforming into a very different man than he had been. He'd never before seriously thought of killing another man as something he could actually do. It was a little frightening, but also cathartic.

Just then he saw someone moving through the rain and heading toward the very tent in which he stood. It appeared to be a youth, a boy, and as he grew nearer McSwain saw that the lad clutched something close to his chest, shielding it from the rain. And it looked as if it might be. . . .

Oh, dear God. Oh, Lord above . . . it *was*. The young fellow, who was coming from the direction of the Sadler camp, had in his arms McSwain's most important possession: the preserved remains of the feline companion he'd called Cicero.

Without a moment's hesitation, McSwain bolted out of the tent and into the rain, heading for the young man, who himself was moving so swiftly that it took a few moments for him to realize he was being approached. When Squire Napier saw McSwain rushing toward him, he dug his heels into the ground . . . ground that was slick and sopping mud, and gave way under his momentum. Squire's feet went out from under him and he fell hard, sinking his rear into the sodden ground. As he threw his arms outward reflexively, he lost his hold on the preserved cat, which arced through the air. McSwain saw it, gave a yell, and threw his arms out to catch it. He did, but lost his own footing and went down face-first in the muck. He held the cat up as he fell, thus going down on his chest and knocking the wind out of his lungs. For several moments his lungs locked and he was unable to draw breath. When the paralysis broke, he gasped loudly, and groaned and rolled onto his side to begin to rise.

McSwain and Squire rose together and faced each other in the rain. They were watched by faces peering out of tents, especially the one from which McSwain had bolted.

"Is it yours?" Squire asked, eyeing the cat now held by McSwain.

McSwain nodded, still sucking hard for breath. "Yes," he managed to gasp. "It is mine. How . . . did you . . ."

"I don't deny I took it, sir. Not for me, but for my sister. She's little, and she's very sick, and she needs to have a toy, something to hold and play with and make her happy while she still has life in her."

"Not this," McSwain said, holding Cicero's stuffed and stiffened form even tighter to his chest. "It cannot be this particular thing."

"Please, sir. She has nothing to take her mind off what is happening to her."

McSwain said nothing. One of the men in the tent called out to the pair and told them to come in out of the rain. He referred to Squire as "son."

"Why, sir?" Squire asked McSwain. "I know I was crossing a line to steal it, but she's my own sister, just a sick little girl, and it's only a stuffed dead cat. You're a grown man! Why would you care about such a thing?"

"There are reasons you cannot possibly know."

"I'll pay you for it, sir. My father will pay you for it."

"You could in no way afford it."

"It's just a dead *cat*!"

"It's far more than that. You cannot know."

A small-framed man emerged from the tent where McSwain had taken refuge earlier. He grabbed the boy's shoulder, pulling him toward the tent. "Friend," the man said to McSwain, "I can't tell you what to do, but I'll not be having folks say that anyone with the last name of Napier doesn't have sense enough to come in out of the driving rain! Come on, Squire, son . . . get into the tent!"

"Yes, sir."

McSwain followed the Napiers into the tent and stood, dripping like a dog fresh from a splash in a farm pond. The senior Napier looked at McSwain nervously. "What is the problem, sir?" he asked. "And why are you holding that . . . thing?"

"I had it before, but I fell in the mud, dropped it, and he got it. I had found it in the next camp," Squire said. "I picked it up because I thought Winnie could play with it. It might make her feel better. Get her

209

mind off things."

"Sir," said McSwain, "this 'thing' is mine. If this boy 'found' it, he did it by digging around in my wagon, uninvited. I had put Cicero away there, stowed and hidden."

"Cicero?"

"That's the name of the cat. It was a pet of mine for years, very precious to me. Very important. And I must not let it be taken."

"Even though it's dead?"

The other men in the tent, listening to the exchange, chuckled among themselves and shared glances.

"It's a situation I can't fully explain. Suffice it to say, that cat belongs to me, and though I understand this boy's motivation in taking it, and even admire it, I cannot let Cicero be taken from me. Even for such a noble cause as brightening the spirits of an unfortunate young girl."

" 'Unfortunate,' " Joe Napier repeated. "Unfortunate indeed, sir. Let me let you meet someone, Mr. . . . Swain, was it?"

"McSwain."

"Sorry."

Napier motioned for Squire to follow and all but dragged McSwain out of the tent. He led the way through the rain to another, slightly smaller tent nearby. At the flap door he called in, alerting his wife that he was bringing in a visitor. The flap parted and a wan-looking woman whose face resembled Squire's peered back at them. She managed a weak smile at McSwain, who she assumed was some new friend of her husband's, being brought in out of hospitality. Then her eyes fell on the sodden, preserved animal corpse clutched in McSwain's hands, and she grew puzzled.

"We'll explain shortly, dear," Napier said, hustling the others into the tent and then following.

The experience shook McSwain. As he had guessed, the person Napier had brought him to meet was the little girl herself, and a more heartbreaking sight McSwain had never seen. The girl was sallow, sickly, her pale skin a grayish hue, her eyes listless and full of sorrow and the tracks of infirmity. The impression made at once upon Zeb McSwain was that little Winnie Napier was a girl destined for childhood death.

Even so, he forced out a smile and put a brighter tone in his voice as he met her. He introduced himself as a man from Tennessee who had come to meet her and wish her the best. The little girl smiled back, but it was clear that what drew her interest was not McSwain himself, but the unmoving cat he held. Winnie pointed a pale finger at the animal and asked in her thin voice if it was a doll.

"It's a cat that used to be my pet, but it isn't alive anymore. I had it preserved and stuffed so I could remember it as it looked in life. So I suppose, in a way, it is kind of a doll. Its name was Cicero."

The girl shook her head. "Cat," she said. "Its name is Cat."

McSwain realized the spot the Napiers had placed him in. Obviously they knew their own little girl well enough to know she would be drawn to the cat as a plaything, a toy. By having him bring it into her presence, they had caused her to focus upon the cat and begin to think of it, as children will, as something that was hers, or might become hers. The other side of the coin was that, in letting McSwain see with his own eyes the dreadful shape the girl was in, he was put into the place of looking like a hard and heartless man if he, an adult, chose to cling to such a seemingly meaningless item as a preserved dead cat while a dying young girl clearly wanted it.

At one level, the situation broke his heart because he knew the Napiers merely were doing what any parent would do, trying to brighten the life of a child who knew mostly grim darkness. On another level, he was infuriated, because the assumptions under which they acted were uninformed ones. It wasn't their fault that they did not know the true significance of this bit of fur and bone and stuffed hide, and that sentiment played only the most minor role in his protectiveness toward Cicero the cat.

Winnie held out her hands, asking without words to be allowed to hold the cat. McSwain looked uncomfortably at Mrs. Napier, who said, "Don't fear. . . . What she has does not spread to other people."

So McSwain placed the cat in the girl's hands and she pulled it to her chest, smiling down on it, unconcerned that it was dampened by the rain and had the musty, vaguely decayed smell that accompanies even well-done taxidermy. As Winnie received the cat, it actually seemed that a bit of color returned to Winnie's face, as if Squire Napier's notion that his little sister would improve if she had a plaything to cheer her might actually have merit.

McSwain knew he'd been manipulated, but the smiles lighting the faces of all the Napier family, including Winnie, all but forced him to search for a way he could let the child have the remains of his old pet. There was a complication inherent in doing that that McSwain alone knew about and was not free to explain.

He thought hard and found the only solution possible. Turning to the Napiers, he asked, "Sir, do you have a small, sharp knife, and, ma'am, might you have a needle and sewing thread you could spare?"

They did. McSwain let the little girl play with the cat for several minutes, then told her he was going to make a gift of it to her. Cat would be hers. But first he had to borrow the animal back for just a few moments. He would bring it back directly, he promised.

Reluctantly, Winnie let him take Cicero back again and he took as well the items he had asked for from the adult Napiers. Noting that the rain had ceased, McSwain asked the family to excuse him a few moments and let him step outside and make a repair on the cat's body, some small thing he'd noticed needed doing and hadn't gotten to yet. It was a false pretext, but it served its purpose.

Someone had stowed some wood under a tent flap and kept it dry through the rainfall, so already a good fire was burning in the sodden encampment. McSwain took Cicero and his borrowed knife, needle, and thread, and positioned himself where he could benefit from a bit of firelight yet work without drawing much attention to what he was doing. He worked first with the knife, then with the thread, and when he was done, examined his threadwork and found it virtually undetectable. Clutching in his fist what he had extricated from beneath the skin of the cat's belly, he walked to the Napier tent and presented the former Cicero, now named simply Cat, to a very ailing little girl, who beamed brightly at him in gratitude. McSwain told her good-bye and departed the Napier tent.

He returned briefly to the tent, wherein he had conversed with the other men, said a quick good-bye to the Pennsylvanians, and expressed hope that he and his new acquaintances would see each other again on the trail or in California. Then he returned to the Sadler camp and his wagon, wherein he found Ben Scarlett snoring and reeking of liquor.

Ben's prized flask, now drained, lay on the bed of the wagon near Ben's flopped hand. McSwain picked up the flask and dropped into it the items he had held in his fist, then stoppered the flask and put it away among his own wagon-stowed gear and goods, hidden.

"I lost something tonight, Ben, and now

you have, too," he whispered to the unhearing drunkard. "Such is life, I suppose. Such is life."

Chapter Seventeen

"It was my fault, and I own right up to it," a hungover Ben Scarlett said the next morning, pain in his head and his voice. The fact that Cicero was no longer present was now known. "I should have chased after that boy when I saw he'd took something from the wagon. But I couldn't see what it was."

"Well, we know now. It was my cat. But don't fret over it, Ben. The fact that you didn't stop him doesn't matter much since I ran into the boy myself after that. All he was trying to do was help his sick little sister. I gave the cat to her, Ben. It was the right thing to do."

"I'll be! I'm surprised. You seemed mighty attached to that cat."

"Yes. I suppose I was."

"Why was that? I know it was an old pet, but it was dead and gone. So why did you keep it so close all the time, and hide it when you weren't around, like it was some treasure? Lord, my head hurts. Why do I do this to myself?"

"It wasn't the cat itself that mattered, really. It was something inside it."

Ben's addled, hurting brain puzzled over that comment. "Something inside it. . . . Love, you mean? Affection?"

"What? *What?*"

Ben was embarrassed. "Well . . . I don't know what you mean by something inside it. I figure a cat has bones and blood and guts and such as that inside it. But that can't be what you're talking about. So it must be something that ain't flesh and blood. Like the cat loving its owner, you know."

McSwain had to chuckle. "You're a strange man, Ben."

"Not strange. Just drunk a lot. You, you're the strange one. No offense meant by that."

"I know, Ben. I know."

"So, what was inside the cat?"

"Something I put there. Something important."

"So you gave that to the little girl, too?"

"No. I got it out in secret before I gave Cicero away."

"You got it now?"

McSwain became conscious of the weight of the flask in one of his pockets. "It's hidden again," he said to Ben. "So I won't lose it."

Ben sighed. "I hate to lose things. You know that new flask of mine? Already lost it. I was drinking out of it just last night and it was in my hand when I went to sleep. Now it's gone."

"Strange."

"Yep. Strange."

"You got to come, Jedd. He's hurt. He's sure 'nough hurt himself."

Jedd Colter looked up from his wooden plate and for a few seconds quit chewing his beans. The person who had spoken to him was Keller Buck, a man Jedd had barely known during his Knoxville years. Buck had been a carriage maker who doubled as a finish carpenter; all across the town of Knoxville and its surrounding region the work of Keller Buck filled parlors and dining rooms and carriage houses.

Jedd sat his plate to the side and looked Buck in the eye. "Who's hurt?"

"Treemont Dalton. Your old partner."

Jedd was on his feet in half a second. "What happened?"

"I don't know for sure. . . . I didn't see it happen. But he must have been either out for a walk or maybe looking for a fishing spot, 'cause he was walking along that little creek running just south of here. There's trees growing along the north bank of that creek, and Tree had stepped out on some roots that grew out over the water. They were wet, and his right foot slipped down through a gap in the tangled-up roots, and he jammed his leg all the way up to the kneecap into that hole and tilted forward so he nearly snapped the knee."

"Lord," Jedd muttered. "Where's he now?"

"Lying on the ground by the creek like a turtle on its back, moaning and groaning. The knee hurts him too much to walk on just yet."

Guided by Buck, Jedd went to where Tree-mont was and found matters just as Buck had described them. Now, though, some of the initial pain had worn away for Tree, but not enough for him to do more than come to his feet and stand with most of his weight on his left, uninjured leg, with his left hand against the tree trunk for balance.

"I done it up good, Jedd," Tree said. "That was the same knee I hurt years and years back, when I was a boy and you and me took a tumble in that cave we'd found. You remember that, I reckon?"

"I remember. You hurt your knee, I busted

up my elbow. I can still feel a twinge in it every now and again."

"Same for me with the knee, even before I went and damn fooled myself up again in that root tangle over there above the creek bank just now."

Jedd knelt beside his friend and studied the injured leg, though he could not really see anything because Treemont still had his trousers on. Knowing he needed to check the knee for bruising, blood-swelling, and the like, he opened his mouth to ask Treemont to drop his pants, though he knew this would inevitably launch Tree into all kinds of highly improper, joking commentary. Then Jedd noticed something that held him silent a minute.

"Treemont, you've broken the skin on that leg."

"Don't think so."

"You have. There's blood coming out around your ankle."

And there was, a small but steady flow. "Lordy!" Treemont declared. "I didn't even notice it."

It was unnecessary then for Jedd to suggest that Treemont divest himself of his trousers. Tree did it right away, dreading but needing to know how much injury he'd suffered courtesy of that pinching, twisting tree root.

Jedd examined the leg. The knee was indeed miscolored and puffing, and Jedd knew at once that Tree was in for a period of convalescence that would probably stretch on for weeks. What really caught Jedd's attention was the source of the blood running down Treemont's ankle, however. It came from two places, on the left side of the calf and from a parallel spot on the right side. Jedd looked at it a full minute before being willing to say aloud what it was.

"Tree, you've been shot."

"Shot? The hell!"

"It's true. You've had a ball pass clean through your calf. Looks like it went in on the left side, went on through, and came out the other side. Was your left side faced toward the creek when you went down into that space in the tree roots?"

"It was, yeah."

Jedd instantly began scanning the terrain on the far side of the creek. The land was relatively clear up to a stand of trees that lined a smaller branch of the creek thirty yards distant. That line of trees and brush must have been the hiding place for whoever put a rifle ball through Treemont's lower leg.

"Why would anybody shoot me, Jedd?"

"No idea. You ain't been getting too close to some other argonaut's woman, or daughter, or sister or somebody, have you?"

"I've tried with a couple, but you know my luck, Jedd. The women get a scared look and run off once they figure out what I'm up to."

"Maybe you tried too hard with one of them, and somebody close to her noticed and decided to put you out of the lecher business."

"Or maybe it was an accidental shot."

"I'm going to go over the creek there and look around, see what I can find that might tell us something. After we get you patched, I mean."

"I'd like to go with you, but I don't think I'll be doing much walking for a spell. I may end up like old McSwain, making my journey to California mostly in the bed of a wagon."

"Treemont, I don't think you'll be going to California right away. I think that knee isn't going to be up to a lot of bumping around in the back of a wagon. And you want that punctured leg muscle to heal up right, too. We'll think about all that later, though. For now let's get you on the safe side of this tree and get a bit of cloth wrapped around those bullet holes."

They'd just gotten Treemont settled on the side of the tree away from the creek when Jedd, glancing around the trunk, caught a flash of gunmetal in the brush across the rill. He came around the tree, looking hard, figuring he'd just located the person who had wounded his friend.

He saw the rifle barrel come poking out through a bush just before it fired. He felt a sharp, cracking pain in his left ankle and fell down hard.

"I'll be drawed up and quartered, Treemont — I'm shot, too!" he exclaimed.

Treemont swore loudly and whoever was across the creek moved, rustling the brush, and then was gone.

Jedd looked down at his shattered and bloody ankle, and wondered what in the blaze of perdition was going on, and who had done it.

"Whoever it was was either a very bad shot or a very good one," Jedd said to Wilberforce Sadler. Wilberforce had come, with Witherspoon, to see Jedd and Treemont and learn the details of their woundings. Wilberforce was evidently disturbed at the fact that someone in his enterprise had been fired upon, even hit, but Witherspoon was an emotional wreck, weeping inconsolably.

Jedd wasn't much surprised by that: he'd seen Witherspoon weep when he saw one of the wagons crush a scampering field mouse beneath its wheels while they were still traveling toward Louisville, Kentucky.

Jedd soon found out there was more to Witherspoon's sorrows than mere upset over the inexplicable shooting incident.

Wilberforce was the one who brought it out. "Jedd, you must realize that your current crippled situation, which is likely to continue for some time yet, considering how long it can take an ankle to heal, puts a new light on your situation with us."

"I grant you, sir, I am of much reduced value to the venture," Jedd conceded. "But I've always healed fast and well from injuries. I've broken many a bone in my day, from fingers to ribs to arms, and never have I been out of commission for long. If you can bear with me patiently for a short time, I am certain I'll be able to carry out the most important parts of my duties."

Wilberforce sighed and shook his head. "That is not realistic, Jedd. You can scarce hunt, scout, or give protection if you cannot even take a step. As you know, our travel has been much slowed and impeded already — mostly through the fault of the late General Lloyd, not you — and we cannot afford to be slowed again. I am sorry, Jedd, but I believe it essential for us to end our arrangement and proceed without you. You will be provided packhorses, extra mounts, and what supplies can be charitably spared, but go on without you we shall."

As Wilberforce said that, Witherspoon moaned loudly and wept harder. Jedd could tell there was no theatricality in it; Witherspoon was authentically distressed. "I'm sorry, Jedd," he managed to say. "I wasn't for it, argued against it, in fact — but Wilberforce . . . but other voices spoke out against me. I'm sorry. I don't want to see you go."

The truth was, Jedd didn't much care if he parted from the Sadler enterprise. He did not consider himself reliant on any particular group, individual, or agreement to make his way in the world. He could go to California with or without the Sadlers.

"What would remain of our original agreement?" Jedd asked, thinking of the provision giving him a percentage of any mining profits made by the Sadlers. "Am I to be penalized because some unknown person chose to shoot me and my partner?"

Wilberforce's smile was cold. "And are Witherspoon and I to be penalized perpetually by having to recompense in an ongoing way a man who was unable to complete his agreed task?"

"It's you who are asking me to separate from you. As I said, given a small amount of time I believe I could complete my side of our bargain without difficulty."

"We can't afford further delays, Jedd," Wilberforce said. He put out his hand for Jedd to shake, but Jedd was not so inclined. Wilberforce shrugged and turned away. "My best to you, Jedd. I hope your healing proceeds apace and that, should you come to California later or should you take a different direction in life, you will find much success in your undertakings." With that, Wilberforce turned and exited the infirmary tent where Jedd and Treemont lay on cots. Treemont grunted disdainfully.

"That man, I believe, is a cheat to the very heart of him." Realizing Witherspoon was still present to hear this said of his brother, Treemont said, "No intention of slurring your family, sir. Just speaking my mind with my usual freedom."

"I have no argument with you," Witherspoon said. "I am more aware than any other man of the coldness of my brother's heart and his focus upon taking care of himself above all others. I want you to know, gentlemen, that I was of the view that your situation should have been accommodated, time given for you to heal, and our journey to move forward as before. I was told just what you were: we can't afford more lost time."

"It would be best at this point to delay in any case," Jedd said. "So much time was lost by General Lloyd that there is the danger of being caught in the winter snows before we complete our crossing. Safest to wait and reach the gold fields in the spring."

"I don't question that you are right," Witherspoon said. "I will express that same view to my brother and see if, for once, reason can prevail over ambition." Witherspoon shook his head and moved his rotund form toward the tent door. "We should never have promised a fast crossing. That was our mistake. By making that promise we put unneeded pressure upon ourselves, the kind of pressure that can lead to hasty decisions and mistakes. Should never have done it that way."

When Witherspoon was gone, Treemont said, "Jedd, that porky Sadler may prove to have some sense and mettle to him yet."

"So he might, Treemont."

Tree chuckled. "You know, Jedd, old Withers there will realize something before long that may make him shift to his brother's side. There'll be an advantage to him in you being left behind."

"I know what you're thinking. Rachel McCall. With me out of the picture, Witherspoon will have her to himself."

Jedd laughed and unwittingly moved his hurt ankle, which brought his laughter to an instant halt. Treemont said, "That's indeed what I was thinking. That woman is smit with you, no question of it. Pure old smit to the core of her. But not so bad as poor Withers is smit with her."

"Smitten, Tree. Smitten. Not smit."

"Beg pardon, schoolmaster. I'm just an unschooled old rover of the wild country. I know very little of book learning."

"Just trying to help you out a little."

"I'm obliged." A long pause, and then Treemont spoke again. "Jedd, you don't think old Wilberforce would have shot us himself as a way of getting rid of us, do you? You know, so he wouldn't have to share any of his gold with you in California?"

Jedd could have admitted that the same possibility had come to his own mind. But he didn't. "I don't think he'd do that, Tree. He ain't that bad a man, surely."

"I don't know, Jedd. Somebody surely did shoot us, and it had to be somebody with a reason. Something to gain."

"Who knows, Tree? But let's you and me agree to be mighty cautious in speculating, especially out loud. These tent walls are mighty thin, and sound carries."

"If it wasn't Wilberforce, then who?"

"Ben Scarlett ran into Jake Carney a short while back."

"Jake Carney? The one who was so mad when you beat him because it made him lose the affection of his woman?"

"The same. Not that he ever really had her affection. He just wanted her and she was looking for a reason not to take him. She let that fight become her reason. She claimed that she couldn't accept a man who would lose in a fight like that. Silly sort of way to think, but like I said, she was looking for a reason."

"You really think he'd kill you after all this time, over something as silly as that?"

"He might. Or he might just try to ruin my life for me. Turn me into a cripple."

"But why would he shoot me, too? I never had any dealings with him, never done him any wrongs, real or 'maginary! And I was the one who got shot first!"

"It may not have been Jake Carney at all. I'm just speculating based on the fact that Ben ran into him. But if Carney was the shooter, and he recognized you out by that creek, he might have decided to injure you so I'd be drawn out there, and he'd have an opportunity at me."

"Well . . ."

"I know it don't sound that convincing. And like I said, it might not be him who did it. The fact remains, though, you and me are both laid up wounded by what was surely the same man. So somebody out there had cause to do it, and Carney's been seen in the area."

"I can't argue with that." Treemont paused. "How long you think we'll be crips, Jedd?"

"I think we'll both be up on our feet a lot faster than old Wilberforce thinks we will. And if the Sadlers don't manage to make hay of not having the general to slow them down anymore, and keep on foot-dragging, I can easily see the day when you and me come riding up on their camp, tip our hats, and go on past and get to California before they do. Even after being left behind here."

"You mean that?"

"I do. In fact, let's just kind of plan on doing that, huh? Because I got a feeling they ain't going to do much better without the general than they did with him. Slowness has become a habit by now. It happens."

"Sounds good to me, passing them by."

"My ankle hurts, Tree."

"My knee hurts. And my leg."

"Just another adventure to tell the grandchildren about."

"If we ever find wives."

"Tell you what, Tree: I'll let you have Rachel McCall."

"Know what? I'd take her. A lot of men would. And since you've got the chance, you ought to take her yourself."

"She ain't my kind. Besides, Witherspoon would hunt me down and gut me if I took his gal. He's a mighty frontiersman, you know. He's got the clothes to prove it."

Treemont laughed and did not speak for a while. Then he looked at Jedd and said, "Jedd, you don't think it could have been Witherspoon who shot us, do you? You know, being jealous over the Widow McCall being smitten with you?"

"The way he was wailing and caterwauling in here a little while ago? No. I really don't think he'd do it. And I doubt he's a good enough shot to put a ball through one man's ankle and through another man's lower leg."

"You're probably right."

Jedd sat up, listening to the night. Treemont slept soundly, not hearing what Jedd heard faintly, but distinctly. He sat up farther, despite the pain it caused him to do so, and listened harder, to be sure he was not merely misinterpreting some natural sound . . . the howling of some beast, or of the wind.

No. It was not that. Jedd listened until he was sure, then lay flat again until the sound grew faint and indistinct beyond the thickening mask of descending sleep. When morning came the sound was gone along with the darkness from which it had been born.

By midmorning, daylight and distraction had all but erased the memory of that sound from Jedd's mind.

CHAPTER EIGHTEEN

Being "laid up" did not suit any aspect of Jedd Colter's temperament other than his enjoyment of solitude. His idea of good solitude, however, had nothing to do with lying on cots in tents or bedrolls in the back of a wagon. Jedd liked the solitude of the forest and plains and mountains . . . and a man had to be able to move to enjoy those.

For days he was stuck in the same tent with Treemont, and as much as the men liked each other, it was not long before each wore out his welcome with the other. Ironically, things outside the tent seemed at last to be moving at a better pace, which only made confinement more irksome, and also made Jedd start to wonder if he might be wrong in doubting the Sadlers would move along faster without the heavy anchor of General Lloyd.

The problems that had led to the long encampment to begin with were finally corrected. Wagons were in good shape, mules had replaced dray horses, and provisions were plentiful. Some of the emigrants wisely began disposing of items they had brought with them that would obviously be problematic once the plains were behind and there were mountains to be crossed. Among the discarded things were a few medical items, including crutches. Jedd and Treemont were made a gift of these, and sheer desperation led them to begin attempting to use them well before they should have done so. No calamities resulted, fortunately, and both men were surprised at how soon they were able to hobble around, swinging their damaged limbs and struggling through the pain the movement caused, enduring it for the reward of mobililty, however slow and awkward.

Treemont did better than Jedd on this score, his injuries being farther up his leg. Jedd was required to be eternally vigilant in not letting his left foot so much as brush the ground, because even a minor wrenching of his ankle was excruciating. Even so, Jedd found some comfort in the fact that Treemont was soon spending as much time as he could bear outside the tent, moving around outside and leaving Jedd a bit of privacy.

Before the Sadler emigrants moved on, Jedd and Treemont were visited by almost every member of the group, so much so that Jedd began to believe he was saying the word "good-bye" more frequently than any other. He made scores of pledges to be sure to look up certain families and individuals once in California, knowing that most of them would be forgotten. That didn't matter. He knew they would forget him, too.

Rachel McCall swore she would not forget Jedd Colter. In fact, she would wait for him, and somehow in California she would find him. She would wait until he had ample time to heal and reach California. Then she would begin her search. If she had to, she would pass through every mining town, every camp, every "digging" until she had reunited with him.

Jedd struggled for a way to speak honestly to her without needlessly hurting her. "Rachel, I don't know that you're looking at our situation the way it really is. I've been separated from the Sadler venture, and truthfully I don't know for certain that I'll even go on to California now." This was a falsehood; Jedd fully intended to go on if for no reason other than finding Emma and seeing for himself how she was faring in her apparently unhappy home. With the thought of Emma, he realized he owed Rachel a fuller bit of truth. "Rachel, the fact is, there's already a woman I care for, and she's in California right now. If I do go on to California, it will be in order to find her. You have a right to know that, given that you seem to have an interest in me."

She managed a weak, sad smile, and it gave way to tears. There was no sobbing, no outright crying, only tears, quietly streaming down her face. Jedd felt wicked for the pain he was causing her, especially since the woman he was talking of seeking out was probably still married and unavailable to him anyway.

"Jedd, I wish you the best in whatever and whomever you choose," she said, voice quivering a little. "But I will not hesitate to tell you that I believe the best for you may well be sitting here beside you right now. I would prove to you a faithful and completely loving wife, true and hardworking and kind. You can find no one else who would give you more of her full devotion."

"Rachel, I can believe that. If only things were just a bit different, I can't say what might transpire between us."

She leaned forward, then hesitated. "May I?"

"You may."

Not since the days he and Emma had held each other close on the drawing room sofa in the big McSwain house on Addington Street had Jedd received such a memorable kiss. He lay back in the lingering glow of it and wondered if maybe he should try a little harder to put Emma behind him.

Not that that could be done. Some things, like shot-up ankles and love, were beyond a man's control.

Jedd managed to get outside and seat himself on a flat boulder the day the Sadler group decamped and left. He was surprised at the sorrow he felt at being left behind, and the resentment that flared toward Wilberforce Sadler for forcing him into this situation. He supposed his real anger should have been directed toward whatever person had shot him in the ankle, but it was not easy to fully hate someone without knowing who the someone was.

Treemont looked at Jedd's ankle, resting before him on the ground. "That can't feel very good, Jedd, having the weight of your foot down on that ankle. Let's get you back on your cot again so you can keep your leg stretched out flat."

"I'm tired of that cot, Tree. And the ankle don't hurt as bad as it did. I'm beginning to think that a lot of the hurting was just from the rifle ball going through, and maybe the bone wasn't injured as much as I'd first thought. If that's the case, I may be able to be up and going faster than I'd expected."

"That may be just some wishful thinking, Jedd."

"Oh, it's wishful, all right. I'm ready to be my old self again. But sometimes wishes come true, you know."

Treemont watched the final wagon roll out of sight. McSwain's wagon, now shared almost always with Ben Scarlett.

"Know what, Tree? McSwain told me sometime ago he'd go along with an idea of mine for him to teach folks to read while the journey to California went along. I believe he really meant it. When I got hurt, though, I figured that would be the end of it, him probably not likely to stick with it without me there to goad him along. But when he came in and said his good-byes, he told me he still aimed to do it, if there were any willing to let him teach them. I hope he does. That would be a right fine thing."

"He's an odd fellow, Jedd, that McSwain. Remember how he used to carry that stuffed dead cat around? That was plain old strange."

"It was. And I think there might have been

more to the story of that cat than any of us knew. And I got a feeling McSwain will never tell that story, just like he'll never tell just what got him thrown out of his job at the college." Jedd shifted his leg slightly and winced. "I've wondered whether or not maybe them two stories might actually twine together somewhere to become the same one."

Treemont gave a spasmodic chuckle. "What? You think he got the axe at his college over a dead cat?"

"No. But I've wondered if it was really the cat he was guarding when he used to carry it around, or maybe something else. Something the cat was hiding."

"Huh?"

"Never mind, Tree. Never mind."

Treemont looked across the horizon and shook his head. "McSwain ain't the only one who's strange, I think."

For two days, Jedd and Treemont were the lone occupants of what had been a crowded campsite. The Pennsylvanian forty-niners had moved out the day before the Sadler group left, so for a time Jedd and Treemont could look across the flatlands and find little to see.

The third day, another emigrant band

moved in and set up camp, pausing in their journey primarily for wagon and saddle repair. Tents sprang up and suddenly Jedd and Treemont felt as if the calendar had turned back and their old fellow travelers were back. But these were new faces, new figures, and there were even more of them than had been with the Sadlers.

Among the newcomers were no less than three physicians, doctors who had practiced together in Philadelphia and found themselves "seeing the elephant" and catching a case of gold fever their own medicine could not cure. One of the physicians was a specialist in injuries of the bones, and when he caught a glimpse of a stranger making his way on crutches toward a tent, he went to him and asked the nature of his injury.

"Took a rifle ball in the ankle," Jedd told him. "I don't know who fired it. My friend I'm tenting with yonder got hit in the meaty part of his calf and also wrenched his knee bad on a tree root."

"Have you had a doctor look you over?"

"Not a real one, no. Just kind of letting things heal on their own."

"I want to look at that ankle. I believe I can bind that up for you in a way that should make it a lot more stable and probably ease some of the pain."

"Sir, I'd be your devoted servant if you could do that."

"I'm a physician, by the way. I work mostly with bones."

"I'm your man, Doctor. Name's Colter. Jedd Colter."

"If we can step into your tent, I'll take a look at that ankle right now. I'll fetch my bag from my wagon over there."

"All righty, Doctor."

"Call me Alistair. I'm Dr. Alistair Blane."

"I'm Jedd. Two *d*s."

"That doctor knows his business," Jedd said later, looking at his own neatly wrapped and lightly splinted foot. "You wouldn't know that just having a hurt ankle wrapped up the right way would make such a difference."

"He didn't help *me* much," Treemont mumbled. "My knee's all stiffened up from his wrapping, but it don't feel any better for it."

"I heard him tell you it'll help it not be so stiff once it heals up all the way," Jedd said.

"We'll see. I'm glad yours ain't hurting so bad."

A lull in conversation. "Jedd, who done this to us? And why?"

"My main suspect is still Jake Carney,"

242

Jedd replied. "I think he shot you to draw me out to the creek where he could get a shot at me."

"What will you do if you run across him on down the road?"

"Settle accounts. That's how Carney thinks, so that's what he'll get from me."

"I hope I'm there to see it, Jedd. I really do. And I'll help. With pleasure."

CHAPTER NINETEEN

Witherspoon Sadler sighed loudly. "I'm going to talk to her. I'm going to tell her exactly what's on my mind, and I'm going to ask her if she feels the same, or thinks she ever can."

"Don't be a fool, Withers," Wilberforce said to his brother, who was clad again in his increasingly frequent buckskin costume. "She's going to tell you what she thinks, all right, and she very well might laugh in your face when she does it." Wilberforce forced the stern tone out of his voice. "Let it go, Withers. Don't put yourself into a position to be hurt by this woman."

"I, for one, think she has a high opinion of me," Witherspoon said. "I've seen her looking my way more than once."

"And I, for one, know she's looking only because she's laughing at you in that fool's getup you insist on wearing."

Witherspoon glared silently at his sibling.

Then: "One day, Wilber. One day you'll learn just what I'm capable of. And you'll be mocking me no more."

"If you don't want to be mocked, Withers, don't make it so easy."

"I'm not listening to you anymore today," Witherspoon said. "I've had enough poison poured in through my ears." He had the tone of a petulant child.

"Ha!" Wilberforce chortled, mockingly. "Going witty on me, are you, little brother?"

"I'm just tired of it all, Wilber. It never ends from you. You seem like you can only feel like a big, powerful man by making me seem little by comparison."

"You? Little? Fat as you are? Ha!"

"See? Again! You can't help yourself, I think."

Wilberforce drew in a slow breath, closing his eyes and quietly shaking his head. "Withers, let's call a truce for a moment. I need to talk to you, anyway. I think I've found us a new pilot to replace Colter for the rest of the journey. Man name of Dorey. Boo Dorey."

"Boo?"

"That's right. Boo Dorey."

"Can he do the job?"

"I wouldn't be having you meet him if he couldn't."

Witherspoon nodded. "Wilber, can we maybe try to be kinder to each other? I could stand for a little more kind treatment myself."

"I can understand that, brother. I realize I am sometimes a harshly toned man."

Witherspoon smiled and put out his hand. Wilberforce looked at it, then tentatively accepted it and shook it. A big grin exploded across his face and quickly he pumped the hand with vigor.

"We'll try to do better by each other, Withers. But please take some advice from me that you truly should heed. Don't go talking to the Widow McCall just yet. And quit wearing that buckskin suit you've got on."

"I'll think about it, Wilber. I honestly will."

It was Boo Dorey who drove former Carolina sheriff Rand Blalock away from the Sadler group and back to the place they had left Jedd Colter and Treemont Dalton. Dorey was crude, gruff, unclean in mind and body. An unpleasant man all around, like most of his forebears, including one who had once crossed paths with Jedd Colter's best-known ancestor, the frontiersman Joshua Colter. Blalock was not easily offended, far from it, but Dorey was too much

246

for even him. Blalock quietly abandoned the Sadler camp and made his way back the way he'd come, preferring to make his way to California with Jedd Colter. He had to ask himself why he was even bothering to go to California at all. He was no gold miner and had no real desire to be.

Blalock was one of those men who were one thing and one thing only. He was a lawman. Almost his entire adult life he had served as either a sheriff or a deputy sheriff, enforcing the rules that keep men civilized. In that capacity he had become a student of human nature and behavior, and had developed virtually an extra sense that warned him when he ran across danger. He could read the subtle signals in how a stranger glanced his way, the way he held his shoulders, his hands, the way his eye twitched and shifted. That experience-generated sense had saved Blalock's skin more than once.

He'd learned another thing through experience as well: the most dangerous men were those who had taught themselves to send no signals of their thoughts and intentions. As a result, Blalock had grown to be wary of all, particularly strangers. Learned to be ready for what he could see coming, and even more importantly, what he could not.

His caution was pricked when he realized he was being followed. He knew it before he even saw the man . . . simply felt his presence back there. Blalock did not wheel about to face his tracker, however, not wanting to introduce an element of confrontation unnecessarily. Whoever was behind him might merely be traveling the same direction and route as he was, for no reason involving Blalock. So he stopped and dismounted without turning, kept his back toward his follower, and took advantage of the moment to empty his bladder, which he'd been needing to do, anyway. Then he turned to get back into the saddle and at the same time take a seemingly random look at whoever was behind him.

The man was afoot, no horse, a ragamuffin of a fellow. Sparely built, hair poking in a dark, shaggy fringe from beneath the sides of his hat, clothing tattered and hanging loosely on him, trousers cinched tightly around his middle with a belt made of rope. His whiskers were dark and had been roughly hacked at to keep them short, but the man hadn't really shaved in a good while. This was one of those fellows whose age was nearly impossible to judge. Blalock guessed him to be a relatively young man who had aged before his time through hard living.

The man saw Blalock looking back at him, paused, and waved hesitantly, smiling. Blalock merely nodded and kept his hand close to the pistol at his belt, just in case. But the stranger kept coming, a little hesitantly the closer he drew, but without stopping short until he was near.

"Howdy, sir!" the man called to Blalock. "How are you today?"

Blalock's intuition did not flare any warnings. He had a sense that this was not a dangerous man. Even so, he held himself wound as tightly as a watchspring, ready to react if the man made any threatening move.

"My name's Ben Scarlett," the newcomer said. "You look familiar to me, sir. Were you in the Sadler group?"

"I was, briefly. But I left it."

"Did you, sir? I did, too."

Blalock saw nothing worth replying to in that. As far as he was concerned, the conversation was at an end. He swung into his saddle and moved on.

Ben Scarlett moved on, too, and because Blalock rode slowly, the pair ended up moving along together. For Ben, at least, silence felt uncomfortable in this situation, so he began to quietly sing. Because Ben had a pleasant voice, Blalock didn't mind it much, but after fifteen minutes or so of music he was ready for some quiet again.

"You mind not singing for a spell?" he asked.

Ben instantly shut up and didn't even speak for a minute or so. Finally he said, "I'm sorry."

"Sorry for what?"

"For singing. I didn't mean to bother you with it."

Blalock shrugged. "Not a bother, not really. You sing well, Mr. Scarlett."

"Thank you, sir. Kind of you to say. But I must have been bothering you some, or you wouldn't have asked me to stop."

Blalock sighed and thought this a silly conversation. "It wasn't your fault. I'd been annoyed earlier by another man, back in the Sadler camp. Fellow name of Dorey. He replaced Jedd Colter as pilot."

"I know, I didn't like him much, either. Jedd, though, different story. I think the world of Jedd. I've knowed him for years, back from the days he lived in Knoxville, where I'm from."

"I've known Jedd even longer than that," Blalock said. "I was the sheriff in his home county back in North Carolina, when he

250

was a boy. I've gone hunting many a time with Jedd and his kinfolk when he was little. I taught him a good deal about shooting."

"No fooling! Well, sir, you and me got a friend in common, then. Jedd's been mighty good to me. And a lot of times, other folks ain't been so kind. I drink a little too much, you see. A lot of people look down on a man who drinks too much."

"Jedd's a good man. That's why I'm heading the direction I am . . . going back to rejoin Jedd and his friend Treemont. I'd rather travel in his company than with Dorey."

"I'm doing the same thing, Mr. Blalock."

"Just call me Rand."

"All right, Rand. And I'm Ben. Like I was saying, I'm doing the same thing you are: going back to get with Jedd again. Because it just didn't seem right to me to be moving on and leaving him behind after he's been such a friend to me, especially now that he's hurt. He bought me supper one time, and sat right down with me, same table in a public restaurant, and had a meal alongside me. Right in front of God and everybody, and he wasn't ashamed to be seen with me, either. Not a bit!"

"I reckon we'll be traveling together, then, if we're both traveling with Jedd."

"I reckon so."

They moved on together, no singing or clumsy silences now. Quiet conversation flowed, much of it about Jedd Colter and the times they had shared with him in years past. And about California, and gold, and their individual hopes for the better life each wished to build. Ben assumed Blalock was heading for California for the same mercenary reasons most others were, and Blalock had no reason to correct the assumption.

Talk also drifted to the subject of others on the way to California, and Ben asked Blalock if he knew, or knew of, Zebulon McSwain and a college in Knoxville called Bledsoe College. Blalock replied that he had heard of the college, he thought, but of this McSwain he knew nothing.

"Well, he's part of the Sadler group," Ben said. "And he's an unusual kind of man. There's something wrong in him, something bad that's happened to him, I think. He was one of the high kings of Knoxville for years, president of Bledsoe College, living in a big, nice house, good deal of money. Had a pretty daughter name of Emma. Jedd Colter was mighty sweet on her for a goodly while. She ended up marrying another man, and I think she and her husband are already in California. Anyway, I'm mentioning Mc-

Swain to you because of something that happened just yesterday. I had been given a nice silver liquor flask by somebody, and it was the finest possession I had. Real silver on it, not just pewter or tin or nothing. That flask went missing, and I looked all over for it, and McSwain — he'd become kind of a friend of mine, letting me share his wagon space — he knew I was trying to find my flask. Said he knew nothing of it. Well, just yesterday I seen it in his pocket while he was teaching his reading school in the evening camp. He's doing that now, teaching folks to read who don't know how. Nice thing for him to do . . . Jedd Colter's idea. Anyway, he noticed I'd seen the flask and instead of giving it back to me, he sneaked it into a different pocket of his coat, where it wouldn't show. I asked him for it later and he told me he didn't have my flask. Called me a drunk and a liar. His very words. 'A drunk and a liar.' Hurt my feelings bad, to tell the truth. I'd come to think of him as a right decent fellow, even if he was a little odd. He used to have a dead cat he'd had stuffed and preserved, and he'd carry it around like it was a live pet. Cat's gone now, though. Young fellow got hold of it and ran off with it to another emigrant camp. Anyway, I don't know why he would steal my flask, knowing it was important to me."

"Maybe he figured it was worth something, being silver and all. Maybe he needed money and aimed to sell it on the sly."

"Pshaw! He don't need money. He's had plenty of it all his days. He didn't need my flask, but treated it like it belonged to him even when he knew I wanted it. Makes me mad, thinking of it."

"Ben, you can't always account for what folks do. As a man of the law I've seen people do things you can't find no good reason for, nor make a lick of sense of. Some of it is as sad as it can be. I saw a young woman who'd had a baby without having a husband, back in my Carolina days, and she laid that baby on a doorstep for a family to take in as a foundling. There was two problems, though: that family had a female cat in her season, and she was howling and meowing top of her lungs all through the night, masking out the little sound of that infant child crying outside the door. And it was wintertime and even though the girl had swaddled the baby aplenty, when they found it next morning . . . you can figure the rest out. When we buried that little baby, I could see the girl who'd birthed her standing at the edge of the woods, watching. God have mercy, how she must have felt!"

"That's a sad tale, Rand. Awful sad."

"It is. And the point of it is, you don't know what makes people do what they do. A lot of times it ain't bad intent. They just follow something inside that goads them on, and that's when they do things that end up being wrong, or foolish, or sinful or whatever label you want to slap on it. Ain't no sorrier animal on this planet than the human animal, Ben. Nor any stupider one. It's a sad fact."

Ben nodded and was thoughtful for a while as he trudged along. "Maybe McSwain had some cause for wanting my flask that was like what you're talking about. Something inside goading him." He paused, then went on. "God knows I know what it is to be goaded on the inside. It's that way with me and liquor. Something in me just goads me to drink all I can get of it, and I can't help myself."

"We all got our own inner goads, Ben. All of us. I believe that."

"I think you're a smart man, Rand Blalock."

The old sheriff shook his head. "Not smart, Ben. Just experienced."

CHAPTER TWENTY

For Jedd Colter and company, the remainder of the journey to California would be completed without ever reconnecting with the Sadler group. This was not for lack of opportunity, because as they advanced, they soon came within overtaking distance of their original band. Jedd considered whether it might be advisable, for the sake of safe travel, to rejoin the Sadlers, but two things killed the notion. The first was his memory of Wilberforce Sadler nullifying their agreement, including the percentage Jedd was to have received from any gold the Sadlers might mine in California. That part of the bargain had been the key selling point for Jedd when he'd sat down for the first time with Ottwell Plumb, but it was gone now.

The second factor that inclined Jedd against rejoining the Sadler band was catching a glimpse of Boo Dorey riding around the perimeter of the camp. His replacement.

He resented being replaced more than he would have expected he would. He knew something of the Dorey family; Jedd's forebears and the Doreys had interacted, unhappily, all the way back to the days before the Revolutionary War. Too much history there. Jedd quietly told his three traveling companions that they would simply pass by the Sadler band and continue on their way. They would reach California first and give the Sadlers ironic greeting when they showed up. Hello, boys! Here to get you some gold, you say? Sorry. . . . We done got it all!

Ben Scarlett, for one, found that comment hilarious, because down inside himself he was quite certain he would find no gold at all. . . . He just didn't have the luck for such as that. Even so, he had decided to align himself with Jedd Colter rather than go back to the camp where a man he'd thought was becoming his friend had stolen his most valuable possession, his silver flask.

"There she is, Jedd, the nation's prettiest widow woman," said Treemont, moving his horse up beside Jedd's. Treemont was keeping more silent than usual, finding it difficult to ride without quite a bit of pain in his knee. It was a sighting of Rachel McCall that prompted his comment.

"I see her," Jedd said. "Why would you mention her particularly to me?"

Treemont gave a scornful little laugh. "Jedd, you may as well quit pretending you don't know that woman has her cap set for you. If you ever decided to take a wife, she'd be a handy choice, because she'd never turn you down."

"I can't see it. I'm inclined to let Witherspoon Sadler have her. Lord knows he'd like to stake a claim on her."

"I wouldn't think you'd look with favor on any good thing happening for the Sadlers, the way they cut you loose just because you had a stroke of bad fortune. It wasn't your fault you got shot in the ankle."

"They didn't cut me out because I suffered bad fortune, to be fair about it. I was cut out because I couldn't complete the job they hired me for. Or they didn't believe I could. Can't say I don't have some resentment over it. But my problem is with Wilberforce, not Witherspoon. Witherspoon wanted to keep me on, but like always, Wilberforce just ran over him."

"He got 'Wilberforced' into it," Treemont said, and Ben Scarlett laughed again.

Blalock sighed and shook his head. This Scarlett fellow seemed a nice enough gent, but something about him wore on Blalock's nerves. Sometimes Rand Blalock wished he could live in a world all by himself.

They rode on, leaving the Sadler camp behind. Ben hesitated, looking back, trying to see if he could spot Zeb McSwain. He could not. Probably McSwain was hidden away in his wagon, as was so common for him. Drinking from Ben's stolen silver flask, most likely.

Enough to make a self-respecting drunkard mad as blazes, Ben Scarlett mused bitterly.

Two days of travel, and it was obvious that Jedd's small and lean group was going to maintain a strong and probably growing lead over the unwieldy Sadler band, which seemed to be moving no faster despite the fact that General Lloyd was no longer around to cultivate inertia.

This suited Jedd mightily; it was important to him on a personal level to leave Wilberforce Sadler in his dust. Despite the continuing bodily pain both he and Treemont endured, and the fact that Ben Scarlett was beginning to suffer mentally and physically from lack of liquor, the quartet of riders (Jedd and Treemont had pitched in to buy, from a small emigrant band they passed, a horse and a cheap saddle for Ben Scarlett) moved on apace.

Ben Scarlett vanished the next night. He walked out into the dark to, as he put it, "perform his necessaries," and did not return. After an hour of absence, jokes began among the others about the apparent "bowel-binding" effects of Ben's new status as a horseback rider, jolting along on his rear end rather than striding on his legs. When that hour stretched to nearly two, the jokes stopped. Jedd grew worried and declared he was going out to look for Ben. Treemont proclaimed he would join him, and it wasn't until the pair was actually readying to rise and go that they remembered their current infirmities and the fact that they were essentially helpless to go after him.

Blalock did not hesitate. He'd spent many a dark night on the hunt for other human beings, some of them being victims, others being criminals who had created victims. He'd almost always brought in those he'd gone after.

"Good luck to you, Sheriff," Jedd said. "It's an ache in my craw that I can't walk out there on these feet to help you."

"Be wary. You never know what direction things may turn in," Blalock replied. "Keep in mind, Jedd, you and Treemont were both shot at, and hit, by somebody. If that somebody has been following, and if he got hold of Ben this night, he could show up here when I'm out looking for him there." He gestured toward the darkness beyond the reach of their campfire.

"You're right, of course," Jedd said. "And be wary we shall."

Blalock stalked away. Jedd and Treemont settled down with guns close by and eyes scanning the darkness. They sat on either side of the fire, backs turned toward the flame and each other so that they could see in all directions and their eyes would remain adjusted to the darkness. And they watched. For anything. Any hint of movement that might indicate Ben's safe return, or other possibilities not so pleasant to ponder.

Another hour passed. No Ben. No Blalock. Jedd grew increasingly worried and Treemont fretted so badly his breath was coming in ragged, wheezing gasps that threatened to hamper Jedd's concentration. Jedd had heard Tree do that before over the years, at times of particular stress.

Then Ben appeared. Slowly. He took form before Jedd's eyes like a ghost, moving slowly in from the darkness, shuffling along on foot. This was no surprise in that he'd left in the same manner, his horse with the other horses in a rope corral. What was a surprise, however, was the look on Ben's face. Jedd saw Ben's face more clearly the farther Ben stepped into the outer perimeter of the firelight. His eyes darted, his lip quivered . . . and Jedd noticed something at Ben's neck, circling it. It was a rope, and the length of the rope strung out behind him, into the dark.

"Ben? What the . . ."

"Jedd . . ." Ben's voice was tremulous and weak, the voice of a very scared man.

"Hello, Jedd Colter!" came a second voice, much stronger, from behind Ben. Jedd looked past Ben and saw the speaker just barely coming into view. The other end of the rope that was tied around Ben's neck was tied around the man's waist, and a shotgun, cut off short, was in his hands, aimed at the center of Ben's back. "You know who I am, Jedd?"

Jedd's hand subtly crept to the butt of his pistol, which lay on the ground beside him. "I know you, Carney. And I'm telling you to put down that shotgun you've got aimed at my friend there."

It was astonishing to Jedd to actually see this man again, a face he'd hoped nevermore to encounter. Carney, who had suffered ill personal consequences stemming from losing a bare-fisted prizefight with Jedd, had hated Jedd ever since. He'd publicly threatened to kill Jedd, and Jedd knew it, but he'd never worried much over it because it seemed unlikely he'd ever run across Carney again.

The narrowing of the funnel, Jedd thought. Once again, the funnel.

Treemont, who had been facing the opposite direction from which Ben and his captor had emerged, had by now turned himself painfully about and was looking across the fire and past Jedd, seeing only Ben but hearing Carney beyond him. Using his rifle as a support, Treemont managed to overcome the pain in his knee and push himself to his feet. He was raising his rifle when Carney shoved the muzzle hard against Ben's back, making him tilt forward from the waist. In that brief period that Ben was bent forward, Carney was barely visible to Treemont, who reacted by instinct. Tree raised his rifle and fired, but he'd not had time to aim, he knew right away the shot was wide of its target.

It was the last thing he ever knew. Carney fired his shotgun, the barrel extending out over the bent-over Ben Scarlett and fanning just above the seated Jedd's head. But the pellets caught Treemont in the upper chest and neck, and he pitched backward with his head nearly blown from his shoulders.

Ben moved more rapidly than he would have thought possible, grabbing the rope behind his head and jerking forward, hard, so that Carney was disbalanced. In a continuation of motion, Ben also came upright again, turning at the same time and knocking Carney's shotgun upward, lessening Jedd's danger momentarily and giving him time to whip up the revolver that had been lying beside him, and with it hammer three slugs into Carney's chest. Carney staggered back and collapsed as Jedd let out the roar of a madman, only just then having realized the fate Treemont had suffered.

Out in the darkness, Blalock heard the shooting and knew he was on a fool's errand out here in the night. He should never have left the camp, should have considered the fullest possible consequences of going after the missing Ben Scarlett, leaving the camp occupied only by two crippled men.

He turned at once back to the camp, and quickly put the bloody story together. To one side lay the corpse of Treemont Dalton, head blown into a hideous pulp. Kneeling over Treemont was a distraught Ben Scarlett, keening like a mourning Indian woman, declaring loudly to the night that it was his fault, his fault, his fault. He should never have left the camp because then he wouldn't have been caught and Treemont would still be alive. Oh, God forgive me, forgive me, please. . . . I'm so sorry. Ben's voice was an incessant, mumbling chatter.

Jedd remained where he had been before, seated with his back toward the now-diminishing fire, staring out at the dark and the barely visible body of Jake Carney. Blalock quietly entered the camp and walked to Jedd's side of the campfire. Jedd did not even look up at him as he spoke in a drained, listless voice. "He's dead, Sheriff. Treemont's dead."

"I know. I know. I'm more sorry than I can say. I wish I hadn't left you gents here alone in the camp."

"Wasn't your fault, Sheriff. Wasn't Ben's. It was *his*." Jedd pointed at Carney's body, visible to him mostly by the firelight-illuminated soles of Carney's upturned boots.

"I'm glad to hear you say that, because you're absolutely right. I've seen this kind of situation before, Jedd, and a lot of folks — a whole lot of folks — do just what poor old Scarlett is doing over there, blaming themselves for a string of events that really was a whole lot bigger than them and their own little part in it. You're right. This is the fault of that dead man lying before us. He is the one who shot you and Treemont out by that creek, and he's the one who shot Treemont dead tonight. Him and nobody else."

Jedd finally looked at Blalock. "I know, Sheriff. I know. But there's a part of you that just keeps asking, what if? What if I'd done this or done that, or anticipated this or considered that . . . ? You can't help it. I'm sitting here quiet, but inside me there's something screaming just as loud as poor Ben is back yonder. It's telling me that Tree is dead, Tree is dead, and there's bound to have been something I could have done that would have stopped it." Then Jedd tilted down his head and wept unabashedly.

"A man can 'what if' himself to his own grave, if he don't stop it," Blalock said. "The best is just to stop with the questions and doubts and go with the tears. Tears can be a strong healing medicine. So go ahead and cry them, Jedd. Go ahead."

Behind them, Ben Scarlett tilted up his head and wailed like a tormented phantom at the brooding sky.

They buried Treemont the next morning,

and Jedd found it easier to think calmly about his lost friend once his body, with its ruin of a shotgun-blasted head, was hidden beneath prairie soil. Blalock found some wood an earlier emigrant had tossed aside to lighten his wagon and with it made a cross, carving Treemont's name into the horizontal piece with his knife. They hammered it into place at the head of the grave; then the three men looked at one another, wondering who should say a prayer.

"I ain't one who is good with words," Blalock said, begging off, then casting his eyes toward Jedd.

Jedd shook his head. "My praying is done silently, in my mind. It never feels natural to speak it out loud."

Ben Scarlett shrugged and said, "I had a great-uncle who was a Methodist preacher, and he taught me how to pray. I reckon I can get through one, if you don't think it hurts the memory of Treemont for a drunk to be praying over him."

"Treemont would think it an honor," Jedd said, smiling encouragement at Ben.

Ben prayed just as he sang: beautifully. When he was done the two other men, and Ben himself, had tears on their faces and a sense of sorrow just beginning to be purged, just a little. But a beginning purge was all it was.

Jedd Colter especially knew he would not stop grieving for Treemont, at some level, for the rest of his life.

CHAPTER TWENTY-ONE

Santa Fe
October 1849

"Folks from the eastern states are often let down when they first see this place," said Jedd Colter as he, Ben Scarlett, and Rand Blalock rode into the streets of the historic old town, a piece of old Mexico transplanted into climes farther north. "It's the sameness of it. Everything's the same color, mostly, anyway. Dirt-colored. Adobe everywhere. Looks like a big old brick kiln to a lot of people."

"I think it's a beautiful sight," Ben Scarlett said. "I've heard they have big parties here, lots to drink. Fandanga-doodles or some such."

"Fandangos, Ben. Fandangos." Jedd chuckled. "Fandanga-doodles. I'll remember that one, Ben."

"There'll be liquor at them things, won't there?"

"Of course. If they happen to have a fandango while we're here. Odds are high that they will. They're common enough. But, Ben, you already have liquor. I bought it for you myself, back in San Miguel. Hell, I even bought you a new flask to replace that one you lost."

"The one I lost was silver. This new one is just tin. And I didn't lose the first one. It was stole from me."

"Let it go, Ben. Best thing you could do is throw the blasted thing away, and don't fill it again. You got to give up the drinking, Ben, unless you aim on dying an early death."

"Lord have mercy, Jedd. . . . You're a Job's comforter, you are!"

"I'm a truth-teller. I like you, Ben. I don't like seeing you killing yourself."

Ben snorted and refused to speak further, letting his horse fall back a little so he was no longer beside Jedd. Blalock rode up on Jedd's opposite side.

Jedd looked over at him. "Treemont would have liked to be here, Sheriff. I've been here with him before. . . . He loved the senoritas. Thought they were the prettiest ladies to be found anywhere. And he might be right."

Blalock was looking at a hump-shouldered, broadly built woman who was sharing the street with them, heading the opposite direction on foot. "I don't know, Jedd." The woman kicked a dog that had just run out of an alley and yapped at her ankles, and Blalock laughed.

"You're looking the wrong direction, Sheriff," Jedd said, eyes on a dark-eyed, dark-haired beauty smiling from a nearby balcony.

Jedd turned his head to see if Ben was doing any woman-watching of his own, but he was not there. He pointed out his absence to Blalock, and both riders turned back the way they had come and began a search for their friend.

It was not hard to guess where to look, nor did it take long to find him. Ben's horse was tied outside a cantina and Ben was inside, happily drinking himself into a fine humor. Jedd was unhappy but not in the slightest bit surprised. Nor did he scold Ben, who was, after all, a grown and independent man who made his own decisions, at least to the extent alcoholic addiction allowed it.

"Have a few swallows with me, men?" Ben asked. "Getting to Santa Fe is a milestone for the California-bound, and we ought to celebrate it."

"Our horses and packhorses and everything we own is outside on the street. I ain't willing to leave it there," Jedd said. "I'm going to see to our situation here, and then I'll come back once the horses are secured and we've got a place to stay."

"Jedd, I got no money for a hotel."

"Ben, you had no money for that drink in your cup until the sheriff and me gave you some. Don't fret. We'll pay for you for a place to sleep."

Ben took a long swig, belched, then wiped at his eyes. In a vaguely weepy voice, he said, "Jedd, I owe you so much. Ain't nobody in this world ever been kinder to me."

"Aw, Ben."

At that moment a bell clanged across the room and a tall Anglo man stepped onto a chair and raised his hands for attention. Many of the cantina patrons began to shift toward the rear of the broad, low-roofed room.

"What's about to happen here?" Blalock asked.

"I got a suspicion," Jedd said. "See the roped-off place near the corner there?"

His suspicion proved correct. "The fight will commence with the next bell in three minutes," the man in the chair declared in a booming voice. "Place your bets with Pablo

272

here behind the table. In an orderly manner, please. Gentlemen! Place your bets!"

Jedd moved forward on his crutch, being drawn back to a time not very long ago in his own life, when he'd toed many a line chalk-scrawled across barroom floors while facing off against some muscle-bound bare-fisted challenger. He didn't miss those days, but part of him remained intrigued with it all: the accouterments of fighting matches, the glint of an opponent's eyes, the feeling of fists cutting through air so fast they made an audible swish.

Ben stayed with his drink, but Jedd and Blalock joined the flow of the crowd, finding a position giving them a good view of the makeshift fighting ring, a mere square of rope suspended about three feet off the floor.

Jedd eyed the man on the chair, who held a bell in his hand, ready to start the fight. The betting was winding up over at Pablo's table. In moments the fighters would be brought out.

Then Jedd remembered the horses still outside, laden with all the possessions of the three travelers, and moved to go. Telling Blalock he would return shortly, Jedd left, with some logistical difficulty led the string of horses down the street, stabled them safely, stowed saddles and bridles in a rented locked storage room in the stable, then buttonholed a passing Mexican youth and paid him and a companion to carry luggage to the nearest hotel. When lodging was secured and luggage put away, Jedd began the difficult trek back to the saloon where he had left his companions. His ankle hurt fiercely; he wondered if he'd managed to reverse some of the healing progress he'd recently detected.

He neared the cantina where he'd left his companions just as a roar of voices rumbled out from inside the place. He surmised the fight had just reached its close — if so, it had been a long and probably fierce one. Bare-knuckle fights that dragged on this long indicated evenly matched opponents, and those were the fights that left men with broken noses and bleeding ears and bruised eyes swelling shut.

Jedd went inside, determined to sit down and get off his throbbing ankle for a while, and to regather with his friends and bring this long day to a close. Before he found a place to perch, though, he saw a bloodied hand being hoisted upward over in the fighting ring, another hand gripping its wrist. The victor being presented and declared to the applause of the rough and mostly drunken crowd.

It was a black man's hand, and even though his view of the winner's face was blocked by the crowd, Jedd instantly was sure that was Rollie Slott up there, another win beneath his belt.

But it couldn't be Rollie. Rollie was far away, back in Knoxville with his brother, Ollie, tending to his aging mother and dreaming of one day having something better than bruised knuckles and pounded flesh to show for himself. The thought of all the distance between him and the world he'd come from, not to mention the distance between a man's real life and the one he longed to have, made Jedd feel vaguely homesick and alone.

Then he thought: What if it really is Rollie up there? He and Ollie talked of their wish to go to California if circumstances ever allowed it — in other words, if their old mother passed on. What if she had passed on, and they had set out at once across the country? As slow as the Sadler group had moved, the Slott brothers could have passed by them unseen at any number of points along the way. Maybe Rollie and Ollie had made it as far, at least, as Santa Fe.

Jedd moved up closer, shifting about until he could see the face of the black man who had just won the bout.

It was not Rollie. This was a stranger, darker-skinned and far more battered than Rollie. He also lacked Rollie's smooth, supple musculature; this man's muscles were knotty and corded, bulging at places against the underside of his torso skin like potatoes trying to push their way out of the sack that held them.

That wistful sadness heightened inside Jedd. It would have been a fine thing to have run across an old face from home, here so far away, where everything was different.

"That was quite a fight," said Ben Scarlett behind Jedd. Jedd turned his head and flashed a quick grin at the now-drunken man. Ben's was an old face from home, just as he'd been thinking about, but in this instance Ben Scarlett just didn't count.

"I figured that out for myself when I came back in," Jedd said. "I was out of here for a good spell of time, and if they were pounding away at it that whole time, I knew it had to be a real knuckle-buster."

"You used to fight, didn't you, Jedd?"

"I did. Eight, nine years back. It's a rough road to travel, Ben. It has its moments, when it's your hand being hoisted up in the air at the end . . . but there's plenty of the other kind of moments, too. And it leaves you aching all the time. Even after the fight is long over and you've healed up. There's always pain remaining."

"I know about that. About pain remaining."

"You used to fight?"

"Nah. That ain't the kind of pain I'm talking about. There's more than one kind, you know. And more than one kind that can remain with you even after you think all the healing's done. That's what makes me drink, you see? Because of the pain that always remains."

"Does the drinking wash it away?"

"Just numbs it. That's all. Numbs it."

Jedd realized then how little he knew of Ben Scarlett's life story. The Ben he'd known had already been a drunkard when Jedd first met him after moving to Tennessee from North Carolina. But there had to be more to him than that. There was a time in Ben's life before the liquor took over, and something in that time of his life had to account for his fall into the swamp of alcohol. Jedd had no idea what it was. Maybe sometime he'd ask Ben about it.

Not tonight. Jedd felt low enough already, and his ankle hurt worse than it had the night after he was shot. He'd be glad to put this day and night behind and start fresh in the morning.

California was calling.

Ben and Jedd collected Blalock, who was himself significantly besotted by this point, and Jedd took them toward the hotel he'd secured for them earlier. Blalock proved out to be a whining drunk, reliving and relaying in unwanted bloody detail the murder of Carver Dalton's family back home, the atrocity that had driven Blalock westward on a search for Treemont so he could give him the bad news.

Now Treemont was dead, too. Blalock bemoaned the harshness and bitterness of human existence, the blatant unfairness of it all.

The drunk old former sheriff staggered away from Ben and Jedd, out into the center of the street, and turned his eyes upward to the sky, an angry grimace on his face. He raised his fist and shook it.

"It ain't right, damn it!" he hollered drunkenly. "It just ain't right that such things happen! You hear me, God? You got no business treating us so mean! You need to stop all that kind of nonsense! You hear me? You need to stop it. I've got half a mind to come up there and kick your . . . your holy . . ."

Ben looked horrified and stared upward

as if expecting a bolt to stab down from the sky and fry Blalock where he stood raging and blaspheming. "He don't mean it, Lord!" Ben said to the heavens. "He's just drunk, Lord. That's all. Everything's good. We're fine down here, thanks. Just fine! Oh . . . and I'm drunk, too. But I reckon you already know that, huh? You being who you are and all that."

"Good God!" Jedd exclaimed softly, incredulous at all this strange behavior and babble from his companions. Then he flicked his own eyes skyward. "And I mean that in a good way, Lord. Just to make sure we're clear on that. And please overlook my two partners here. . . . They know not what they do."

Then to his companions, he said, "Gentlemen, let's move on to our lodgings for the night. After many a night in a bedroll on the ground, we're in for rest on some real beds for a change, and I believe I'm ready."

They lingered in Santa Fe for enough days that Jedd began looking for the Sadler band to come rolling into town behind them. They did not. Jedd and company moved on.

In Albuquerque, Colter and company found even more comfortable lodgings than they had enjoyed in Santa Fe, and decided to settle in for the winter. There was no particular reason to rush to California as long as they could reach it by the start of the mining season. The three men found basic labor in the town to sustain themselves, Ben working with a grocer, Blalock with a local marshal as a jailer, and Jedd as a clerk in a gun shop. Low-paying work all around, but the men were glad for a change of pace. Ben even cut down on his drinking, though he was far from giving it up. The fact that Albuquerque had fandangos even more frequently than Santa Fe kept Ben around enough liquor to defray any ambition toward teetotalism that might have stricken him from some unexpected fount of inspiration. Not that such was likely to happen in any case.

The winter passed and still the Sadler emigrants did not appear. Jedd considered backtracking to investigate, fearing disaster might have struck them. Knowledge that he had been deliberately severed from that group kept him from doing it.

Also the fact that he found himself worrying about Rachel McCall. Strange that he would be thinking of her, because he didn't really care about her. Did he?

He was forced to admit to himself that he wasn't really sure of the answer to that question. It was odd, and unsettling.

The winter dragged on, but when 1850 rolled around, California called all the more clearly. Jedd and his companions traveled between the route generally known as Cooke's Wagon Road, and the Gila River. They passed the town of Socorro and tracked along the Rio Grande into Mexico, then turned at the Diego crossing and traveled to the Two Buttes. The journey continued from there, along trails becoming all the more worn and well known because of the volume of traffic the rush to California had brought to them.

It was April 1850 before the three men reached Los Angeles, and some weeks beyond that before they were in the heart of the gold country.

What had begun as an adventure with a group pledging to set a new record in crossing to California had turned into a long, slow, yearlong journey, and Jedd Colter found himself lacking any ambition to repeat it anytime in the near future.

It had taken him a long time to reach California. Now that he was here, he was inclined to stay awhile. He wished only that Treemont had survived to complete the journey with him.

■ ■ ■ ■

PART THREE:
SCARLETT'S LUCK

■ ■ ■ ■

CHAPTER TWENTY-TWO

August 1850

Rand Blalock was a sheriff again. He still could hardly believe it, but it was true.

Well, not entirely true, old boy, he reminded himself. He wasn't a full-fledged, authentic sheriff, just a local marshal in a mining camp that was growing into a town, a jurisdiction he could very nearly spit across if the wind was in his favor. And even though his official title was marshal of Scarlett's Luck, California, he thought of himself and referred to himself as sheriff, and most everyone around him did as well. Including his law enforcement staff, which consisted of a single deputy, Jedediah Colter, who received no pay beyond being allowed by Ben Scarlett to pan out a few flakes of gold for himself on Ben's claim.

Blalock downed the final swig of his morning coffee and stood. He'd been seated on the edge of his sagging bed, a rough straw tick suspended from a simple frame by rope slats. He staggered forward clumsily across his cabin floor; the pressure of the bed frame against the underside of his thighs had put his legs to sleep. He grimaced as he moved around, suffering from the painful tingle of blood reentering the deprived vessels.

His eyes drifted upward and he shook his head as he eyed the underside of what served inefficiently as a roof for his little log dwelling. It was merely an expanse of canvas spread over a central elevated ridgepole running horizontally down the middle of the cabin, end to end. Blalock had been known to refer to his fabric roof as his "rain strainer." This little cabin, like many in Scarlett's Luck, was a relic of the camp's beginning, the period when prospectors had only just started to swarm in profusely in response to spreading news of the latest discovery of gold. This find had been made in a small creek by one Ben Scarlett, a newcomer from Tennessee. Scarlett, one of the hardest-drinking men around even by mining camp standards, had ridden into the area in company with Rand Blalock and another fellow named Colter. That they had come at all was surprising to some, because Colter and Blalock had presented little evidence of serious mining ambitions. For that matter, neither had Ben Scarlett.

Which was where the "luck" in Scarlett's Luck came in.

The story of how Ben Scarlett made his find would become part of mining camp lore carried down through the years. Ben had been drunk one afternoon — no surprise there to any who had come to know him — and had been making his way toward a thicket of trees to relieve his bladder when he'd encountered a little creek he'd not even realized was there. Sufficiently intoxicated that the narrow little step-over rill was enough to flummox him, Ben had come to a halt, stood listening for a moment to the liquid flow of the creek, and had wet himself where he stood, drenching himself from crotch to cuffs.

Embarrassed, he'd looked around and mumbled a drunkard's prayer of thanks that there had been no one nearby to see him shame himself. Then he'd peeled off the wet pants right there on the spot, leaving on his long underwear to retain a modicum of decency. He knelt and washed his outer trousers out in the creek. Then into the water he'd gone, full body, sitting down as if in a bath and letting the running water wash out his urine-soaked underwear as best it could with the garment still on him. He'd pulled his wet pants back on over his equally wet legs, and stumped back to the tent that served as his first California home. The tent had been a gift from Jedd Colter, bought at a premium in a mining supply store. In his tent Ben had stripped down to his shirt, hung his wet garments up to dry inside the tent, and taken a nap.

Upon awakening two hours later, Ben had stumbled over to the entrance of his tent and stepped out into the waning day, having completely forgotten he'd stripped down earlier. He looked around, stretched with elbows cocked out beside him at shoulder level, and yawned broadly and loudly. Then he'd heard a youthful feminine scream and, immediately after, the chiding voice of a man who was running toward him, none too happy.

"Sir! What in blazes are you doing, showing yourself so! My twelve-year-old daughter is down there in that wagon, and this she does not need to see! Cover yourself, man! Have some decency about you!"

Ben looked down and was visually reminded, with horror, of his nakedness. His hands groped downward, covering himself, and he backed into his tent, apologizing profusely. He quickly pulled on his underwear, then scrambled to get his trousers on with equal haste — but abruptly he stopped.

Something was glittering back at him. Yellow flecks caught in the fabric of his pants, throwing back the last remaining rays of sunlight streaming in through his west-facing tent door. Ben's mind was seldom quick, liquor having slowed it. This time, though, he knew right away what had happened, and that the golden dust caught in the cloth of his pants had to have been trapped there while he was washing the garment clean of urine.

He'd found gold. He, Ben Scarlett, world's must unprivileged and unlucky man, had become the only man in history to find California gold because he'd peed in his own pants.

In subsequent days, word spread of the new find, as it always did. Ben established his claim, but before long had neighbors all around him. When details of his odd route to success became known, what started out being called Scarlett's Creek became Scarlett's Wash, then Scarlett's Camp, and finally, Scarlett's Luck.

Ben liked the sound of that. He'd never thought he'd be considered a lucky man. And his luck continued, day by day, as he began to adjust himself to the discipline of kneeling by Scarlett's Creek and swirling gravel and sediment in his pan. The dirt was kind, and paid. He was steadily gaining wealth, however modestly, for the first time in his life.

In September of 1850, statehood came to California. By that point, Scarlett's Luck had become an actual town, governed by a board of "mining commissioners" who oversaw much more than mining. As some mining camps were prone to do, Scarlett's Luck attracted more than its share of undesirables, leading the commissioners to seek an appointed officer to maintain a measure of law and order. When the sheriffing background of Blalock was discovered, he was offered the post, and took it on condition that he be allowed to hire a deputy to assist him. Jedd, who had never sought to work as a lawman, was offered the job and on impulse accepted it.

It was to be a more fateful choice than he could ever have foreseen.

It was by no particular design that so many of the emigrants from the California Enterprise Company of East Tennessee drifted into Scarlett's Luck and established claims there. In California, news of a new strike drew miners from all over, both newcomers and those well established in other camps. So Scarlett's Luck gained new residents derived from any number of recently arrived emigrant bands.

Some of the Sadler group who came to the new mining town did not know that the Scarlett whose name had become attached to the place was the same one who had traveled with them. Others knew exactly who he was and came in part because they could not resist seeing with their own eyes how success and good luck would affect the bedraggled drunk with whom they had passed almost all the way across a continent.

Crozier Bellingham was one of the latter variety. He'd heard the story of Ben Scarlett's undignified way of discovering gold in his little creek, or at least one version of it, and knew he had to learn the full details. This, he knew, would have to find a place in his novel of the gold fields. Probably in a disguised, renamed form, but still the same story. And he wanted to get it right. He also wanted to see Ben again, and Jedd Colter, who reportedly was living in Scarlett's Luck as well. There were stories of the Sadler journey as it progressed after Jedd's departure that Bellingham wished to share. And he wanted to know what had happened to

Jedd and his partners on the final leg of the trip. And if it was true that Jedd's friend Tree Dalton had been killed.

Bellingham had another reason for wanting to go to Scarlett's Luck as well. Now that the California Enterprise Company of East Tennessee had completed its venture, it was officially inert and inactive, if not fully dissolved. Bellingham's part, however, was at an end. He'd filed his last report back to the Knoxville newspaper, simply averting his attention, as he'd taught himself to do, while Wilberforce Sadler worked over his report with a censorious and self-serving pencil before allowing it to be posted off to Tennessee. Bellingham had no idea exactly what was being published under his byline once Wilberforce got through with the copy, but he tried not to worry over it. He was gone from Knoxville now and did not anticipate a return. The newspaper reports did not matter. What mattered was his own, Sadler-free project, his planned novel. He already had a title in mind for it: *Schuyler's Luck*. Anyone in the know would easily guess from whence that title was derived, but it wouldn't matter. He would fictionalize it sufficiently to separate his story from the real-life tale of Ben Scarlett and his remarkable stroke of pants-wetting luck.

Jedd Colter had built his own cabin within sight of Blalock's, but had taken it a step or two further than Blalock had by riving wooden shingles and putting a real roof on his dwelling. He offered to help Blalock do the same, but the old lawman was prideful and didn't want to be seen as trying to keep pace with somebody else's progress. He'd put on a real roof when he was ready; until then, his tent-cloth covering would suffice.

Jedd was behind his little hut of a cabin, building himself a boxy outdoor oven from native stone, the day Bellingham arrived. Because of Jedd's deputy status, he was well known in Scarlett's Luck, so Bellingham had encountered no difficulties in obtaining directions to where Jedd could be found. It was a Sunday afternoon and Jedd was enjoying a time of solitary work. He wasn't much of a stonemason, but it was a pleasure to try his best to do a good job at it. . . . So he was none too happy to hear the muffled thump of someone knocking on his cabin door. Though he wasn't inside, the sound carried around the cabin. He walked around the cabin to see who was out front, still limping badly on his injured ankle, but now moving about without a crutch or cane.

"Hello, Crozier," he said, feeling surprise but not showing it. "Where did you come from?"

"Jedd, sir. How are you?"

"I can't complain. I won't, anyway. I reckon you heard about Ben Scarlett's turn of good luck."

"I have. That's part of what brought me here."

"Come on around back. I'm building an oven back there. You can tell me all that's going on with you and the others."

Bellingham found a handy stump to sit on. He couldn't stop grinning. It was honestly good to see Jedd Colter again. Jedd went back to his stone laying. "Got your book wrote yet?" he asked Bellingham.

"Still involved in the planning," Bellingham replied. "It's something I want to do right, when I do it."

"I can understand that. Sadlers won't be involved, right?"

"The Sadlers won't know a thing about it until everybody else does. When it's published."

"You're confident you can find somebody to publish it?"

"I am. Because I know how good it will be. And because this nation is still full of excitement about gold in California. And stories like Ben Scarlett's are just what people love to read."

"So it's Ben's story you'll tell?"

"It's likely to be the frame around which the novel is built. Names changed, some details different, of course. No pants-pissing in it."

Jedd grinned. "That's the best part, though."

Bellingham laughed. "I know, I know."

Jedd worked awhile longer in silence. "Got a bottle inside, if you'd like a drink."

"I'd like one, but I think I'll pass. Get yourself one, if you want."

Jedd did, and when Bellingham saw it, he changed his mind and accepted one as well, served up in a cracked china teacup. Bellingham sipped slowly.

"Have you gone to see her yet?" Bellingham asked Jedd, knowing it was a potentially delicate question.

"Who do you mean?" Jedd asked, knowing perfectly well to whom Bellingham was referring.

"McSwain's daughter. The one you told me about."

Jedd felt some irritation at the personal question, and wondered if talking to Bellingham would result in his most personal life affairs being fictionalized before the entire world in Bellingham's planned book.

"I ain't been to see nobody," Jedd replied, a little sullen but trying to hide the fact. "I was named deputy marshal in this mining camp, and I've tried to keep close by in case something happens."

"Has anything happened?"

Jedd shrugged. "A few fistfights. Two knife fights. A bit of gold theft. One fellow shot at another and missed, but killed his own dog with the shot. Nothing you'd want to write about, I don't think."

"It's the little things that bring life to stories. The touches that make them feel real. Verisimilitude, it's called. Verisimilitude."

"Sort of like, very similar to the real thing. Real life."

"Bang! Right on the nose!"

"I'm so smart I scare myself," Jedd said, and Bellingham laughed.

CHAPTER TWENTY-THREE

Now it was Jedd's turn to ask a question. "Speaking of McSwain, how did things go with him the last part of the journey? And where is he now?"

"It was kind of strange with him. You know how things are between him and Wilberforce, with Wilberforce heading up the college board that took away McSwain's college and his job. Well, after you were gone, Wilberforce became more and more belligerent with McSwain, calling him a thief and a scoundrel, right in front of the entire camp. Challenged him to return what he'd taken."

"Did he explain that any further?"

"No. That's all he said. 'Return what you took, you damned thief.' And McSwain denied he'd ever taken anything from anyone. Wilberforce laughed at him, but there was nothing funny in how he did it. You know what I mean. One of *those* kinds of laughs."

"Yep."

"And Witherspoon scolded him for making such a display of it all, told him to leave McSwain alone. Wilberforce called Withers a 'fat fool.' Witherspoon just glared back at him, trying to look bold and strong, and you could tell it."

"Was Rachel McCall nearby at the time?"

"Oh yes. Oh yes. Witherspoon couldn't stop himself from glancing over at her, over and over. He was showing off for her, standing up to his brother like that."

"I can't help liking Witherspoon," Jedd said. "Wilberforce I can do without. He's the one who broke the deal we had, after my ankle got hurt."

"I know. I don't like him, either. Nobody does, I don't think, except maybe his wife. And I can't swear that she does."

Mention of Wilberforce's wife reminded Jedd about the painter of portraits, Dupont Gale, who had joined the Sadler wagon train along the way. He asked about him.

"He got shot. Santa Fe. I don't know the details, but I think he'd tried to talk a senorita into letting him paint her, and her man misunderstood what he was asking. Pulled out an old flintlock pistol, of all things, and shot him right through the head."

"Gale is *dead*?"

"Believe it or not, no. That pistol ball punched right through his brain, but it didn't kill him. Put him down, but he was still breathing, eyes still looking around, he was even speaking some. Saying he was going to paint again. Damnedest thing I ever saw, I have to admit. I don't see how he survived it, but he did. Last I saw of him, he was still living, anyway. He was left with a doctor in Albuquerque who took an interest in him because it was so unusual, him surviving such a thing."

"I hope he makes it."

"So do I. Hey, one more thing about McSwain. A strange thing that happened one night, right at the time Wilberforce cut you off from working for the enterprise . . . right after your ankle was ruined."

"It was hurt, not ruined. It's healing well now. But go on with your story."

"McSwain was out in the camp, just talking to some folks, seeming more cheerful and less distracted than he usually did. Well, from out in the dark there came the sound of someone singing. A man's voice, off a far distance away but still carrying in on the breeze, faint and strange. It raised chills on my flesh. The song sounded . . . well, I suppose you'd have to say it sounded foreign. The singer had a brogue, an accent. I don't know accents well enough to tell you what kind it was. Maybe Scottish. Maybe English . . . but no. No. I've heard Nigel Straw speak, and this accent didn't sound like his. I think it was maybe Irish."

"Did everyone hear it?"

"A lot did. I heard it clear, and McSwain heard it. When he did, it changed him, right away. Sent him pulling back inside himself like a turtle going inside its shell. . . . I don't know how else to put it. He heard that singing voice coming in from out in the dark, and he quit talking, quit looking anyone in the eye. . . . Then he stood up and went back to his wagon and crawled inside. Nobody saw him the rest of the evening. But that voice out there just kept on singing. Sounding so strange and foreign and . . . well, fearful."

"I know," Jedd said. "I heard it, too, just like you did. There in my tent with Treemont. It raised bumps on my flesh."

"Do you know who it was?"

"I don't. Do you?"

Bellingham's gaze drifted and settled on a lizard making its skittish way across a rock. "Not exactly . . . but I may have an idea of

300

why he was out there, and why McSwain reacted to the sound of him like he did. Something Ferkus Varney told me that night. He heard the voice, too, and it rattled him. I could see that it did, and later I asked him about it.

"He was in a humor to talk, I suppose, because he told me that he recognized the voice as belonging to an Irishman who had visited with Wilberforce Sadler behind closed doors. Varney hadn't been privy to the meeting, but he was so curious about this man that he slipped into a closet nearby that had one thin wall, the other side of which was part of the wall of Wilberforce's office. In there he was able to hear enough conversation between Wilberforce and the Irishman to let him know that something very bad was being worked up between them. Something involving McSwain."

Jedd frowned in thought. "It had to relate to the troubles of Bledsoe College. Right?"

"Indeed. Varney told me that Wilberforce was talking to the Irishman about the theft of something from the coffers of Bledsoe College. Wilberforce wanted whatever it was to be retrieved from the thief — McSwain, it would seem — and returned. Varney took that to mean returned to Bledsoe College, no doubt then to be absorbed, along with the other assets of Bledsoe, into East Tennessee University."

"This Irishman, then, was being hired by Wilberforce, whether as an individual or on behalf of the board of Bledsoe College, to find McSwain, and retrieve whatever McSwain stole."

"That was Varney's understanding."

Jedd took a seat on a nearby rock, resting his still-healing ankle. "Crozier, whatever arrangement Wilberforce made with this Irishman surely must have been a lucrative one, if we are to believe it was his voice we heard making music out on the plains that night. Because that would mean he was sufficiently motivated to follow McSwain all the way across the country to complete his assignment."

"Yes. So either Wilberforce had promised him a high level of pay indeed, or . . ."

Jedd saw where Bellingham was leading. "Or whatever McSwain had was so valuable that it was worth traversing a whole nation to get his hands on. Because once he got it, he could keep it for himself."

"Exactly," Bellingham said. "You and I are thinking along the same lines, Jedd. But the big question becomes, what is it that McSwain took? It had to be highly valuable, portable, and small enough to fit . . ." Bellingham paused, looking at Jedd.

Jedd completed the thought. "Small enough to fit inside a dead cat."

Bellingham gave a vigorous nod. "Meaning there was far more than just sentiment at work when McSwain kept that stuffed cat of his in hand nearly every minute. He was protecting his treasure.

"He ended up giving that cat away. . . . Did you know that, Jedd? Right in there just about the time you and Treemont got shot beside that creek. McSwain gave the cat to an ailing little girl in that emigrant camp that set up right beside ours."

"I didn't know about that, no. But I can tell you this: the way he was clinging to that cat, he must have taken out what he'd hid inside it and stashed it somewhere else. Otherwise he'd never have given it up. Know what I'm thinking?"

"Gold? Jewels?"

"You and me think just alike, Crozier. Jewels . . . almost has to be. Something that can be very small but still very valuable. Something that could be hid inside a stuffed dead critter."

"Or a drinking man's flask."

Jedd's querying look led Bellingham to expound a little. "You remember that flask Ben Scarlett was so proud of, and then it

303

went missing? Well, it went missing right at the same time McSwain gave away Cicero to that little girl. So I think McSwain took that flask, popped his diamonds or whatever they were down the spout, then either kept the flask on him in a pocket from then on or kept it hidden in his wagon."

"That's as good a theory as any, I reckon."

"Oh . . . Jedd, one more thing about that Irishman. Something good to know that might help you identify him if he shows up in these parts. He has a notched ear. Like somebody cut him with a knife or something. Ferkus Varney saw it when the man came to see Wilberforce."

Something about that rang an alarm in Jedd's mind, but it took him a couple of minutes of thought to remember where he'd run across a notch-eared man before.

It had been that evening at McSwain's house on Addington Street in Knoxville. The night Ben Scarlett had gotten caught nosing around in the rubbish behind the house, and had surprised an armed man, who had fled. Jedd recalled that Ben had said the fellow spoke no words — a measure to keep his accent from being heard, maybe? — and that he'd possessed a notched ear.

McSwain indeed had been in danger that night, Jedd could see. He was grateful that old Notchy apparently had not made a second visit to the house after Jedd and Ben were gone from it. If he had, McSwain would probably not be alive today.

Jedd and Bellingham had another drink, and Jedd moved the conversation to other subjects: California statehood, the speed with which wilderness could become a small town, then a town not so small, and the steadily improving mechanics of placer mining and the inevitable development of new mining technologies.

"You think McSwain has gone to see his daughter, Jedd?" Bellingham asked as conversation finally began to wane.

"No idea, Crozier. It wouldn't surprise me. I know he's fretted over her a good deal. Didn't like her husband."

"I'm trying to remember the name of the town they live in here. . . ."

"Bowater."

"I've heard of it. Never been there, but heard of it."

"I've not been there, either. I expect that may not hold true much longer."

"You're going to go see her, Jedd?"

"I think I will. I've come a mighty long way, after all, and it was her being out here that was a big part of the reason for it."

"What will her husband think, you knocking on their door?"

"I think that when he sees me, he'll wish he'd treated her better, if what I've been hearing about his sorry ways proves to be true. Which I hope it ain't. As much as I wish she'd never married that coot, and as much as I wish the marriage would just kind of wash away like mud off a slick rock, I don't want to think it's because she's been mistreated by her own husband. I'd rather him just strangle to death on his cup of coffee, or something. Get out of the way convenient-like and easy."

"Nothing's ever easy, Jedd."

"I know. Hey, where is Zeb McSwain living now that he's in California? You got any idea?"

Bellingham shrugged and shook his head. "Nobody seems to know. He pulled away from everybody else and just vanished off on his own, sort of like he did on the way here when he was hiding out in his wagon most of the time."

"Yeah. And I'm not sure how he got away with all that hiding out as well as he did. Not pulling his own weight and all. Just letting himself be hauled along like a piece of baggage. How did he get away with it?"

Bellingham said, "I think it was because Wilberforce was glad to have him out of sight and out of mind. He didn't want him along on the journey at all, you know. It was Witherspoon, not Wilberforce, who agreed to let McSwain buy his way into the journey."

The conversation made another shift, Bellingham inquiring about just what had happened to Treemont Dalton. Jedd told him the sad story and fell into a quiet reverie. Bellingham could see that his welcome was beginning to wear out and knew it was time to leave and find his way to the nearest semblance of a hotel. But he hated to depart from Jedd's place with the mood so somber.

Bellingham helped himself to a little more whiskey; Jedd did the same. To brighten the atmosphere, Bellingham raised his cup. "To California, and Scarlett's Luck, and Emma, and the memory of Treemont Dalton. A fine man."

"Hear, hear!" They drank.

That night, Jedd Colter sat upright in his bed and stared into the corner of his cabin, mind racing.

He hadn't dreamed, but something had arisen in his mind. A memory, one that returned with the clarity of a mountain stream the moment it poured into his semi-consciousness. It hit his mind with enough force to waken him.

"I know him," Jedd said to the empty cabin. "I know old Notch-ear sure as the world. I fought the son of a bitch, in Missouri. Calahan's Beer Garden. I remember it well."

Clear the memory was, but not pleasant. Few memories were that derived from Jedd's days as a bare-fisted fighter when he was about twenty years of age. He associated those days mostly with pain, sweat, and blood, with a grating roar in the ears that came partly from the howling, violence-loving crowd around him and partly from the ringing of his skull by his opponent's fist. He remembered the smell of chalk dust and tobacco smoke, the stink of his own sweat and his opponents', and the even-worse stink of the sweaty crowd encircling the pugilists. These memories raised little nostalgia in him. He'd been glad to put fighting behind when that time came. He was happy to let most of the memories of those days fade.

The memory of his bout with notch-eared Declan Finnegan was one of the worst of them. He'd lost that fight. Jedd Colter usually won his matches, but that one had gone badly. He would never forget the power of the jolt of Finnegan's right fist, jarring his jawbone and knocking a tooth loose inside his head. He'd awakened on the filthy floor of Calahan's Beer Garden with that liberated tooth swimming around in a mouthful of his own blood. He spat it out as he got up, and a saloon girl had fainted at the sight of blood washing down his chin like a red waterfall.

Jedd cupped his hands behind his head and leaned back against the wide, pit-sawed, on-its-side plank that served as a headboard on his homemade bunk. He relived the fight with Declan Finnegan and pondered the oddity of having run across the man again after all these years, even if only indirectly.

Just another verification of his narrowing funnel theory, he supposed.

At the time he'd been set up to fight Finnegan, he'd known nothing of the man except his reputation as a fighter who would do whatever it took to win. "Watch him close," Treemont had warned him. "Old Irish there has been known to sneak a metal slug into his fist so he can break jawbones easier. So I've heard."

There had been no hidden metal slugs during Jedd's fight with the Irishman, but he'd gone down hard nonetheless, having carelessly given the fighter an opening when a pretty saloon girl had blown a kiss Jedd's way and distracted him for less than a second. When he'd come around again, spitting blood and a knocked-out tooth, he'd made a pledge to himself to steer clear of Finnegan in the future.

In terms of fighting, he'd kept that pledge completely. But it appeared likely that it had been Finnegan who was outside McSwain's Knoxville home that night. . . . Finnegan with a gun in his possession, a threat to McSwain. Why? Who had put him there? Would the board of trustees of a respected college actually do such a drastic thing as hire an assassin? Actually try to do in a collegiate president under their hire?

Not just a president, though. A president who apparently had stolen from his own college, stolen at a significant level.

Sitting there in the darkness, Jedd decided it was time to find McSwain and, if he could, finally get to the bottom of this thing. It was impossible for him not to care about McSwain and what might happen to him, considering McSwain's support of Jedd and the simple fact that he was Emma's father.

Jedd decided he'd just have to see Emma, too. He owed it to himself, particularly after traversing the entire country to be where she was. If her husband didn't like him coming by, the scoundrel would simply have to deal with it.

Jedd lay back down and rolled over. He closed his eyes, but it was an hour before he slept again.

CHAPTER TWENTY-FOUR

San Francisco

The man sat back on the outdoor bench and appreciated the shade of the awning above him. The awning was attached to a slightly fire-damaged and abandoned dry goods store and extended out over the wide boardwalk that had become a place of business for the man kneeling at the first man's feet.

"And how did you come into the knowledge of the boot-making trade, might I ask?" the first man said. He was a lean fellow, fair skin but weathered, and appeared to be bald, or mostly so, because he wore a scarf tight around his head and showing no evidence of a padding of hair between the cloth and his flesh. One of his ears had a triangular piece missing from it, cut out as neatly as if a surgeon had removed it or a tailor had taken a pair of good scissors to it.

The kneeling man, who was studying the

reading on the tape measure he'd just wrapped around the other man's foot at the highest point of his arch, said, "It was family training, sir. My uncle was the best boot maker in Knoxville, Tennessee, in his day, and he taught me all I know. Well, most of it. What he didn't teach me, experience did. I've made many a boot for many a foot in my time, and I believe that when the final product is on your own feet, you'll see the benefit of that experience."

"Confidence!" the boot maker's customer said. "I like that in a man! Knoxville, did you say?"

"Yes, sir," replied the other. "That's where I come from. Me and my brother, Rollie, we both traveled from there to here, and been in San Francisco just shy of three months now. We'd probably have come sooner if it hadn't been for needing to take care of our mother, who was old and ailing. It was after she passed on that we were free to leave Knoxville."

"Aye, aye," the other man said. "I've been to, and left, Knoxville myself. It was from the Knoxville area that I set out just last year to come here."

"You ain't a-foolin' me, sir?"

"Not a bit of it, Ollie. Not a bit."

"Well, I'll be! They say it's a small world,

and I reckon it must be."

"Aye, and smaller yet it will become as the years go by, my good man."

"Sir, I hope you don't mind me saying that, from the sound of your speaking, I'd never have guessed you for a Tennessee man."

"Oh no. I was in that state only briefly. On business, shall we say? Where I come from is a long way indeed from Knoxville in Tennessee. I'm an Irishman, friend Ollie. I spent my youth in the old country and came to America to build both future and fortune."

" 'Future and fortune,' I like that, sir," Ollie Slott said. "I'm going to remember them words, and tell them to Rollie. He'll like them, too."

"Is Rollie a boot maker as well?"

"Oh no, sir. No. Rollie's a strong man, powerful with his fists. He fights. Fights for money."

"A fighter? No!"

"Actually, sir, it's yes. He's been at it for a few years now. He don't lose often, Rollie don't. He's best known back home, but it won't be long before he's known just as well out here. He's been fighting some since we got here, and he's won every one of them."

The Irishman stared across the street at a

dog slowly sauntering up an alleyway. There was a cat at the far end of the alley, but the dog was too old and slow to care, and so was the cat. The dog strode past the feline as if not even sensing its presence.

"Rollie Slott. I'll remember the name," the Irishman said. "You know, Ollie, I've done some fighting for pay in my time, too. I wonder if your brother and I have ever crossed fists. I've fought a few Africans over the years."

"Sir, might I ask your name? I'll need it anyways to make sure I get your new boots safe to you without a hitch."

"I am Declan Finnegan."

"Sir . . . I might have heard of you. I think maybe you did fight Rollie once before, years ago. I think maybe you won that fight."

"If he is the man I am thinking of, I believe you are right. It was a hard fight, and I very nearly got the worst end of it. It was a lucky punch on my part, as I remember it, that brought your brother down. Nothing I can boast in . . . just good luck." Finnegan looked squarely at Ollie. "I respect your brother, Ollie. I respect any man possessing the level of skill he possesses. I might have prevailed over him before, but I'd guess that if we faced off again, I'd not be so lucky."

"I'll tell him I run across you, sir, and pass on your greetings, if that would suit you."

"Please do, please do. And one other thing I'll ask you about. You are from Knoxville. Perhaps you know an old friend of mine who I believe came to California. He was president of a college there in your old city, but I think no longer is."

"Zebulon McSwain, sir?"

"The very man! Do you know him?"

"I'm familiar with him, sir. I'd not call him a friend, him being in a station of life far above my own."

"He is an old friend. I hope to find him. Can you help me?"

"I'll try, sir. Where could I get word to you if I find him?"

Finnegan provided the name of a well-known hotel, and Ollie promised to send word to him if his path and McSwain's should cross. Even as he did so, he wondered if he was being prudent. This Irish fellow seemed cordial enough, but Ollie didn't really know him. And Rollie always did tell his brother he was too quick to put his trust in strangers.

Ollie told himself it didn't really matter. The odds of encountering Zeb McSwain were tiny. Nothing to be concerned about.

Bowater Gulch, California

It was said that the feminine population of California in this year of 1850 was under eight percent of the total, and Emma Wickham had no problem believing it. She lived in a world in which it seemed every traveler coming down the road, every visitor knocking on the door, and every face of a customer in her husband's camp store was inevitably male.

Emma remembered what her expectations had been at the time she'd married Stanley Wickham and their move to California was still ahead of her. She'd anticipated life in an exotic, perfect country where warmth and sunshine prevailed. Her home would be fine and modern, rivaling the best dwellings of the big eastern cities. Accustomed to the rugged and gritty little frontier town of Knoxville, Emma would make sure they lived in a far more sophisticated setting, a place where there was culture, music, art, theatre. And they would have money, Stanley's family money combined with that which he would make in business, in abundance, and with that they would enjoy a life of security, good food, good clothing, good living in general. And for Emma there would be friends, countless friends, other women of like status and situation, sharing with her the joys of privilege.

How different the reality had proven to be! They lived not in a sophisticated community, but a little mining town where the greatest artistic and cultural endeavor was a little out-of-tune brass band made up of amateurs who routinely slaughtered every melody they attempted. Her house was, admittedly, one of the biggest and sturdiest in town, but even so it was a haphazard combination of conflicting construction techniques: log, frame, stucco. To Emma's eye it appeared absurd, an architectural joke.

As for the army of female friends she had anticipated, there was no such group. There were hardly any women around at all, and of the few there were, several were Mexican, two were "Celestial," or Oriental, one was Indian, one an Australian. The Aussie drank hard and swore harder, and Emma found her intolerable. With the others she simply had little in common.

There were a few other women who were more like Emma in age, background, and so on, but some of them were dance hall girls, saloon ladies, even prostitutes. Only Ellie Briggs and Sadie Cooke seemed to Emma like women she could enjoy a friendly, sisterly relationship with. Ellie was the dearer friend of those two, but she lived far enough away to make visiting difficult. Sadie, though nearer, wore on Emma's nerves after only a short while. Too prone to chatter. And too envious of Emma, whom Sadie perceived as a rich mansion-dweller. The oddities of Emma's helter-skelter house were fully lost on Sadie, who admired the place and envied Emma for it.

Emma had the distinct feeling that Sadie also envied her for her husband. She had never seen another woman put on such a blatant display of flirtatiousness than did Sadie when Stanley was near. Schoolgirl giggles, ridiculous attempts at silly humor (which Stanley always laughed at, fulsomely), batting eyelashes, and movements clearly designed to be provocative. But what really wore on Emma was the fact that Stanley seemed to like it all, even encourage it. Sadie was a beautiful young woman, unmarried, but Emma knew she herself was more beautiful than Sadie. And why was Stanley paying heed to a flirty woman-child such as Sadie, anyway? Did he not love his own wife?

Even now Stanley was not present. Off to San Francisco, he'd told her when he left the prior day. Another meeting with Wilberforce Sadler. "More discussion of the bright days ahead of us, my love," Stanley had said to her. *My love.* His words.

Therein lay the true misery of Emma's life: her own husband did not love her, and she knew it, whatever endearments he might occasionally speak. Further, she was quite sure he had been with other women since their marriage . . . sure enough she had even confided that conviction to her father. To Zebulon McSwain's credit, he had not responded with a "told you so" attitude but had simply grieved with her in her pain and disappointment. She wished now she had listened to him when he'd encouraged her to let Stanley Wickham go and take Jedd Colter as her husband instead. But Jedd had been a poor man who didn't seem to have much by way of financial ambition, and Emma had not been able to accept the prospect of life without abundance.

Sometimes she tried to persuade herself that things weren't so bad, that if Stanley didn't really love her, well, neither did she really love him, so what was the difference? She'd married him for security, not love, and secure she was. At least there was that. Things were not as she wanted them to be, but in her community she was reigning queen, if such a status existed, and other women, the few there were, envied her position.

It should be enough, she told herself. Yet it wasn't.

Emma's hopes at the moment were pinned on the plans Stanley had been talking about involving Wilberforce Sadler, the Knoxville businessman Emma had known all her life. Sadler, along with his funny lump of a brother, was in California now, San Francisco, and according to Stanley, was interested in pooling resources with him to create the biggest and most visible string of mining camp stores in the new state.

Mining camp stores were the most central and important institution in any mining community. Virtual community centers, selling every kind of imaginable item, from groceries through pickaxes. Liquor, too.

In the vision of Stanley Wickham and Wilberforce Sadler, Wickham and Sadler Supply stores soon would fill the gold country, stocked with the best goods the owners and operators could find at a discount price. That discount would be passed down to the customers, undercutting competing merchants and ensuring that virtually every gold pan, pick, shovel, and commercially produced rocker and long tom would come

from a Wickham and Sadler store. Along
with clothing, fabric for house curtains, iron
stoves for kitchens.

"You think we are well off now, Emma,
you wait until our stores are open and running!" Stanley told her one rare night when
he seemed to actually be in a mood to
involve her in his life and plans. "You, my
dear, will be the richest woman in all of
California! That's my promise to you,
Emma. And my promise to myself is this: I
will someday be governor of this state. You
may rely on it." And for a few days, the
excitement she had known in the first days
of their marriage had returned.

"Do we have sufficient money to carry our
part of the cost?" she'd asked Stanley, who
always kept her in the dark regarding the
specifics of their financial life.

"Everything is in place," Stanley had said.
"The resources will be there when they are
called for." Typical vagueries, giving implica-
tions rather than hard information. Emma
had known that was the fullest answer she
was likely to receive.

Stanley's talk about his plans had been
lessened of late, but Emma still was hopeful. She knew he'd had at least three meetings with the Sadlers, particularly Wilberforce, and had also been in conference with

bankers and attorneys and land agents from San Francisco and Los Angeles.

Something was brewing. Stanley, at least, was working to make things happen. The life Emma had hoped she would have when she'd passed over Jedd Colter, who truly loved her, in favor of one who had married her for her beauty and her willingness to be bought by the promise of wealth and luxury — that life of success and worldly fulfillment might even yet come about for her. Stanley Wickham might fulfill her hopes even yet.

"I'll be happy then," she had whispered to herself one evening when Stanley was away, ostensibly on "business" but more likely consorting with some cheap strumpet in a neighboring mining camp dance hall or some roosting place of soiled doves.

"My husband the governor," she had said to the darkness. "My husband the leader of men, the wielder of power, the possessor of great wealth. Yes . . . then I'll be happy."

But when she'd fallen asleep that night, she'd dreamed she was walking through a meadow alongside the Holston River at Knoxville, her hand clasped in Jedd Colter's. In the dream, the happiness she wished for was already there, not something merely to be wished for in a faraway future, but already in her possession, clasped in her hand and Jedd's, together.

CHAPTER TWENTY-FIVE

"I can't deny my concerns, sir," Wilberforce Sadler said to Stanley Wickham. "I am beginning to wonder if you do indeed have the resources needed to carry forward your end of our bargain."

Wickham was a thin man with lush brunet hair that swept up from his brow and stood mostly straight up, but with a backward tilt that made it look as if he had faced into a stout wind to dry it. Wickham looked Sadler squarely in the eye and nodded. "You need not worry. Those resources will be in hand soon."

"That kind of vague promise rouses my concern even more, given that we are in a land with a steadily growing population of men who are confident they will soon be wealthy with only a minimal putting forth of effort. Hopes rise fast in California and die even faster. From where do you expect to gain these 'resources' you are so confident of? Do you expect to encounter the fabled mother lode in your privy pit?"

Wickham laughed fulsomely at Sadler's unimpressive joke, desperately wanting to lighten the atmosphere in the room and establish rapport with this man who held his hope for the future. This was the first time Sadler had treated him with such ambivalence and vaguely hostile doubt. It was hard to blame him, because time was running out.

Given the rapid pace of development in California's gold fields, it was crucial that the chain of mining camp stores be put in place soon, or the opportunity would be seized by others. But so far all Wickham had been able to do was make promises. He'd put forth no actual money toward their project.

He thought of his father-in-law and cursed him silently. Zebulon McSwain held the key to Wickham's hopes, and the power to crush them. Without the diamonds that McSwain possessed, a portion of the famous Finnegan ancestral jewels, Wickham could not fulfill his pledge to Sadler. Not unless he did make some major find of gold, as Wilberforce had just joked about. Unlike some, though, Wickham knew better than to treat luck in the gold fields as a destined certainty.

He could not assume he would be one of the fortunate few blessed with the same kind of luck that had come to old Ben Scarlett, making Ben's name famous across all California.

No, no birds in the bush for Stanley Wickham. He could count only on the bird in the hand . . . even if the hand belonged to Zeb McSwain.

It was a highly frustrating situation, the diamonds so close, yet so unreachable.

Those diamonds had been given to Bledsoe College of Knoxville, Tennessee, by one of Ireland's wealthiest men, Samuel Finnegan, since deceased. Eccentric in the way of some men of wealth, Finnegan had been long fascinated by the growth of the American nation, and imagined himself tied to it. The simple fact that so much unsettled land existed on the North American continent had captivated Finnegan, resident of an island encompassing far less terrain. He had become a strong foreign proponent of what, five years earlier, a noted American editor had labeled the "manifest destiny" of the United States — and this though Finnegan had never set foot in America. His fascination with the country was given from afar, but was as strong as if Finnegan had been a native-born American.

And so, against the wishes of some of his sizable family, he had declared that he would make a major gift to benefit the people of the United States, particularly those forging into new frontiers. Finnegan had put a handful of his family diamonds, jewels of long, complex history and immense value, into the custody of his son, John, the only one of his children whom he fully trusted, and sent him with them to the United States and the state of Tennessee, there to present the diamonds to a college called Bledsoe. Samuel Finnegan chose Bledsoe College because he had read some of the early writings of the college's founder, the late Reverend Eben Bledsoe, and liked the man's ideas. Eben Bledsoe had written of the necessity of education for the prosperous growth of a nation and asserted that the frontier of any growing land must not be neglected in provision of such education. The fact that Finnegan had personal connections to the settlement of the Carolina-Tennessee frontier through the Scots-Irish only heightened his interest in playing benefactor to the college, and this despite its Presbyterian roots in contrast to his own Catholicism.

Wilberforce Sadler stared Wickham in the

face, unflinching and fierce. "I'm going to ask you something, Stanley, and I expect a straight and honest answer." Something in the way he said "Stanley" sounded mocking, making Wickham feel small and unimportant.

"Ask, then."

"Very well. Is it the Finnegan diamonds you are waiting on?"

Wickham did not want to answer, feeling unsure where the answer would lead. But he was trapped.

"It is," he admitted.

Wilberforce Sadler froze a moment, then nodded. "I feared as much."

"I will have them."

"Why do you believe so? Why would Mc-Swain steal them, flee his own town, and travel all the way across the country, hiding them, then just hand them to you?"

"I *will* have them."

Wilberforce shook his head firmly. "I see no grounds to share your confidence. Mc-Swain took a great risk, criminalized himself, to get those diamonds into his own hands. It is hard to think he would simply give them up. And hard now for me to believe we are going to be able to carry through with the plans we have made."

"I . . . I promise you, Wilberforce, I will, I

will, obtain those diamonds. I will succeed because I am willing to do more than simply ask for them. I will exert pressure on my revered father-in-law to make him turn them over. Then we can proceed without delay."

" 'Exert pressure,' you say. You are unaware, my friend, that pressure has already been exerted. Even before McSwain fled Knoxville, I had hired a capable and ruthless man to provide, shall we say, encouragement to him not to try to cling to what he had no right to have."

"But it hasn't worked?"

"It hasn't worked."

"I am assuming that this 'ruthless man' threatened McSwain in some manner."

"He did. Yes."

Wickham looked Sadler in the eye. "Then perhaps the wrong person was threatened."

"What do you mean?"

"I hardly dare say." And Wilberforce Sadler knew right away what Wickham was thinking.

"You would do that? Your own —"

"If it will put the diamonds into our hands and enable us to move forward with our plan, then yes. Yes indeed, I will do it. In the end it will benefit her, too, you know."

Wilberforce felt the dominant status in

the conversation shift from himself to Wickham. What Wickham apparently was ready to do was startling, even troubling . . . but Wilberforce could not deny the practicality of it. It might make the crucial difference. McSwain might prove to be one of those men who are more responsive to threats against loved ones than against themselves. And because the actions would be Wickham's, not his, Wilberforce's own conscience need not be sullied.

Sadler money alone was insufficient to properly launch the sprawling series of big camp stores that were planned. And Wickham's in-hand financial resources were not enough of a supplement to make the crucial difference without themselves being supplemented. So Wilberforce, despite being stunned and even appalled by what Wickham obviously had in mind to motivate McSwain, could only hope the plan worked.

"Fifteen days, Wickham," he said. "You have fifteen days to cause this to happen. After that, all previous bargains are nullified. Are we of a common understanding? You may as well agree because you have no choice to do otherwise."

Wickham reluctantly nodded. "We are." The handshake that followed was devoid of enthusiasm.

Wickham had more to say, though. "There is one thing I must insist upon: Emma cannot know of my part in what will happen involving her. She cannot know that I would condone such a thing. If she did, it would be the end for us. She would never abide my presence again. And I could not abide that."

"You are a man with a gun-steel conscience, Stanley."

"I am a man who is willing to do what must be done. And it won't really matter in the end. She's not going to be hurt. Scared, certainly, but not hurt."

"We may hope."

Near the Scarlett's Luck mining camp, California gold country

One week after Ollie Slott fitted a notch-eared Irishman in San Francisco for a new pair of boots, Jedd Colter had the oddest of feelings as he set out on his horse in the direction of the mining camp known as Bowater Gulch, or sometimes merely Bowater. Though he was alone, he could not shake the feeling that Treemont Dalton was riding beside him. Jedd found himself glancing over time and again, ready to make some comment to his old friend, only to find no one there.

Yet he was there. Jedd could feel his presence, and welcomed it.

Jedd was out today in his capacity as deputy, acting in response to an odd and highly questionable bit of intelligence he had received from Ben Scarlett. Jedd had strong doubts about this effort. Was it a waste of time? His mind kept drifting to the possibility that he might make better use of his time and travel by riding all the way to Bowater, where Emma lived. He might be able to see her this very day if he would only do that.

Common sense restrained him. Seeing Emma might also involve seeing her husband, and that wouldn't do. Jedd had no carnal intent in paying a call on Emma, but he doubted that Stanley Wickham would believe that. A confrontation with Wickham was nothing Jedd wanted today.

He did want to know, though, the truth about Wickham's treatment of Emma. If he was misusing her, hurting her, treating her unfaithfully, Jedd would not stand by unresponsive. He would protect the woman he had not been able to cease loving.

Not today, though. He had other duties to perform, however unlikely they might be to possess any validity. One had to take information received from Ben Scarlett with a grain of salt, considering that Ben had an active imagination that was fueled in large measure by alcohol.

As he rode toward the remote area Ben had told him of, Jedd's mind did continually drift back to Emma, though. He wondered what an initial approach to her would be like. Would she receive him with welcome and happiness? And what would he say to her? *Emma, I crossed the country just to make sure that old Stanley isn't being unfaithful to you and maybe laying the old cane switch or hickory rod across your shoulders every now and then.* It was going to be a clumsy matter to address, whenever and however it happened. Jedd knew he needed to give himself plenty of time to prepare his thoughts before he actually went to her.

Jedd reached a peculiar boulder that jutted out into the dirt road. Jedd slowed the pace of his horse and moved forward slowly and about thirty feet beyond the boulder, found the landmark Ben Scarlett had said he would find: a footpath that met the main trail at a ninety-degree angle and ran up the flank of the hillside to Jedd's right.

Jedd eyed the little path and wondered if he could ride his horse up it. More prudent to dismount, he decided. He'd lead his horse by its reins and climb the hill on foot because of the narrowness of the passage. He was grateful for how quickly and thoroughly his ankle had healed. Hardly any pain now, and what pain there was was lessened by the support given the ankle by the fine pair of boots Ollie Slott had made for him back in Tennessee. The boots had been damaged by the gunshot that had hit Jedd's ankle, but recently he had put that boot in for repair with a shoemaker-turned–gold miner who was living and mining at Scarlett's Luck. The man had done a good job and the repaired boot was nearly as well fitted as it had been when Ollie Slott presented it to Jedd.

Halfway up the hill, lost in concealing brush, Jedd heard a guttural sound in the undergrowth to his left. His well-trained senses told him it might have a human origin. With that thought, Jedd reached to his side and touched his newest possession: a Colt Dragoon, one of the newer pistols available and a growing favorite among those fortunate enough to have one. Jedd owed his own good fortune on that score to none other than Ben Scarlett, who had enjoyed a particularly good day with his gold pan a few days back and had used the proceeds of it to buy a gift for a man who had been good to him when others had not.

Jedd had protested the gift as too grand to be given him by a man who had seldom possessed two coins to rub together. Ben was insistent, though, and Jedd, once he'd seen and held the Colt, felt his resistance give way. "A good marshal's deputy needs a good pistol," Ben had said. Jedd had nodded and accepted it.

The noise Jedd had heard beside the trail proved to be feline rather than human in origin. The cat scurried off furtively, and Jedd continued on, leading his horse up the claustrophobic pathway.

According to Ben Scarlett, he should soon reach a small, basinlike valley, in which a handful of small cabins would be visible. Ben, who had explored the area after being told there was a hidden store of stolen whiskey up the trail, had promised Jedd that he would see something strange about those cabins but had declined to tell him what it was. This had annoyed Jedd to some measure, but as Ben obviously had intended, it had intrigued him, too.

He abruptly reached something that Ben had not forewarned of. The trail forked, one branch veering left, the other continuing straight ahead. Jedd paused, trying to decide which branch to follow. Beneath his breath, he swore at Ben Scarlett in absentia and kept to the branch that appeared to continue the main path.

He found no basin of a valley, no mysterious cabins. He cursed Ben's name again and continued on down the back slope of the hill he'd climbed, and came out on a wagon road that he recognized. This was a road that connected the area now occupied by Scarlett's Luck with the longer-settled site of Bowater, the latter being to Jedd's left, the former to his right. He sighed, paused to rub his somewhat sore ankle through his boot, mounted up, and turned right to go back to Scarlett's Luck, having forgotten for the moment about that second branch of the trail he had not explored.

Even if he'd recalled it, he might not have climbed back up to explore it. He'd always liked Ben Scarlett at some level, but the man was a drunk and therefore unreliable. The old sot might literally have dreamed up that supposed hidden valley and strange cabins. Jedd had better things to do with his time than pursue the illusions of a drunkard.

CHAPTER TWENTY-SIX

A combination of nature, experience, and heredity had given Jedd Colter the ability to detect — usually — when he was alone and when he was not. Often he simply knew when another was near and could not have said exactly which of his senses had provided the information. He'd pondered the matter before and had surmised only that it was almost a supersense created through some undesigned special combination of the usual five. That special sense had failed him a little earlier when he'd mistaken an animal sound for a human one, but such failures were not the norm.

Whatever it was that told him of it, Jedd detected the presence of the other man before any noise, visual evidence, or scent presented itself. Having gone down that hillside trail to the Bowater Road, remounted, and traveled about an eighth of a mile back in the direction of Scarlett's Luck,

Jedd had been stricken with a muscle cramp in his left leg, the same sort of cramp he and Ollie Slott had discussed at some length on a Knoxville street in a time not particularly long past, but which now felt like five years gone. Halting his horse, he dismounted and tethered it off to a branch and paced about, massaging the cramping calf muscle of his right leg.

The other man emerged from brush to his left and leveled a scattergun at Jedd's midsection. Jedd's hand whipped to the butt of his Colt Dragoon. He did not draw, however, stopped by the threat of that scattergun aimed at his gut. As fast as he might draw and shoot, he could not hope to do so faster than the other man's trigger finger could squeeze.

"You've got the drop on me, friend," Jedd said, lifting his hands slowly. "What do you want from me? I have no gold."

The man who had him in his sights was as young as Jedd himself, perhaps a year or two younger. He was slender nearly to the point of wiriness, but muscular. His hair was dark and he wore a mustache a month overdue for some grooming. He stared at Jedd with eyes that did not flinch or falter, though Jedd did see them flicker down for a moment to scan the roughly made tin badge

Jedd wore. Blalock had made badges for himself and his deputy when they'd taken on their humble law enforcement roles in Scarlett's Luck.

It was only then that Jedd noticed the other fellow was wearing a badge as well.

"Since we're both lawmen, I wonder if maybe we've got a misunderstanding here," Jedd said, keeping his hands up.

The scattergun lowered just an inch or two. "Maybe. Just maybe. What's that badge you're wearing?"

"It's homemade, is what it is. Not by me. By Mr. Rand Blalock, marshal of Scarlett's Luck mining camp. I'm his duly appointed deputy."

The scattergun muzzle dropped six inches this time. "Pleased to meet you, Dooley," said the man holding the weapon.

Jedd was amused but didn't let it show. "No, no . . . I'm *duly appointed.* That's what I was saying. Name's Colter. Jedd Colter. Not Dooley."

"Sorry about this scattergun, Dooley. I thought you were someone else."

Jedd started to correct the name error again, but in a moment of insight realized he was dealing with a man who was hard of hearing. "Who are you, sir?" Jedd asked slowly, and noticed that the other's eyes fixed upon his lips as he spoke. No question about it: hard of hearing.

"My name is Tom Buckle. Tom like the cat, and Buckle as in what holds your belt together. I'm a lawman like you are," Buckle said. "In my case, I'm deputy marshal of the town of Bowater Gulch. Though I prefer merely to shorten it to Bowater. It sounds a little more appealing to these Yankee Maine-born ears."

Maine. Jedd had never encountered anyone from Maine in his life, not that he knew of. It explained why Buckle's speech sounded odd to his ears.

Jedd eyed the badge on Buckle's chest. It was no homemade item like the one Blalock had given him. Buckle's badge had a silver sheen and glimmer, not to mention a neatness of form far surpassing that of Jedd's crude tin credential. Buckle saw Jedd looking at it and grinned. "My marshal had badges crafted by a silversmith in San Francisco. It is as fine a badge as any man of the law could want to wear. I'm quite proud of it."

Jedd said, "Mine's hammered out of common tin by an old-time North Carolina mountain sheriff. No words nor images on it. Nothing to be proud of in the badge itself, but knowing the man who gave it to me and trusted me to help him, I'm proud of mine, too."

"Ayuh, sir. You think right-headedly." Seemingly having decided that Jedd had passed whatever test he had just put him through, Buckle slid his scattergun into a saddle scabbard. "I am pleased to encounter another man in my position. It's providential, certainly, because I am in need of the help of a capable fellow lawman at this moment. Are you aware that there is an informal agreement among the various towns and camps that official representatives of the law in those places will provide one another mutual assistance when called upon?"

"It's not been discussed with me, but I would presume such is the case even without being told of it," Jedd answered.

"Ayuh, good. Because I feel the need of help just now, Dooley, and you appear to be just the man to provide it."

What Tom Buckle had to say to Jedd came as a surprise. He presented to Jedd almost exactly the same scenario that had led Jedd out onto this trail to begin with, the scenario Ben Scarlett had incompletely described to him.

Buckle's version was incomplete as well,

but fuller than what Ben had described. And more chilling.

"Up ahead there is a trail that goes up the ridge, and the trail divides at one point. The straighter portion continues on over the ridge to the older road that now leads on over to Scarlett's Luck. The other, I'm told, leads to a small valley where there are secret cabins built in such a way that they serve as pens of a sort. Disguised pens, made to blend into the landscape."

"Pens for what?" Jedd asked. It was at this point that Ben's description had fallen short.

Buckle looked squarely at Jedd. "I don't know if you are a man of a sensitive nature or toughened to this hard world we live in."

"I'd say I'm right toughened. It takes a lot to stir me up."

"I'm of the same nature. Toughened to the bad, welcoming to the good. But what I think is going on in that valley with its secret cabins would stir up any man with a sense of decency and civilization about him, even the most toughened. Ayuh, it might."

Jedd frowned. "Did you say 'ayuh'? Does that mean yeah, or yes?"

"Ayuh . . . uh, yes. Yes, it does. I'm sorry for my Yankee drawl. It is hard for many to understand me. On the same score, I find it

343

nearly impossible to comprehend the speech of South Carolinians and Georgians. I have met several of both since I reached this place."

"That's the thing about California: because everyone comes here from everywhere, it's like a kettle where we're all stirred into the same stew. But tell me about these cabins, or pens."

Buckle looked and sounded very solemn as he spoke. "You are aware, I suspect, that there are places in the world where human beings, particularly females, are bought and sold like cattle and treated worse than such. Enslaved. Used and misused. There are bad men in Mexico, and farther south, who are involved in this. But not just them. All around the world are those willing to trade in humanity as a commodity. I'm not speaking here of slavery as we ordinarily understand it and which is so prevalent through the South and elsewhere. The kind of slavery I'm speaking of involves women. Women, young and old, of any race, who get washed away in a terrible river of human trade, stolen away, sold, resold, hurt. And worse."

"I've heard of such but know little about it," Jedd said. "Are you telling me that it's going on here?"

"I know nothing for a certainty," Buckle replied. "What I am told, though, is that a small valley overlooked by the western end of this ridge has little prison cabins and is used sometimes as a holding location for women either being moved down to Mexico — where they are transferred like so much merchandise to men who serve as brokers and continue the process until these sad souls are turned over to masters, abusers — or taken to the coast, where, at secret bays and inlets, they are put on ships and carried to Asia, to Europe, to some of the large islands that are like small nations to themselves. There are bad men of all peoples and races and nations, Dooley. Men who relish the destruction and domination of others in all kinds of ways. And others, less wicked, perhaps — or perhaps equally so — who are willing to serve as the vendors, agents, and suppliers for those evil ones, willing to give them what they want. It is that, specifically, that I am told goes on, at least sometimes, in this valley we will visit. Ah! Here we are at the base of the trail. It is a closely grown trail, just a narrow path, and nearly impossible for a rider to traverse. We shall best be served to dismount and walk on foot."

"I know," Jedd said. "I came down this

very path earlier, all the way from the main road across the ridge. Looking for this very valley you've been talking about, with cabins that I was told would be missing something I would spot right away. It was a drunk who told me about it, and I had no idea whether to believe him. But he said nothing about the use of those cabins as human pens. Maybe he didn't know about that, or didn't believe it, or just didn't want to spread a story he hadn't verified. He's an oddly moral fellow for a drunk. He's Ben Scarlett, the very man whose find of gold led to the mining town of Scarlett's Luck."

"So you've already traveled this path. . . ."

"But saw no valley, no cabins. I did, though, see the fork of the trail, and could only travel one of them. The one I chose, this same one that we're at the base of right now, took me only to the ridgetop and down to the road we met on. The other, I reckon, must have been the one leading to the valley."

"Ayuh. We'll know soon enough. I suggest you lead the way, Dooley, since you have more familiarity with this bit of terrain."

They advanced onto the trail and began climbing toward the top of the ridge.

"I need to let you know that my name's not Dooley," Jedd said as they moved along.

"My name is Jedd Colter."

"Well . . . why did you say before that your name is Dooley?"

"I didn't. I said I was duly appointed as a deputy in Scarlett's Luck. You misunderstood me. Bad ears?"

"Ayuh. Especially this right one. A gun went off too close to my ear almost a year ago, and I've been waiting for the full hearing to return ever since. I despair now of it ever doing so."

"I'm sorry."

Buckle pursed his lips and shook his head, thinking. "Duly appointed," he said. Then he grinned. "Know what it sounded like to me? Dooley Poindexter. That's what I thought you said, Jedd. I do hope you'll beg this Yankee's pardon."

"We Poindexters are generally forgiving types, especially to the deaf," Jedd said with a chuckle. Buckle laughed heartily, but stopped abruptly.

"I'll be!" Buckle said. "I didn't notice that!" He was looking back down the short distance of inclining trail up which they had progressed. They were still close enough to the Bowater Road below to see it, and Jedd followed Buckle's gaze to look at the far side of the road.

"I didn't notice it, either," Jedd said. "And

for a man who prides himself on his keen eyes and woodcraft, I've got no excuse I can name."

"Shall we go back down and have a look while it's still bright daylight? Perhaps it has a bearing on what we're looking for."

They headed back down the trail and across the road to the thing that had drawn their attention.

CHAPTER TWENTY-SEVEN

The name on the grave meant nothing to Jedd Colter, but the fact that it was located not in a proper graveyard but in a small clearing beside the road, and the fact that there was a smaller grave beside it, was intriguing.

"Just a child," Jedd said to Tom Buckle. "Always a sad thing, the grave of a child."

Buckle squinted at the words on the wooden marker, read them aloud. " 'Winnie Belle Napier, Born 1841, Philadelphia, Pennsylvania, died California, March 1850. Loved by her Maker and her family. Nine years of blessing to her parents.' Lord, Jedd. That's enough to make a man weep. And why do you reckon that little grave is there beside hers?" Buckle asked. Jedd knelt beside the tiny grave to take a closer look.

" 'Cat,' " he read aloud. He heard Buckle give a loud, wet snort and looked up to see the young lawman wiping tears from his face.

Buckle spoke in a breaking voice. "Jedd, you know what that must mean? She had her a cat that she loved so dear that it died right along with her, and they buried them side by side." Buckle actually sobbed out loud then.

Jedd marveled at the unexpected display of emotion from a man who didn't give an initial impression of being likely to be sentimental, and who had already declared himself "toughened" to life's harsher realities. It became a clumsy moment for Jedd, because Buckle proved to be, unfortunately, one of those men who look and sound hilariously comical when in grief. Jedd chuckled against his will at the sight of the tear-gushing man and tried to disguise the chuckle as a cough. It didn't matter, really, because Buckle's bad ears hadn't heard it, anyway.

The moment of out-of-place jocularity brought out a mischievous sense of dark humor that occasionally surfaced in Jedd. He looked at Buckle, who quickly got control of his weeping out of embarrassment, and said, in a dead serious tone, "Buckle, I believe it didn't happen like you said. I think that cat there killed that little girl. She was sitting there, petting on it, cooing at it like a gentle little dove, and that

Satan of a cat up and went for her throat and tore it right out. Poor little Winnie Napier died with that cat hissing and spitting at her while she bled to death. And with her last flicker of life, Winnie put her hand on a stone lying near her and brought it down on that cat's head and killed it dead just as she died herself. They buried them side by side. That's what I think happened. Or maybe they hanged the cat for her murder."

"No! You don't mean it!"

"Oh yes, oh yeah. I mean, ayuh."

"That all sounds mighty unlikely, Jedd."

Jedd astonished himself by maintaining his dead-serious composure a little longer. "Unlikely? No, sir. That was exactly how my little sister, Molly, died. Seven years old and her cat tore out her throat. Nearly removed her head from her shoulders. Mama was never the same after that. Molly never got the chance to kill that cat with a rock, though. She was indoors when it went after her. No rocks."

Buckle, his face blotchy and damp from his earlier tears, sputtered and stammered, then looked deeply at Jedd's face. Jedd could no longer hide his mirth and laughed explosively in Buckle's face. Buckle began to glower.

"Damn you, Jedd Colter — or Dooley Poindexter or whoever the hell you are!" Buckle growled. "You're making a jest out of me, damn you!"

Jedd shook with laughter. "I'm sorry, Buckle. I couldn't hold back from it. You looked so durn funny sitting there blubbering in the saddle. I just had to rag on you a little. I never had no sister named Molly, nor one named anything else. And if I had, it's danged unlikely she'd have died from having a cat tear her throat out."

By now Buckle was catching Jedd's mirth, and looked as funny in laughter as he had in tears. Both men happened to glance down at the burial site again, realized it was very inappropriate to be laughing at such a solemn place as this, and turned to start back up the inclined trail again.

"Really, though, what do you suppose is the story about that cat buried beside her?" asked Buckle when a few minutes had passed and the laughter was done.

"A pet, I guess," Jedd replied. "It is strange they both died at the same time, though, if that's the case."

"I guess we can't know."

"I guess not." They strode silently a few more minutes. "It's an odd thing, people and animals and how attached they can become. I knew a man back in Tennessee who made the journey with my emigrant group to California. He had a cat, an old pet of his, that had died and he had it stuffed and preserved, and kept it with him about all the time. He held and petted and scratched on that dead cat like it was still living. It was an odd thing. But he's a bit of an odd man. I almost married that man's daughter back in Tennessee. He was president of a college there for quite a few years."

Jedd halted suddenly and stared straight ahead, thinking hard about something Crozier Bellingham had said about McSwain . . . about jewels stolen from the coffers of Bledsoe College and probably smuggled across the country by McSwain, possibly inside the preserved carcass of Cicero the cat. And how McSwain, after clinging to that cat for hundreds of miles, had suddenly passed it on to someone else. A little girl on her way to California with her family, in fact. An ailing little girl.

"What'd we stop for?" asked Tom Buckle.

Jedd started to tell Buckle that perhaps he knew the story behind the cat buried beside the little girl's grave after all. But he shut up even before he started, realizing telling the tale wouldn't be worth the effort, just a distraction from what they had come here for.

"Well, at least finish what you were telling me before. The college president and so on."

"His name is McSwain. His daughter married a man named Wickham, and they live in Bowater, of all places. Your own mining town."

Buckle gaped at Jedd. "Stanley Wickham?"

"That's the man. You know him?"

"I know who he is! Everyone for miles around knows Stanley Wickham. He's a merchant of mining and dry goods and has the best house in Bowater, though it isn't much to look at. Something of a hodgepodge. Wickham's wife, though . . . now, there is beauty to any man's eyes! Did I hear you say you almost married her?"

"I did. But it . . . it didn't happen."

"I must say it's your loss, then, because Stanley Wickham is the envy of every man in a dozen different mining camps for his wife's beauty. Here we are in a state with not enough women to fill a teacup, and who but a mouse of a man like Stanley Wickham has the finest one in several states?"

"Life ain't fair, Buckle."

"No, it's not. And what makes it worse in Wickham's case is that he seemingly doesn't appreciate what he has. The man is reputed

354

to have climbed into the nests of many a soiled dove. A woman like he has deserves better than that. Sorry even to tell you that, Jedd."

"I already knew. To tell you the truth, Buckle, I have every notion of seeing Emma when I can. It's most of what drew me to California. I've got to see her and know how she is. If her husband is hurting her, I will not stand by and let it go on."

"I can't fault that, Jedd. But to change the subject a moment . . . we've reached the fork of the trail."

Jedd looked down the trail branch he had not taken before. "Shall we ride down to that valley, assuming we find it?" Jedd asked Buckle.

"I'm inclined to stay on foot. Easier to stay quiet, low, and out of sight on foot. Why don't we hobble the horses here and come back for them later?"

"I think that's a good notion, Tom."

They went on, more tense now, wondering how much truth there might be in the rumor they were chasing. Jedd asked Buckle a question that had been bumping around the back of his mind for several minutes now. "Tom, why did you have to buttonhole me, a deputy marshal from another town, to help you do this? Why did your own marshal not come with you?"

"Well, Jedd, because he is occupied more with his mining than his work for the law. I often feel that I was hired to do his duties for him while he gathers up his flakes and dust and guards his claim."

"Like we talked about, life ain't fair."

"No."

They went on. Jedd, experienced at reading landscapes, could tell from a subtle difference in light, breeze, and atmosphere that they were approaching a depression in the hilly land. The valley of cabins, most likely.

A few paces on, Buckle said, "Jedd, you asked why my marshal did not come with me. I'll ask the same question back to you."

"My marshal, man name of Rand Blalock, doesn't know about any of this, doesn't know I'm out here today. It was me who Ben Scarlett talked to about it, Blalock not being there to hear it. So I came on alone, in case it turned out to be nothing. And also because I wasn't certain just what I would do . . . whether I would come up here or go on to Bowater to find Emma."

"Jedd." Buckle had stopped in his tracks and pointed ahead. "A cabin. Just one. You see it?"

Jedd looked and shook his head. "No. I see at least five of them."

He was right, though it took Buckle much longer to see them. "So it's true," he said.

"At least about there being cabins in this valley, yes. And Ben was right about the cabins . . . something missing."

"I think I see. No windows. No doors."

"But some missing chinking here and there . . . to let air through, I guess."

They stood silent for more than a minute. There was no sound at all but a light breeze.

"Do you think anyone is down there?" Buckle asked.

"I don't think so. Let's go down, quietly, and see."

Buckle drew back, nervous. "There might be someone guarding the place, if there are people in any of those cabins."

Jedd shook his head. "What I smell isn't the scent of humans."

Buckle sniffed the air. "I don't smell anything."

"It comes from spending enough time hunting, tracking, trapping. And from being a Colter. They say that, in the earlier days of my family, Joshua Colter could smell the scent of deer long before he could see them. And do the same with people."

"So, if those cabins don't hold people, then what?"

"Ever heard of bull and bear fights,

357

Buckle?"

"Ayuh. Saw one once. Fearsome bloody thing, ayuh, is a bull and bear fight."

"Well, I think those cabins are maybe there to hold bears captured for use in bull and bear fights. That's what I smell. Bear spoor."

"No women held here, then? Just bears for the fights?"

"That's what I'd bet we'll find. I'm going down to look. If there's ever been people held here, I'll be able to tell. But I have to say, Tom, even though I know the kinds of things you talked about really happen, women and girls being captured and hauled off to be misused by bad men in other places, I doubt it happens much compared to most things. I think it's more likely there's something not quite that devilish going on here."

To Jedd's surprise, Buckle's eyes filled with water again. He frowned, tears brimming over. "It may not be as uncommon as most would think," he said, his voice quaking a little. "And don't think that it can only happen somewhere else."

"Tom, what's going on with you? Is there something about all this that cuts close to the heart with you? Did you maybe know a woman who —"

"I can't do it, Jedd. I can't. I thought if I had somebody with me, I could get through it. But I was wrong. If we go down there and find that there have been women held here after all, I . . . I don't know what will happen. I don't think I could bear being there, knowing . . ."

"Knowing that somebody who matters to you was hurt in a place like this . . . if this proves to be that kind of place. Am I right?"

Buckle nodded fast and couldn't look at Jedd any longer. His eyes and face were wet now. "You aren't the only one who has lost a beloved woman, Jedd," he said. "In my case it was my sister. Taken from us too young, and in circumstances no woman should ever have to face, anywhere, anytime. The kind that the rumors say might prevail in that valley there."

"I'm sorry for whatever happened, and whoever it happened to. You needn't go down there with me, Tom. I'll take a look and then I can tell you."

"I'm not going to wait. I'm going to go on back home, Jedd. I don't even want to know what you find, not today. You can look me up and tell me sometime later."

It was clear to Jedd that, whatever had happened to Tom Buckle's lost sister, it had had a devastating effect. The man was wrecked, shaking now as if the California day had just gone as cold as a Canadian winter. Buckle's tears came hard, but this time Jedd had no impulse at all to laugh at his grimacing expression.

"Go on, if you need to, Tom. I'll get with you another day and we'll talk some more. As much or as little as you want to."

Buckle nodded and managed to pull himself together a bit. His emotions settled enough for the tears to stop.

Jedd shook Buckle's hand and began trudging down into the valley. Ten steps down, Buckle called to him, "Wait just a second." He trotted down and joined Jedd.

"What is it, Tom? Have you changed your mind?"

"No, just wanted to ask you something. When I first saw you today, the first thing that caught my eye was the sun glinting on your badge, which is what drew my interest. The second thing was the man beside you. I saw him while you were at a distance, but when you reached the place I was, you were alone. Where did he go?"

Jedd gazed in amazement at Tom Buckle. "There was no one riding with me today. I've been alone since I rode out of Scarlett's Luck."

"Oh no, there was a man there. To the left

360

of you, and then you both were out of sight behind the trees a few moments, and when you came back into view and were close to me, he was gone."

"It's a mystery, then. I can't explain it," Jedd said. He glanced to his left and mentally added, But maybe you can, Treemont.

Chapter Twenty-Eight

As Jedd walked down into the valley, his nose told him that his early assessment was likely to prove correct. The faint but musky scent of bear spoor increased the closer he grew to the first log structure. He was soon close enough to see that the cabin had no roof designed to shed water. A rain would simply pour in between the logs — more evidence that this was a structure intended to pen an animal, not hold a human. The roof was made in two sections, side by side, the larger of them spiked down onto the top run of logs, the other lying like an upward- and outward-opening trapdoor, hinged on one side to the top of the wall, meaning the cabin's only real entrance doubled as a section of its roof.

Jedd peered between two unchinked logs and determined that the structure was uninhabited at the moment. He clambered up one side and with effort lifted back the trapdoor entrance, letting it swing down against the outer wall. He dropped inside the cabin.

No question about it. . . . A bear, or maybe more than one, had been held here sometime in the past two or three months. The smell remained strong to a nose as sensitive and experience-trained as Jedd's, and he found hair snagged in the bark of the logs and plenty of bear droppings on the earthen floor.

He climbed out, closed down the door, and moved on to the next cabin, where he repeated the same kind of exploration and found the same results. No evidence was there of anything but use of the structure for the captivity of bears. Confident now that he would be able to give a reassuring report to Tom Buckle the next time he saw him, Jedd moved on to the third log structure and entered in the same manner.

In the shadowed interior, he saw something. Kneeling, he plucked thick hair of a bear from a splinter on one of the logs. He rolled it between thumb and forefinger, then tossed it aside. On the ground he saw droppings and examined them. Bear.

He saw more hair, caught like the previous bit in the rough splinters of the log. He plucked it out as before, pinching it idly between his fingers. He was about to toss it to the earth when he glanced more closely at it, and froze. He brought it to his nose, sniffed it. Then something on the ground near his knee also caught his attention, and he picked that up.

"Oh, dear Lord," he whispered. "Dear God above."

Three days later, Stanley Wickham found himself looking at a gnarled, calloused hand he would be expected to shake within a few moments, an act that would seal and close a grim and wicked deal. The idea of touching that hand, and agreeing to that which he himself had just put forward to be done, made him feel as if his gorge could rise and erupt.

Had he really fallen this far? Lost this much of his integrity and decency?

He didn't like to admit it, but he knew the answer was yes. His future depended on the plans he and Wilberforce Sadler had made, and those plans in turn depended on him getting those diamonds of Zeb Mc-Swain's into his hand. And in order to clasp those diamonds, his hand had first to grasp that of the steel-eyed man before him, and ugly things had to be done.

Wickham would not seal this arrangement, though, until certain matters were firmly established. "You do understand that she cannot, *cannot,* know my involvement in this," he said. "No matter what happens, no matter what is asked or demanded or attempted by her or anyone else, she cannot know. *Must* not. Ever."

"Understood, sir, understood. I've told you a dozen times already, eh? You're not dealing with fools here."

"If I repeat myself, it is for emphasis. She cannot, must not, ever know."

"She will not."

"Equally important is the fact that she must never be placed in authentic danger, or be allowed to fall into the hands of anyone who might believe her to be one of the other slatterns who might be in that place, on their way to . . . uh, adventures abroad."

"I will see to it myself, Mr. Wickham. She will not be allowed to become part of the common flow of that particular river."

"I will hold you to that, Turner."

"I would expect nothing else, eh?"

"Repeat to me those conditions I have emphasized to you."

"There is no need. I know your expectations and will fulfill them."

"Repeat the conditions!"

"Very well. She must not know you are the one who hired us to take her, and she must not be harmed or allowed to be taken away with the other women of the pens. She cannot be allowed to become what my associates and I usually term as, eh, 'product.' "

Wickham nodded. "Yes. And you will see to these conditions yourself. Not delegate them to others who might not exercise the full diligence."

"I will see to them myself." With that, the man named Turner reached out and grasped Wickham's hand and without waiting for the latter's cooperation, pumped it with vigor. He smiled a greenish tan, yellowish smile. Though Turner dressed well in overly formal clothing, his decaying teeth belied his attempts to play the sophisticate, the urbane man of business and culture.

When Wickham had left, Turner spoke to an ugly confederate beside him, a heavyset Mexican man who made no pretensions to elegance at all. "Oh yes, Paco. I will see to her myself. Several times, I will see to her with an intensity with which she has never been seen to before, if I judge her husband rightly. It will be nothing she will soon forget, my friend." Then he laughed, hard and loud. And added: "Fear not, amigo. You, too, will have your chance to 'see to' this woman. She is a beauty, a great beauty. You will like her."

Paco laughed the laugh of an imbecile, nodding broadly.

As a sideline enterprise at his big camp store in Bowater, Stanley Wickham had established a stage line to run between seven of the larger mining camps in the district. In one of the coaches of his own line, he made his journey back to Bowater after the ugly and unpleasant meeting just concluded with the unwashed outlaw named Turner. They had met in a thicket in the middle of a remote, wide meadow, away from any camp or residence, insurance for Wickham against anyone hearing or seeing him with such unsavory characters. What he was doing required the utmost secrecy and the most wrenching rejection of human morality and decency Wickham could imagine. He'd never have thought he had it in him to arrange for the kidnapping and short-term imprisonment of his own wife. It would be a horrific experience for her, but if the former Texan criminal named Turner could be trusted to keep his word and not let Emma be hurt, molested, or — heaven forbid it — swept away by accident with the usual flow of human traffic that passed through the place she would be held, she should come through without harm.

Besides, Wickham told himself alone in his stagecoach, Emma was no weakling. She was strong. He said it aloud: "Strong!"

"I beg your pardon, sir?" the stage driver called down to his passenger.

"Nothing, nothing," Wickham said. "I sneezed, that's all."

Wickham did not plan to return home tonight. There was another meeting to be carried out, this one with a man less unpleasant than Turner, but likely just as criminal. Wickham had found him through the guidance of people he knew who were accustomed to dealing with such types of folk, and he was counting on him to fill in a crucial missing piece of the puzzle Wickham was being called upon to solve. If he was lucky, the task was already done.

He had to find Zebulon McSwain. He knew his father-in-law was in California — McSwain had told Emma that much on his own, through a letter she'd received weeks before. But where in California? Wickham was at a loss as to how to find him in such a growing, amorphous society, where the wilderness sprouted new mining camps and towns like an untended Georgia garden patch sprouting summer weeds. McSwain could be anywhere.

The man Wickham had finally settled upon to find McSwain came highly recommended. Peter Coggin had come to California from St. Louis, where he'd earned a name for himself as a locator of missing persons and a retier of broken interpersonal cords. Like so many, he'd come to the golden frontier to leave behind his former ways of life and business, but had drifted back toward older ways when gold proved more elusive than the promoters back East had promised. Wickham had hired Coggin and impressed on him the urgency of locating McSwain quickly, though he'd not told the detective the reason for the urgency.

It made him chuckle blackly to imagine how it would have been if he had told Coggin what he was up to. *"Mr. Coggin, it is crucial that you find where my father-in-law is quickly, because I have only a few days to complete the process of having my own wife kidnapped by a gang of ruffians accustomed to catching and selling women like livestock, generally shipping them off to places they never return from. Nothing like that is going to happen to my Emma, I've been promised, but still, I must have her out of the way for now so I can let her father know he must deliver to me the endowed diamonds he stole from a college in Tennessee . . . diamonds I can pretend to use to pay off the 'kidnappers' while in reality keeping them for myself so I can join my business partner in setting up a string of mining camp stores that will put us among the richest men in California. Oh, and then, of course, I will run for governor and win, and my wife will never know it was actually her own husband who had her stolen away and penned like an animal, to be used as bait to draw out her father."*

He'd told nothing of that sort to Coggin, of course. He'd instead told Coggin that it was his wife who was so eager to find Mc-Swain, because McSwain was an ill man and was pridefully but unwisely trying to live on his own. The Wickhams were ready to take him in and provide him the best of care and comfort, and see him through his illness. So please do hurry, Mr. Coggin. Find him quickly so we can go to him.

Coggin was a punctual man and was already awaiting Wickham at the little saloon located behind a dance hall, where they'd agreed to meet. The broad grin on Coggin's rounded face as Wickham approached him encouraged Wickham mightily.

"Good luck?"

"Good luck. It isn't difficult, generally, to find a man if he hangs his name out on a shingle in a busy city. Mr. McSwain has opened a school of sorts in San Francisco, teaching uneducated adults to read, as best I can tell. Odd line of work."

"He's an odd man. Many academics are."

"Oh, I do know that, sir. I do. I've dealt with many of them in various cases over the years."

"San Francisco. I'd hoped he might be closer than that. Maybe holed up in one of the nearby mining camps. Did you see him?"

"I saw a man exit the door of his building and lock it behind him, so I presume that was McSwain. He did not appear to be ill from what was visible."

"It's a condition of the pancreas. Not a particularly visible ailment."

"I see. So what now? Will you visit him?"

"I have more work for you." Wickham reached beneath his waistcoat and pulled a sealed envelope from an inner pocket. "I wish you to deliver this to Mr. McSwain in two days' time. No sooner and no later. Two days' time. I am not inclined to explain why. . . . A personal, family matter is involved in the timing."

"I understand. I respect the need for

privacy on the part of my clients, including some degree of privacy in regards to what I myself know. All I ask is that you assure me that, in delivering this and following your timing, I am not unwittingly being involved in any criminal activity."

Wickham, a good liar at all times and a decent actor when he had to be, managed to look both shocked and amused at the same moment. He threw back his head and laughed. "Criminal? Oh, sir, certainly not. I am simply handling this in accord with my wife's wishes, and certain preparations she is making to receive her father into the bosom of our home."

"It is fine of both her and you, Mr. Wickham, to perform this kindness for her father. I commend you for it. And certainly I will put the letter in Mr. McSwain's hands at precisely the time you have told me to. Will I need to wait for him to read it in case he wishes to send back a response to you, for me to deliver?"

This was a question Wickham had not anticipated and therefore he had no ready answer. He answered off the cuff. "I think not. I believe that when he reads that letter he will come to us on his own, very promptly indeed."

"Shall I accompany him?"

"No, sir. Once you have put that envelope into his hands, what we need of you will have been accomplished."

"Very good, sir. Now, the matter of my payment . . ."

Wickham brought out a snap-top pocket purse, filled with carefully weighed and measured gold dust. Coggin accepted it with a smile, put the envelope into a coat pocket, and took his leave of Wickham.

Wickham bought himself rum and sat back, letting himself relax as much as possible, the first time he'd even tried to do so since his tense meeting with Wilberforce Sadler.

He had changed his immediate plan. He would go home tonight and be with his wife, because the kidnapping would happen the next evening and it seemed right to be with her tonight and try to give her a cheerful evening before life turned decidedly uncheerful for her for a period of time. It was all planned and timed, and he hoped to the high heavens that nothing went wrong. He'd never been involved in anything more important, or more dangerous, than this. It racked his nerves.

And, unfitting as it was to do it, Wickham prayed. *Dear God, do not let her be hurt.*

Whatever may come, please do not let her be hurt.

He ordered another drink and checked his watch to make sure he did not fail to be at the right place, at the right time, to meet his coach and driver for the journey back to Bowater and home.

In the night, he rolled over and saw her beside him, sleeping soundly, quietly, her face a beautiful sculpture of nature in the moonlight through the window. He almost, almost reached out to touch her, but drew his hand back.

If he touched her, he might weaken, feel pity for her, and decide to spare her from what was ahead. And if he did that, there would be no diamonds from her father, no business venture with Wilberforce Sadler, no massive volume of wealth, fame, and power. No coming day when he would settle his backside into the chair of the governor of this new state of California.

He could not abide that, so he did not touch her. He let her sleep and hoped her dreams would be good ones this night, because at this time the next night, the nightmares would be upon her. Not as dreams, but reality.

Could he do it? Could he really go through

with the process he had already started rolling?

He rolled over, turning his back to her. Yes, he could do it. Because he had to do it.

He had to.

CHAPTER TWENTY-NINE

"Do you know the definition of 'fool,' ma'am?" the man named Turner asked the woman who cowered in the corner of the covered log pen, her face encased in a cotton sack so she could see nothing. A piece of cord cinched the sack in tightly around her neck. With her ability to breathe already greatly limited by the sack, the tightness of the cord rendered it nearly impossible.

Emma McSwain Wickham made no reply, which angered Turner. Though he was too tall to stand up fully in the low-topped, cabinlike structure, he worked his way closer to her. She cringed back from him. He laughed and commented upon her fear.

"I believe you think I'm going to strike you for your rudeness in not answering a simple question," he said in a mocking, scathing tone. "Well, I am not a man content to leave expectations unfulfilled." With that he drove a fist into her jaw, rocking her head back hard against the log wall, making her cry out in shock and pain. The blow had been rendered all the worse because she had not been able to see it coming, to know where it would land.

"Well, my dear Emma — you don't mind me calling you Emma, do you? Certainly with what transpired between us last night, we should be free to speak as the most intimate kind of friends, eh? — perhaps now you might be inclined to be a little more responsive and a little less rude."

"Please . . . please . . . ," she managed to say with what little voice and breath she could find beneath the tightness of the neck-encircling cord. Her wrists were bound together, and those bonds were linked by a second cord to her similarly tied ankles. It was short enough that she would be limited to a bent-over posture even if she managed to get on her feet. So far, since being thrown into this log prison the prior afternoon, she had not dared try to get up, anyway.

"Please, did you say? What a polite word, 'please'! Very well, then, if you want another, you may have it, since you asked so nicely." And he hit her again, and laughed. She sobbed beneath the masking cloth.

"I am an accommodating host, am I not?"

Turner said. She sobbed again. He gave her another blow, this time on her shoulder, but harder. "I asked you a question, Emma."

"Y . . . yes," she murmured.

"Yes what?"

"You are . . . an accommodating host."

"Ah, now, that's how two friends should interact," Turner said. "An open, ready dialogue, answering each other's questions politely. Eh? But there is still one question you have not answered. My first one. How does one define a fool?"

"I don't know . . . sir," she replied, so softly she could barely be heard.

"Oh my, how badly this land needs improvement in education! Not to know the definition of 'fool' . . . my, my." He paused and sighed overloudly, like a bad stage actor. Then went on. "A fool, my dear, is a man who would hire a criminal captor and broker of women to seize and hold his own wife, yet expect that such a man will be true to his promises regarding what he will and will not reveal to her. In short, Emma, a fool is defined as your own husband."

She understood better than she was willing to admit to herself that she did, horrible as it all was. Unwilling to give this evil man the satisfaction of letting him break her down, though, she bottled the horror she felt and did not let him see.

"Please, can you explain more clearly what you are saying?"

Turner laughed. To him, the delight of his evil trade was the control it allowed him to exert, the power over others. The power to break and ruin women, leave them shattered. He did not know what had made him the way he was, and he did not care. Power was pleasure to him. Dominance was his delight.

"I made a promise to your husband that I would not tell you that he is the one who hired me to kidnap you and bring you here. He is using you for bait, you see, to draw your father to him, bringing him something he wants and needs very badly. And you think that I am a bad man, eh? Who is the worse, the man who makes no claim to any goodness, who does what he does with full knowledge and acceptance of the evil of it, or the man who pretends to be upright, a leader of others, someone to be admired and followed and handed power . . . and then is willing to see his own wife brought to such a place as this, to put her into the hands of me, and of Paco. Because I may tell you, dear Emma Wickham, the treatment you received from me last night is pale and mild, absolute kindness, in comparison to what Paco does. When ugly Paco puts his hands on a woman, the woman wishes to die, begs to die. And sometimes she does."

Emma put her hands to her face, pressing the cloth of the sack mask against it. Her tears soaked into the dirty cotton fabric with its stains lingering from the tears, sweat, and spittle of prior victims of Turner and his partner.

"Please . . . can you remove this mask from me? I can scarcely breathe . . . please. I will not run. I promise you I will not even try."

"Promise, you say. Promises . . . the very thing I was talking about. I made promises to your husband. I promised him I would not tell you what I already have. Promise broken. I promised I would not let you be in any way violated. I have violated you myself. Promise broken. I promised him I would not allow you to become part of the regular flow of female traffic that passes through this place. That promise I have not broken. Yet. But it will be broken. You are a great and stunning beauty. You would be worth more than any woman I have ever sold from this place. I cannot just pass you back to your worm of a husband for the meager fee he is to pay me. Oh no. That would turn me, rather than him, into the very definition of a fool."

"What is going to become of me?"

He sighed once more, and swore. "I have to see your face again. . . . It is too fine a face to be hidden beneath that stinking cloth. So luck is with you, my dear. Your request is fulfilled."

He went to her, untied the cord around her neck, and whipped the sack off her head. Her hair pulled upward with the sweeping away of the cloth, then cascaded down around her face and head, piling on her trembling shoulders. Though the light inside the log pen was dim, she blinked as her eyes adjusted to it after the darker shadows inside the sack mask.

"Ah yes, a fine face. Fine beyond any I have seen. You are truly a beauty, Emma! Truly a beauty!"

"I asked you what was to become of me."

"I am a merchant, my dear. Like any merchant, I sell a product that others wish to have. In most cases those others live in other lands than ours, though not entirely so. They are invariably men of wealth. . . . That is assured because only the wealthy can afford to pay for the product I sell. It is product of the highest quality."

"This product . . . it is women?"

"And girls. Yes."

She looked at him, trembling harder, her eyes pooling. "Is that what you plan for me?"

"It's what a man of business and trade, when he is in my particular trade, must plan for the finest specimens of his product. There are men in this world who would pay a literal fortune to possess such a one as you."

"But it's wrong. It's so very wrong." Tears streamed as she said it.

"I have never been much concerned with the idea of wrong. Right and wrong is a concept for mothers and nannies and policemen and preachers . . . and I am none of those things, nor ever will be."

"Oh, dear God," she whispered, and lowered her head so she would not have to look at him while she wept. At length, though, she looked at him again. "You said my husband did this to me? Had you take me?"

"It was not his intention for you to be sold in trade. This was simply an easy way, a convenient opportunity, to put you away for a time, get you out of sight and into a place you could not escape, so that during that time he could persuade your father to provide him the ability to pay the ransom. There is no real ransom, of course, beyond the fee I agreed upon to provide my services. The 'ransom' your father brings is intended, by your husband at least, to go to no one else but himself. For what specific purpose, he did not say."

"I know his purpose," she said, a rising anger and sense of husbandly betrayal steeling her and giving her control over her tears. "He plans to use what my father gives him to expand his business, with a partner, and create his own empire and increase his wealth."

"A worthy ambition. To that extent, anyway, he is not a fool. To the extent he believes I will be content with a simple fee, when there is clearly far more wealth at play here than has been offered to me . . . to that extent he is a fool indeed. What sort of wealth is it your father possesses?"

McSwain had given his daughter a limited confession of his crime in a past letter. She had destroyed the letter after reading it, as he had instructed. It hardly seemed to matter, in this place with this foul man, to maintain secrets, though. "He stole diamonds that had been given to a college in Tennessee, a college he served as president."

"Diamonds! Wonderful things, diamonds . . . immensely valuable, easily hidden, easily turned into cash or put to currency in their natural state. . . . Diamonds are among jewels what you are among women, Emma Wickham. Diamonds I will be glad to possess, so I send a salute of thanks out to your father for bringing them to me."

"He's brought nothing yet, I am sure. And if he does bring them, they will get no farther than the hands of my husband. . . . God! To think my own husband has . . . has . . ." She looked helplessly around at her prison, not knowing just where she was or how close to any of the world she knew, because she had been blindfolded when she was carried here.

"Are you telling me, dearest, that our friend Stanley Wickham would cling to jewels before he would save his wife from a life of carnal slavery to some foreign despot . . . is that your point to me?"

"It is."

"So much the worse for him, then. And especially, so much the worse for you. Should he decline to cooperate, it will be shocking indeed to Mr. Wickham when pieces of his wife begin appearing in his mail . . . fingers, toes, an ear, an eyelid, even an eyeball . . . maybe even portions of a more, eh, *delicate* nature, might you not think? Hmm?" He actually chuckled.

Amazingly, Emma managed to hold her emotions. "Is there no end to the evil in you, sir?" she asked Turner.

He looked upward and rubbed his chin in an exaggerated aping of a man thinking hard about something. Then he looked her in the face, smiled, and said, "No, my dear. I think there is not."

He left her alone then, but neglected to put her sack hood back on her again. An inexplicable kindness or an oversight, she did not know. But it provided her the chance to see how the outward-lifting trap exit functioned, and the chance to examine the bonds that held her wrists and ankles. She pondered trying to reach her ankle bonds with her fingers, then realized she had been tied in such a way as to not allow her to do so.

She was trapped in this hell, and could see no way out on her own. "God," she prayed, "send me rescue. In the name of your power and holiness, oh, God, send me rescue."

She could not tell whether the prayer rose any higher than the low, flat ceiling of parallel logs above her.

She could only sit there, praying and hoping and hating Stanley Wickham, a man she had tried hard to love but who had given her back only betrayal, abuse, and seeming loathing. If only, if only, if *only* she had listened to her own heart and to her father and chosen Jedd Colter instead! She would not be here, hopelessly trapped and betrayed, and surely destined for some foreign port to become the plaything of some man even more wicked than her own husband.

Send me rescue. The prayer rose again and again. *Send me rescue, God. Hear me in my dark prison and send me rescue.*

But no one came except the ugly and unwashed Mexican named Paco, who dropped into the pen as the sun was beginning to set and approached her with a bitter, nauseating smile.

After that it became unspeakable.

Paco did not forget to remask Emma, and he tied the cord around her neck too tightly, forcing her to struggle for air all the night long, and experience no real sleep. The mask was not removed again until the next day around noon, when she was finally given food . . . something she thought initially was squirrel meat served on stale bread until she found part of the pinkish tail of a rat among the minced meat. She was so hungry she ate it anyway, her bonds having been adjusted enough to allow her, with straining effort, to reach her mouth with the food, though not to also reach the knots at her bound feet. These men were experienced and wickedly clever in the machinations of captivity. She washed her pathetic meal down with dirty water given to her in an even dirtier wooden cup.

They left the hood off for good this time, but never did they untie her. Through one of the cracks between logs making up her pen, Emma saw a woman being led out of her pen by Paco, who held a rope that was tied to her still-bound ankles. With no freedom to move her feet, she could only hop, and when she apparently progressed too slowly to suit Paco, he cursed and yanked at the rope, pulling her feet from beneath her and sending her slamming to the ground. He cursed her again, loudly, and kicked her until she managed to somehow get up again. Then he led her to a little clearing within full view of all the other cabin pens, and stood by while she did the best she could to perform the basic private functions demanded by nature, this with her hands and feet still bound. It was an inefficient, ugly affair, and the woman, who looked to be at least part Indian, wept in humiliation throughout. A slightly crippled Mexican girl, Rosita, whom Emma would later learn was Paco's illegitimate daughter, performed the cleanup, which consisted of harshly dashing two bucketfuls of water on the pathetic and shamed woman. Paco turned the rope over to his daughter to take the woman back to her pen.

Through the gap in the logs, Emma watched the sad woman reach her pen. Her guardian managed to get the trap open at the top without letting go of the rope, then got back down and with unexpected strength helped the woman hoist herself up the wall and then fall inside the log prison. The trapdoor was closed down and pinned closed with a heavy wooden rod, and suddenly Emma heard a rattling of her own pen's door.

It was Paco. He had come for Emma. It was her turn.

Emma lifted up her face and screamed in unmuted anguish.

CHAPTER THIRTY

The job of town marshal of Scarlett's Luck, California, ended for Rand Blalock and transferred to his deputy, Jedd Colter, with the death of Blalock's horse. It wasn't the mere fact that the horse was dead that ended Blalock's job, because other horses could be had. It was the way it died and a resultant effect of that death that turned the tables in new directions.

Blalock was riding, the horse merely plodding, down the muddy main thoroughfare of the mining camp, when deep inside the horse's heart, something shuddered, wrenched, sped for five seconds, then halted for all time. The aging beast's heart gave out, causing its legs to give out immediately after. The horse simply stopped walking, stood unmoving a few moments with Blalock in the saddle wondering what was happening, then collapsed as if its legs had turned to air. The left side gave out before the right, however, so the horse fell at a tilt and Blalock's left leg was pinned beneath it and broken. He decided even before they got him out from under the horse that his career in law enforcement was over. He was too old for this kind of nonsense.

"I don't even know why I came to California," he would later tell Jedd Colter. "The only reason I tracked down your wagon train was so I could tell Treemont the bad news about his kinfolk. . . . Now Treemont's dead, too. I just don't know why I bothered to come this far. I never had any ambition to look for gold."

"The point is, you're here," Jedd would tell him. "Maybe there's a reason, maybe it's just something that happened for no reason at all. But you're here, and it's a good place, and you may as well settle in and enjoy all you can of it."

"I used to be the wise one, Jedd. Now it's you."

"It's like I've said oft before. It ain't wisdom. It's experience."

When Blalock's horse died beneath him and broke his leg, neither Blalock nor anyone else noticed that his tin badge had gotten knocked free and fallen onto the ground. It was Ben Scarlett who later spotted and retrieved it, and so as not to lose it before finding a chance to return it to its owner, he pinned it on his vest and forgot about it. He'd taken to wearing a cast-off cravat he'd found crammed between a rain barrel and an alleyway wall, and having no idea how to tie it, he'd managed to leave one end of it hanging down oddly, covering the badge so that forgetting it was there was easy to do.

Ben was walking up the same street Blalock's horse had died on on a Tuesday morning when a youthful fellow walked up to his side and said, in a Pennsylvanian accent, "Excuse me, sir. Are you the sheriff here?"

Ben looked down at the boy and was struck by the notion that he'd seen this face before. Just where or when, he had no idea.

"Me, sheriff? Ha! No, son, no. I'm just the local drunk. The one they named the town for."

"Oh. I saw your badge there and just thought —"

"Oh, that. That belongs to the local marshal. He lost it when his horse died out from under him t'other day, and so I put it on my chest till I could find the opportunity to give it back to him. Not that he'll be needing it, though. . . . He quit his marshal job when his leg got broke under the falling horse."

"Oh." The youth obviously had followed only part of Ben's hurried narrative.

"Son, my name's Ben Scarlett. I've seen you before, somewhere."

"I don't know. . . . I haven't been in California for long. I came with my family in a wagon train out of Pennsylvania."

"Me, I'm from Tennessee. Knoxville. I was a drunk there, too."

"My name's Squire Napier," the boy said. "I'm from Philadelphia. My father . . . stepfather, really . . . wanted to come to California to find gold and have good things happen to us. So far there hasn't been much good. My sister was sickly all the way here, and died. She's buried by the roadside between here and the town of Bowater. We buried her cat beside her."

"Cat?"

"Yes, sir. There was a man in another wagon train who had a cat that had died and he'd had it stuffed and mounted. He was kind enough to give it to Winnie — that was my sister, Winnie — so she'd have something to play with and keep her spirits up with during the rest of the trip to California."

Ben looked more closely at Squire's face,

and it all came back. This was the very boy who had sneaked into the wagon that night McSwain's dead cat had been stolen — the very lad who stole it, in fact.

"I'll be, son. . . . I know who you are, and I was there in that wagon the night you sneaked that stuffed cat out."

Squire studied Ben but did not recognize anything familiar in him.

"I'm pleased to see you again, Squire. Sorry about your sister, though." Ben paused. "Hey, son, why were you looking for a lawman? Is there trouble?"

"Maybe. I don't know. I was down by Winnie's grave this morning, laying some pretty leaves on it for her, Winnie always having been partial to pretty leaves. And I heard a woman screaming up beyond a ridgetop nearby. Sounded dreadful. I climbed up a path there to see, and . . . well, I need to tell a lawman about it, I think."

"Come on. We're going to go find Jedd Colter, you and me. He's the law now that Rand Blalock's leg is busted. I know that very ridge you're talking about, I think, and I suspect you're right about there being trouble up there. Jedd will know what to do. He'll deal with it."

It was a most unexpected reunion. Ben

found Jedd finishing a plate of beans outside his little cabin, and at the same time, found none other than Zebulon McSwain and Crozier Bellingham with him. Also another fellow, twenty-some-odd years old, if Ben had to guess. He didn't know this one.

When Bellingham and McSwain saw Ben, greetings were hearty, though McSwain seemed to be quite burdened over something. When he laid eyes on Ben's young companion, the look of burden bearing became one of confusion.

"You're the Napier boy, I think?"

"I am, Mr. McSwain. The one whose sister you gave your cat to. That was mighty nice of you, sir. That cat cheered her in her last days."

"I . . . I saw her grave by the roadside. I'm quite sorry little Winnie was lost to your family. And I'd come to feel a certain closeness to her myself. It was to see her grave that I traveled to this area. Someone had told me of seeing a girl's grave by the roadside, and remembered the name was Winnie, and that a cat's grave was beside hers. The last name he didn't recall, so I was compelled to come see for myself if it was the Winnie I knew. I regret that it was."

Jedd glanced over and saw that Bellingham was scribbling furiously in a notepad.

He smiled at the feeling of familiarity the sight roused in him.

The man who was a stranger to Ben walked up and introduced himself. "Tom Buckle, Mr. Scarlett. I'm pleased to meet the man who managed to find gold by washing out a pair of peed-in britches."

"I'm pleased to know you, Mr. Buckle."

"Call me Tom. You'll be seeing me more around here. I'm Jedd's new deputy. Been doing the same duty over in Bowater, but since Jedd's boss was knocked out of commission and Jedd advanced to the full town marshal's role, he's asked me to work for him, and I've accepted. I'll be moving to Scarlett's Luck in the next little while."

"I wish you well. Welcome to our town."

"To hear that from the very man whose name the town carries means much to me. Thank you, Ben."

Ben turned to McSwain. "How did you come to be here today?" he asked.

"I've been to my daughter's house, over in Bowater. I was called there by a man sent by my son-in-law, who gave me very distressing news. Emma has been taken."

"Taken?"

"Kidnapped. She is being held for a high ransom that Stanley, her husband, claims inability to pay. He has asked me to pay it in his place."

"Can you do it? I guess I'm asking, do you have the means?"

"It happens that I do. How I came by it is something about which I can hold no pride. But have the means I do, and I am ready to pay that ransom if it is necessary. But I was not willing to do it without talking it through with Jedd. Stanley was quite insistent that I not leave his home and that I begin taking steps to immediately obtain the diam— uh, to obtain the resources in my possession, which at the moment are safely locked away in a vault in San Francisco. There was something odd in it all, though, something that set me on edge and made me insist upon speaking to Jedd about it first. The fact that he insisted on being the one to whom I should present the ransom, rather than me giving it directly to whomever has Emma . . . that worried me."

"Me as well," Jedd said.

McSwain nodded. "That is why I insisted on coming to Jedd before making any major actions. I trust Jedd's judgment on such matters."

Jedd said, "And my judgment is that before anybody starts handing over ransom payments to somebody like Stanley Wickham, who I think is about as trustworthy as a riverboat gambler — and I'm aware I may be misjudging him because of Emma — there is a place that merits a look first. A place that could be relevant to any situation involving a missing woman in this area. You know the area I'm thinking of, Ben, if you'll put your mind to it."

Ben frowned. "The ridge . . . the one I told you about, where there's cabins with no doors?"

Jedd nodded, then spoke. "I went to that place, Ben, and Tom here went with me for a part of the way. There was cause to believe that those odd little cabins were put there to serve as pens for bears caught for the bull and bear fights, but a closer look showed there'd been human beings kept there, too, and recent. I found a woman's comb inside one of those cabins. And in more than one of them there were droppings that were not of bears. Looked to be human spoor."

"But nobody there when you were looking around?"

"Obviously not. I doubt I'd be here and alive today if there had been. But here's the crux of it all: there's strong rumors in these parts that somebody has been using that place as a holding spot for women being sold abroad for evil purposes, sold to bad men of wealth and power. A well-established operation, the rumors have it, going back well before California became part of the United States. So when a woman goes missing, as Emma has, you have to consider at least the possibility that she's gotten snared into that particular net. God, I hope not, but I think another look at that valley is called for." Jedd turned to Bellingham. "A question for you, Crozier. You are a man who spends his time asking questions, listening to answers, and listening as well to what's going on around you. Since you've been in California, have you heard much rumor regarding the enslavement and sale of women through Mexico by land and the California bays and ports by sea?"

"I've heard it talked of frequently," Bellingham said. "And lately, more such talk than when we first arrived."

"Do you take the talk seriously?"

"I must admit that I do. There is a ring of grim truth about it, and such a prevalence of it, that I have to believe there may be at least some truth there." He paused. "I can say one thing with confidence: such a trafficking does go on. It exists. Whether this valley with its cabins is part of it, I have no idea. But the trafficking is real. It occurs."

"Yes, it does," Tom Buckle said.

"I'm going to go with you, Jedd," Ben said abruptly. "I ain't no lawman, but I'll go, if it would help anybody caught up in such a bad snare as that one."

"I appreciate that, Ben. But it ain't the place or situation for you."

Ben looked down at his ragged, liquor-ravaged form and nodded sadly. "I ain't much count to nobody, I don't reckon."

"Don't forget why you brought me here, Mr. Scarlett," young Napier cut in. He'd been so quiet that he'd almost faded into the background.

Ben's face came alive again as remembrance struck. "That's right! Jedd, considering all that's going on here right now, and what you're about to do, you need to hear what Squire here has to say. He was visiting his sister's grave over at the base of that ridge, where the trail is —"

"I know the spot," Jedd said.

"— and he heard something. Sent a chill through me when he told me of it. It must have chilled him, too, because he was looking for a lawman when he found me. He saw I was wearing this. . . ." Ben pulled back the long sash of the wrongly tied cravat and yanked Blalock's badge from his vest and handed it to Jedd. "Found that on the street where Marshal Blalock's horse died on him."

Jedd pocketed the badge and turned to Squire. "Talk to me, son."

Squire told his tale of the woman's scream from somewhere beyond the top of the ridge. When the brief story was done, Jedd looked at his new deputy. "Tom Buckle, welcome to the first day of your new job. And this time I'm afraid you'll have to not back off from going into that valley with me, no matter how hurtful it might be as regards your late sister."

Buckle looked Jedd in the eye. "I'd not miss it, not this time. I'll go in her memory, and for the sake of this man's daughter . . . and the woman who should have been yours."

"Hear, hear!" McSwain said. "Jedd, if Emma is up there, you find her, and you bring her back . . . to both of us. And I'd like to come with you while you do. I'm no lawman and I know I'm no more likely than our friend Ben here to be of true help, but she's my daughter, Jedd. And if she's been taken by such rabble as that, I have to be there."

Jedd replied, "I've said here that I think we are obliged to take a new look at that valley, but as regards Emma, I actually doubt she's there, Zeb. She's missing, but there's been a ransom demand. And the kind of folk rumored to be holding prisoners up in that little basin valley don't take women to hold them for ransom. They steal women to sell them. If they had Emma, there never would have been a call for ransom."

McSwain nodded. "I'm not sure there really has been an authentic call for ransom, Jedd. The only mention of ransom that's been made was made by Stanley Wickham. He had no letter, no note to show me. Only his word that such a demand has been made."

"Wait . . . are you hinting that you believe Wickham would have his own wife kidnapped to try to get money out of you, Zeb?"

"I would not put it past him. The man is a snake and I never should have stood by while Emma married him. I have tried to make my peace with the notion of him as her husband, but there are alarms that sound in my mind every time the mere thought of the man passes through it."

"I'm the same way about that, Zeb," Jedd said. "But all that to the side, I think it's best you stay here with Ben, for now. Squire, has your family settled in these climes?"

"My father has a mining claim about three miles from here."

"Maybe you'd best get home, then."

"I'll . . . I'll wait with Mr. Scarlett and Mr. McSwain. I want to know how this all turns out."

Jedd nodded, then to Bellingham said: "Crozier, you're keeping silent. I'm hoping you don't have a notion that you'll be going along with us on this. If we find somebody up there, it probably won't turn out to be a good time or place for note-taking."

"You will talk to me afterward, though? This could provide an important theme and bit of plot for my novel."

"Talking about that novel openly now, I see?" Jedd observed.

"No reason not to."

"I'll talk to you at any length you want after this is through."

"Then I'll stay put here with the others."

"Good man, Crozier."

Jedd and Buckle armed themselves, and Jedd removed his deputy's badge and handed it to Buckle. Then he put the marshal's badge previously worn by Blalock on his own chest.

"Jedd Colter, town marshal," he said. "I never would have thought it."

"I hope you don't find her in that place,

Jedd," McSwain said. "But if you do, bring her back."

"You can count on it, Zeb. Deputy Buckle, let's go."

"Yes, sir, Marshal Colter."

CHAPTER THIRTY-ONE

There was time to plan, that much she had to admit. Penned up as she was, there was nowhere she could go and little she could do, so she spent much of her time studying her claustrophobic prison, trying to identify weaknesses, possible escape avenues. . . .

And it all came down to one thing: to escape this place she had to have a knife. With a knife she could cut her bonds, and with a knife she could, just maybe, work the blade up through a gap and pin the tip into the sliding wooden bar that held the trapdoor entrance-exit closed. She could work the bar free of its holders and push the door up and open. And simply climb out.

If she had a knife. And there was no knife in this little place. She'd already scanned each crevice, each gap, each corner, in the wild hope that, somehow, someone at some past time had left a knife, a broken blade, even a piece of broken glass, that she might be able to reach and use. Nothing. That hope was fading.

And there was no new hope rising to replace it. Without a way to cut her hands free, there was no hope. None at all. She would be here until they took her to the next place, wherever that place would be. A port, a dock, a wagon rolling toward Mexico . . . or maybe just another wooded valley filled with cabin prisons. She could not know.

She stared out through the biggest gap between two logs and pondered the fact that only a hand's width of wood separated her from the outer world. That, and a few strands of twined fiber. If she could just . . . if she could just . . . she could not even finish the thought, because there simply was nothing she could "just" do.

The bar moved and the door lifted open, and Turner was there. He knelt, smiling at her in a way that sickened her. "You amaze me," he said. "In a situation such as this, yet you still remain as beautiful as any woman could be. Unwashed, unkempt . . . but beautiful. That's a rarity, you know, a woman who can maintain her beauty through such hard circumstances."

"Are you really going to . . . to send me

away? To some strange man somewhere else?"

"This is my trade, my dear. My life. It's what I do . . . send women off to strange men somewhere else, in exchange for the money they pay me."

"But you are wasting me. Wasting me on a stranger! Why do that? I could be . . . I could be *yours*!" And somehow, she made herself smile at him.

He seemed surprised, actually struck wordless a few moments. Was the woman beginning to lose her mind through the effects of deprivation and worry? He'd been at this dark game long enough to have seen it happen before, with others, this shifting of the captor from enemy to friend. He'd never allowed it to go far, though he had used it to his own advantage sometimes.

None of those other mentally disintegrating and desperate women, though, had been what Emma Wickham was: the essence and summation of feminine beauty . . . perfection. He'd had other women be drawn to him in a wild hope that, somehow, he would turn from captor to benefactor for them. Yes, but none of those had been anything close to what it would take for him even to consider taking them for himself in anything more than a momentary, lust-venting way.

Emma Wickham, however, was different than any other. She was one, the only one among all he'd seen, whom he might consider as a woman he could make his own, in some personal and permanent way. He might actually, at some previously unexplored level of himself, be able to love her. Love. Not a word or concept he was accustomed to thinking of, even believing in. For him there had never been anything but power, domination, violent passion . . . never love. Love was a fiction of fools.

He was not fool enough to believe he was at this moment in love with this imprisoned beauty. But he did see in her something that made him think love might actually be a real thing, after all, something at least possible between two people. That alone was enough to set her apart and make her special and important and worthy of his attention.

As he pondered all this, he moved toward her, eyes locked on hers. He reached her, leaned forward, felt her bound hands groping at him to embrace him as best they could within her rope-limited range of motion. She could not achieve it, of course, but the resolve with which she had tried actually moved him. A man who had thought himself beyond the reach of normal human emotion . . . he had been *moved.* It was a novel and somewhat unsettling experience.

She was trying to reach him, trying to kiss him, but again her restraints kept her from success. He looked at her deeply, smiled, then pulled away, not even kissing her or even wanting to. He had already vented his carnal passions upon this woman. Now he wanted something more, and different. And higher. That had never happened before, and it was more than he could deal with.

He turned away from her and wordlessly left her alone in her log prison. He closed down the door and barred it shut, then moved on to the pen of another woman, one he felt free to use and treat in the way he was accustomed to using and treating women. Women who did not waken things in him that had nothing to do with power and lust and domination.

It would be another two hours before he noticed that, somewhere along the way, the knife he carried in a sheath on his belt was gone. He looked for it in a wild fashion, appalled that it was missing, but try as he would, he could not find it, nor imagine how it could have been released from its holder without his awareness.

He'd dropped it, he finally decided. It lay

somewhere amid weeds or stones, out of sight, lost by accident. It had to be. Had to be.

She could not have said exactly how she'd done it. She'd followed her instincts, used subtle shifts of her body, her head, to cause him to move responsively, and she'd thus managed to maneuver him, without his awareness, into a place where she could knock the knife he always carried free of its sheath. It had fallen beside her leg and she'd managed to mostly cover it with her skirt. Turner had left her pen without awareness that his knife was missing. An hour, then two, had passed without him returning to look for it.

Amazing. She'd prayed for a rescuer to be sent, and it appeared that the rescuer who had come had been . . . herself.

But merely having that tool in her prison was hardly a guarantee of escape. Her tied hands would not quite reach the knife, and even if she managed to get it in hand, she was unsure of being able to work into a position allowing her to apply blade edge to rope. The way these men bound their prisoners was diabolically clever and thoroughly thought out. The bound ones were allowed just enough range of motion to keep them always trying to wriggle out of their cords, thus preserving their muscles and bones from the atrophy that would come if they were held utterly still. Yet the range of movement was so small that almost nothing could be actually achieved. Even eating required bone-straining effort.

Emma had moved her skirt enough to expose the knife to her view again, and had changed position as far as it seemed possible to let her come close to reaching it . . . but close was not enough. Straining, exerting, she tried to will her bones and joints and muscles to achieve impossible levels of flexibility, movement, and range . . . her fingers creeping closer and closer, but never quite reaching . . .

And suddenly a scuffling and scrabbling above, on the top of the pen, told her he was back, and it was too late. He obviously had discovered his knife was missing and realized where he'd lost it. No hope now. He would retrieve the knife, probably punish her violently, maybe tighten her bonds, and she'd have lost the only feeble chance she'd found to help herself.

She closed her eyes as the trapdoor folded back and feet thumped down on the floor of the pen. She waited to feel his rough hand grasp her. It did not, and Emma dared to open one eye. . . .

It was not Turner who had entered, nor was it Paco. The person was Rosita, Paco's daughter, the crippled girl whose duty it was to crudely bucket-wash the soiled bodies of the prisoners after they'd voided themselves.

Emma opened both eyes but did not look directly at the girl, whose age was hard to guess. She supposed Rosita, who appeared half Mexican, half Anglo, to be perhaps fourteen or fifteen years of age. Despite her youth, her eyes had the hard glare of an older, life-toughened female. She stared unflinchingly and silently at Emma.

"He has killed one of you," Rosita said, her voice soft and her Mexican accent light. It surprised Emma to hear her speak; her impression had been that Rosita was a mute, Rosita having never spoken in her presence earlier. Emma had not even known the girl's name until she'd heard one of the other prisoners call to the girl while she was leading Emma to the place where she "washed" the women with hard-dashed bucketfuls of water.

"Who has been killed?"

Rosita knelt before Emma. "She was a young woman, like you. Gringo like you, with hair like the silk of corn. But she was

411

crippled, as I am, with a badly formed foot. Senor Turner went to her pen to make his use of her, and he had not known she was crippled. When he saw her withered foot, he cursed her and hit her and called her a 'twist-foot hen.' She tried to rise and he hit her harder. There was a broken splinter of wood on the wall of her pen and she pulled it free of the wall and went at him with it, hoping in her anger to stab him. He kept her from it and pushed her to the ground, and hit her about the head again and again with his fist. She cried out for a time, and then she was silent." Rosita paused. "She will be silent forever now."

Emma had no idea who the murdered young woman was, having barely caught glimpses of the handful of other prisoners in this compound of covered log pens. Even so the fact that someone in the same victimized position as she had fallen victim to such purposeless violence moved her, and a tear rolled down her dirty face. There were tears in Rosita's eyes as well, but her look was less a sad one than one of determined fury.

"A 'twist-foot hen,' he called her. 'Twist-foot hen.' As if she had chosen it for herself. As if she had made herself crippled just to give him annoyance. Damn his devil's soul!"

Emma was growing puzzled. "Why have

you come to me to tell me all this?"

Rosita drew closer, eyeing the space between Emma and one corner of the pen. Emma scooted over some to make more room, and Rosita sat down beside her, their sides touching.

"I tell you because you are his favorite. I always can tell the favorites of him and my father. . . ." She paused and spat as though admitting her kinship to Paco made her mouth taste foul. "There have been many favorites among the 'product' for both of them. But for Senor Turner there have been none like you before. He looks at you in a way different than he has looked at any other woman or girl ever held here that my eyes have seen."

"But why have you come to me?"

"Because he killed the crippled one. The one who was like me. And because he called her what he did. It fires a fury in my heart — 'twist-foot hen.' Damn him! May the mighty God damn his soul to the eternal flame!"

"Even so, why have you —"

"I have come to set you free," Rosita said in the faintest of whispers. "Because if you are free he is deprived and made sad. He does not deserve to be happy. If I take you from him, his happiness is gone. And . . ."

She paused and looked earnestly at Emma. ". . . and you can take me away from here, hide me, and help me escape them. I hate them, hate them both . . . what they do, what they say, what they are. I hate my father, but Senor Turner, Diablo Turner, him I hate most. He is the one who led my father into such dark ways."

This was all stunning and fully unexpected, despite whatever prayers she had prayed for rescue. Emma could hardly find her voice, but did. "Yes, Rosita. We will both get away from them and this place. First you must cut the cords on my hands and feet. There is a knife beside me that I have been unable to reach."

Rosita quickly found and picked up the knife. "This is the blade of the diablo," she said, astounded. "How do you possess it? He is never without it."

"I was able to knock it free of its sheath when he was in here. I pretended to want him to come to me, and when he reached me I was able somehow to free the knife. I hid it beneath my dress but was not able to reach it with my hand, because of my cords. But you are here now, and you can use it."

Rosita was deft and fast, and within a minute Emma's bonds were severed. She had hardly realized how tightly she had been tied until the pressure of the cords was released. The relief was sufficient to bring tears to Emma's eyes.

"Bless you, Rosita. . . . God bless you! Now we will leave this devil's ground behind us, together."

"Adios, Diablo! Adios, *mi padre*!" Rosita whispered.

"Yes," Emma said, nodding and smiling at the teary-eyed girl. "Let's go, Rosita."

CHAPTER THIRTY-TWO

The human devil named Turner was ruthless and without morals, but not without sense. He'd been at his trade long enough to know that such activity could not forever be kept hidden, particularly in a place where every piece of land was destined to be scoured over by gold hunters somewhere along the way. The ruse of also using the pens to hold bears trapped for the violent bull and bear fights that were common entertainment in the mining camps had proven, so far, a successful one. Profitable, too, though at a lesser level than the trade in women.

All past success in covering up the truth aside, Turner was aware of the recent increase of rumors regarding the use of the site as a way station in human trafficking. The secret could not be kept much longer. He thought it likely that the women held here now would be the last at this particular station.

No matter, really. There were other such stations across the frontier and even in the big cities back East. Some were remote clusters of cabins and pens like this one; others were underground in the literal sense, built in caves and tunnels and the like. Turner knew of one station in Kansas that was located beneath an esoteric, purportedly "religious" community that excluded outsiders and was known for its eighteenth-century style of life and the habit of its members of excavating huge cellars beneath their homes, churches, and even barns.

The real purpose of those cellars was known only to a few, and even in a case or two where word had gotten out where it should not have, the damage had been controlled by the network of traffickers of which Turner was but one part. Turner knew that at least two county sheriffs in Kansas were possessors of "cellar maidens" provided to them in exchange for averted eyes and closed mouths. Turner knew this because at one time he'd been a part of the "religious" community with the prison cellars for unwilling females destined for hard lives and harder deaths as the chattel of rich and depraved men. Turner sometimes referred to his time in that strange little Kansas community as his "religious days."

Turner had moved on to his "business days" by now, and as a man of business, he attended his share of meetings. One such was to happen this day, in an empty cabin near an already played-out parcel of mining claims that had been abandoned to the Mexicans, who in turn had abandoned them to the Chinese. Turner was to meet with a certain Chinese gentleman who had hinted he could provide Turner with some of the finest "Celestial" maidens to be found outside the old nation itself. If all went well, Turner and his network of fellow traffickers would be able to offer up a new and profitable line of "product" to those around the world with a taste for the Orient.

Turner trudged through the little basin with its smattering of log pens, halfheartedly casting his eyes about for his lost knife as he went. He'd stopped expecting to find it; probably it was simply hidden beneath brush, leaves, and the like after an accidental loss, but it wasn't worth the effort to turn over every bit of rubbish in this camp to find one knife. He could tell by glancing through the unchinked pen walls that all the women were still in place . . . all but one, that is. The crippled girl he'd beaten to death earlier obviously was no longer part of the count. He grimaced as he thought of her, not because of regret, but because faulty "product" always set his teeth on edge. Not much chance for profit in cripples, blinders, deaf-mutes, and the like. The demand for such was simply not strong enough to make it worthwhile to waste time and pen space with them. Good riddance as far as Turner was concerned.

Thinking of the gimp-footed girl whose life he'd ended caused him to think of the polar opposite of flawed "product," the lovely Emma Wickham. He was still debating inwardly about whether to go ahead and send her on through the trafficking pipeline or keep her as his own personal trophy and toy. The latter option had its appeal but would present challenges, too. He would have to guard her, protect her, keep her hidden . . . almost impossible for a man in his position to do. Any of the other captives he would be ready to abandon at any time, if flight was necessary, but Emma would be in a different category. Still a captive she would be, but no longer "product." She would be *his* captive, *his* possession.

He went looking for Paco to remind him that he would be absent for a time, but he found the big Mexican asleep and snoring and opted not to wake him. Paco slept with a pistol nearby, and had a dangerous tendency to snap it up and level it if anyone awakened him unexpectedly. He'd even fired it off at Turner a time or two before he was fully awake, though luckily Paco was the worst of pistoleers and seldom hit any target he aimed at. Still, Turner was in no mood to dodge bullets, and let Paco snore on.

Turner went to the little stable shed where he and Paco kept their horses, saddled and bridled his chestnut-colored gelding, and rode out onto the little trail that led down to the road between Scarlett's Luck and Bowater. He glanced at the strange little pair of roadside graves, one for a little girl, the other apparently for a cat, and shook his head in bemusement. One saw a lot of unusual things in California these days.

Turner was well away from his camp of captives when the door of Emma's pen pushed up and open. Emma climbed out, eyes peeled for any sign of Paco. She knew Turner was gone because she'd caught a glimpse of him on horseback, riding out, and because Rosita had overheard him telling her father that he was going to meet during the morning with a Chinaman about "business."

"We have to let the others go," Emma said to Rosita as the younger woman followed her out of the pen. Rosita nodded, but whispered, "Speak softly. My father is a stupid bull of a man, but his ears are keen. And before we free them, there is something I must do, or it will not matter."

"What?"

"My father always sleeps this time of morning. I will be back in minutes. . . . Wait for me, and free no one else yet."

Emma watched Rosita limp away toward the area where Paco had pitched his tent. The terrain did not allow her to see the tent, but two minutes later the Anglo-Mexican girl reappeared, coming back toward Emma with a smile on her face and a more game step despite her lameness.

"Is he asleep?" Emma asked.

Rosita laughed. "Oh yes. He sleeps. And will sleep on now, very soundly."

"What did you do?"

"I know that we are commanded to do no murder," Rosita said. "But I do not believe it is murder to end the days of such a wicked man as my father."

"Dear Lord, Rosita, did you —"

"He had slept outside his tent, which made it easier. More room to swing the pick

I found. Something a miner had left leaned against a tree somewhere that my father had found and taken for his own. I stood over him, straddling his chest, and I took careful aim and swung it down as hard as I could. My strength was greater than I had known. . . . The point of the pick went through the top of his head and came out his mouth."

"Oh God!"

"I confess . . . ," Rosita said, then paused. "I confess that I laughed to see it." She laughed again then, and with her finger pointed outward from her mouth, imitating the emergence of the pick point. "Do you believe I have sinned, Senorita Emma?"

"Only in laughing at it, perhaps." Emma looked around at the prison pens. "For the other part, the doing of the act . . . no. No, I don't believe you sinned."

Turner reached the abandoned cabin without difficulty and tied his horse off to a branch. He checked to make sure his pistol was loaded — a standard precaution anytime he was about to meet with anyone he did not already know to be a safe person for him — and continued down to the open door. It was open because the door itself had been removed for use in some other miner's habitation.

"Mr. Li, sir, I am here!" he called as he walked down toward the cabin. "I believe I am slightly early, so I must ask your pardon."

A smiling man stepped into the doorway with a shotgun in his hands. This was no Chinaman. . . . Instead the tall fellow, sandy-haired, had a decidedly European look.

"Pardon is granted, sir," the man said in a brogue Turner recognized as Irish. He'd had a few Irish maidens among the "product" he'd move down the line through the years, and some of his fellow traffickers were Irish as well. "Please do come in . . . and forgive Mr. Li if he doesn't greet you. He is at the moment quite occupied in being dead."

Turner stood frozen, trying to make sense of this. He could not take his eyes off the shotgun. "Come closer," the Irishman said.

When Turner did come closer he saw that the man had an oddity in his appearance: a missing section of his right ear. Turner paid little heed to that, the shotgun still occupying his attention.

"What's this here?" Turner asked, raising his hands to shoulder level to demonstrate that he had no weapons in hand, nor any plan to draw the one in his holster. "What happened to Mr. Li?"

"I'm afraid I had to kill him," the Irishman said. "Name's Finnegan, by the by. Declan Finnegan. And you, if I had to guess, are one Mr. Liam Turner, from Atlanta by way of Kansas."

Something in the Finnegan name was familiar to Turner, but he could not recall just why. But how did Finnegan know him?

"You very well may be right as to my identity, sir," Turner said. "But I am at a loss as to how you know me. And why it is that your name has a familiar ring in my own ear."

Finnegan lowered the shotgun a little and motioned Turner to come on in. When Turner entered he caught the strong smell of blood in the little structure, and saw the corpse of Li cut nearly in half and lying near the place where a stove had once sat when this cabin was in use by miners. The degree of damage to the body caused him to look again at the shotgun, noticing then it had been cut down in length, heightening its destructive power at close range.

"Why did you kill him?" Turner asked. "It had been my hope to enter into a business arrangement with him."

"Aye, and what a convenient thing it is that you have brought up the matter of business at this particular moment!" Finnegan said, for some reason sounding even more Irish now that his voice was amplified to Turner by the cabin walls around them. "Because it is in the realm of business that I have familiarity with you, sir, and perhaps you have heard of me as well. We work for and with some of the same folk, you and I do."

Turner was unsure what to say. He could not trust this man, did not dare even lower his hands as long as Finnegan had that shotgun, and certainly could not begin talking freely about his particular line of thoroughly illegal and immoral work without knowing who and what Finnegan was.

"I have put you in an awkward position, Mr. Turner," Finnegan said. "Perhaps I can improve it. I am Declan Finnegan, member of an old and noted Irish family. My grandfather, Samuel Finnegan, was one of the isle's wealthiest men, and used his wealth to finance a collection of the world's most excellent and costly gems, including what became known as the Finnegan ancestral diamonds. Samuel Finnegan was a man of the highest moral and religious character, a great believer in the American cause and philosophy of freedom, and a particular supporter of education and academia. He attracted to him other men of great wealth and note, some of them of a decidedly lower level of moral conviction and quality than he was himself. He scarcely seemed to notice it. . . . It was his way to think highly of others unless compelled by the clearest evidence to do otherwise. I, on the other hand, was able to see the underlying and veiled characters of some of his peers quite easily. Perhaps because I shared, by nature, some of the same values . . . or lack thereof." Finnegan paused and laughed, and Turner dutifully did the same, though he as yet hardly knew what Finnegan was coming around to. Finnegan went on. "In time I was taken under wing, so to speak, by some of my grandfather's wealthy peers who were at what most would see as the bottom rung of the moral ladder. Men who used their wealth to finance their own debaucheries and degenerate pleasures . . . the very things that appealed to my own spirit. It was through my association with one of these men that I found a place for myself in the trade which we share, the vending of fleshly companionship both willing and unwilling to those capable of paying for it, and willing to do so. As I worked, I heard certain names spoken — yours among them — and began to understand the scope of this business of ours."

"One moment, sir . . . I have not said that I am involved in this 'business' you talk of."

Finnegan smiled darkly. "No, you have not. But we both know what we know, aye, brother?"

Turner merely looked at him.

"The role I began to play most frequently in the trade was that of corrector and punisher. As you know, secrecy is of the utmost importance. Some, though, are less able than others to maintain that secrecy. It became my assigned task to track down and forever silence those proven unworthy to the secrets they were given to hold. Those who did not hold them well." He paused and tossed his head in the direction of Li's corpse.

It was beginning to seem pointless to Turner to pretend ignorance of the things Finnegan was talking about. "I was to talk to Mr. Li about some Celestial girls today. Perhaps it is best that meeting didn't happen, if he is . . . was loose of lip."

"His lack of discretion caused many problems, here and in almost every place the trade extends its reach."

"Everywhere, then."

"Aye, so it is. With scarce an exception."

"It was to deal with Li that you came to California, then? Or were you here already?"

Finnegan stood his shotgun in the corner now, apparently having decided Turner wasn't a threat. Turner lowered his hands gratefully, shoulder muscles aching.

"Have you heard people speak of so-called divine providence, Mr. Turner? Something generally perceived when events and timing and seemingly unconnected circumstances come together in a noticeably fortuitous manner?"

"Of course."

"Well, my experience in past months might lead me to suspect there is a similar kind of providence that is far, far removed from the divine. A 'dark providence,' you might call it. Because though I was bound to come to California in any case on the matter of our friend Mr. Li, it so happened that I was given yet another reason to make the same journey. I was hired to find a thieving college president, or former college president, from Tennessee. He had taken items of great value that had been given to his college for its use in advancing education in areas where it is too often lacking. It so happens the giver of that gift was my own grandfather, Samuel. The gift he gave was a selected number of the extraordinarily valu-

able Finnegan ancestral diamonds."

"So it was your kin who sent you after this thief?"

"It was not. It was the man who had chaired the board of that college's trustees. A man named Sadler. Along with his brother, he sponsored an emigrant band to travel to California under the piloting of a Carolina-Tennessee frontiersman named Colter. And interestingly, one of the emigrants who went with that group was none other than the thieving college president himself, a man named Zebulon McSwain. He came both to flee from his crime back in Tennessee, and to see his daughter, a young woman named Emma, married to one Stanley Wickham, owner and operator of the camp store in Bowater."

Turner's mouth dropped open as he saw the most unexpected connections falling into place. Finnegan, into his story, did not notice Turner's startlement.

"I followed the Sadler group across this broad nation, but never found good opportunity to attempt to recover the diamonds from him. To my knowledge, he still has them. It is still my hope to gain them back from him."

"And return them to the college from which they were taken?"

"Of course not. On any road, that college no longer exists in the same form it did. No, when I get my hands on those diamonds, in my hands — Finnegan hands — they shall stay."

Turner was in a quandary. That he should have encountered this particular man and discovered such an interconnection between their lives and purposes was remarkable. Perhaps there truly was some kind of "dark providence" such as Finnegan had mentioned at work here.

Or perhaps it was all a matter of them both being involved in the same grim line of work.

Whatever the truth about such matters, one thing was clear to him: he and Finnegan had one more thing in common than Finnegan knew about. When Wickham had put his wife into Turner's hands, Turner had begun to think of those diamonds that Emma's father possessed as being something he would take for his own. With Emma under his control he held a powerful ace in this particular game.

But now here was this Finnegan, his own ambitions centering on possessing those same diamonds. That would not do. They could not both possess them.

Moving fast and without warning, acting

on the impulse of a moment, Turner swung about, swept up Finnegan's shotgun from the corner, and shot the Irishman squarely in the center of his face.

The results were ugly, and when the red mist had settled across the already-bloodied room, Turner saw from the corner of his eye that something had landed on his shoulder. He reached up and pinched it up between thumb and forefinger.

An ear. Finnegan's ear.

Feeling the typically human burst of revulsion at the gruesome thing, he almost flung it away, but something about it made him take another look.

Odd. There was a notch of flesh missing from the ear. Not shot away by the blast that had just killed him, either. This was a long-healed-over wound.

Turner decided then that maybe a notched ear, obtained in such an unusual fashion, might make for a good souvenir of this strange, violent day. He rubbed the raw, just-severed base of the ear against the fallen Finnegan's sleeve to get the worst of the blood off it, then put the ear into the side pocket of his own jacket.

He took from Finnegan's body the pouch bearing his shotgun ammunition and accouterments, and Finnegan's boots, which

Turner had noticed. They fit him well. He hefted up his new shotgun and left the cabin that was now spackled with a generous interior coating of blood and aerosolized flesh. He walked back up to where his horse was tied, unhitched it, mounted, and rode back up toward the Bowater Road.

CHAPTER THIRTY-THREE

Jedd Colter rose slowly from the kneeling posture in which he'd been, examining the corpse they had found near a tent in the now-empty valley of log pens. He shook his head as if to clear it and looked at Tom Buckle. "Tom, I've seen some dead men in my time. That one there, though, is about as dead as I've ever laid eyes on."

"Or hope to again," Buckle said. "A pickaxe through the topknot and out through the mouth! Lordy, who would even think of such a way to kill somebody?"

"Somebody who wanted to be very sure the dead one really, surely, truly was as dead as he could be. Somebody you might say was *motivated.*"

"What do you reckon he'd done to have somebody that mad at him?"

"Tom, if this here was the kind of place the rumors say it was, and if this gent here was one of the ones involved in holding women captive here, it might be best that we don't know all he did to earn that kind of death."

Buckle frowned, thinking. "Jedd, you reckon there's any chance that the ones who killed this man were the very women who'd been held here?"

"The thought had crossed my mind. The pens are all empty, after all, but you can tell there's been people living in them. Somebody tied up with cords that are still in the pens, but severed like somebody cut them with a knife. What if those women got loose somehow and surprised this man who'd been their jailer, so to speak? Maybe caught him sleeping, or knocked him cold and took the pick to him while he was out. However they did it, and whoever it was, it looks like somebody stood over him and swung the pick down at the top of his head while he was lying on his back."

"I wonder if any woman could do such a thing."

"A woman can do anything a man might do, if she's pushed to it."

"I suppose so." Buckle looked at the body again for a moment. "Jedd, did you notice that it looks like somebody's carved on the corpse some?"

"I did notice. It's all the more reason to

think it was probably one or more of the women here who did this. You'll notice that his, uh, privates are gone. Cut off and probably lying out in the weeds around here somewhere, if a wild dog or something ain't already made off with them. What I'm getting at is that cutting off of the privates is something you'd only do if you were trying to make a point, know what I mean?"

"Something somebody would do who was, like you said, *motivated.*"

"Very motivated." Jedd nudged Paco's body with the toe of a boot Ollie Slott had made for him in a different lifetime.

"What now?" Buckle asked.

"Let's track these women. We need to find what became of them and what's gone on up here in this place." Jedd looked at his deputy. "Your sister, you said?"

"That's right. My little sister. God, when I think what she must have gone through."

"Don't think about it. It's past for her. Think about the ones who are still suffering from such things. They're the ones who need the thought and the help now."

"Ayuh."

"Tom?"

"What?"

"You're going to have to break yourself of that 'ayuh' nonsense. The word is 'yeah.' Or just plain old 'yes' will do."

"Ayuh. I know. I'll try."

It was not difficult to find the direction the group of women had gone. Their tracks told the story, and the experienced trailsman Jedd Colter was able to read it.

They'd trekked down to the Bowater Road and paused by the grave of Winnie Napier and "Cat," probably to puzzle, as everyone seemed prone to do, over why a grave was at such a place and why a cat was buried with a human.

Then on up Bowater Road they had traveled, heading toward Emma's town. If Emma had been among the captives, might she be taking the freed group of them to her home? Jedd considered the element of oddity that would be added to his long-anticipated visit with Emma if it wound up being done in the context of a lawman investigating the flight of hostages from what was essentially an illegal prison compound.

Life could take a man on strange journeys, he pondered. He'd gone from being a free-roaming trail guide and outdoorsman to being a mining town marshal, and little to none of it had really been planned.

He and Tom rode toward Bowater, and

Jedd turned and said, "Tom, the way I have it figured, sometimes life is something that kind of cooperates with your plans and hopes. Happens *with* you. Other times it's just something that happens *to* you."

"You're a philosopher, Jedd."

"No need for name-calling, Tom. No need at all."

Though neither he nor former marshal Rand Blalock knew it, Liam Turner and Blalock had purchased their individual horses from the same horse trader. The horses, though born in different years, had come from the same mother, sired by the same stallion. And both had exactly the same hereditary defect of the heart that had already dropped Blalock's horse beneath him on the main avenue of Scarlett's Luck.

When the heart of Turner's horse finally lost its life-long struggle to continue beating, Turner was at the edge of Bowater, some miles from Scarlett's Luck. The death of Turner's horse mimicked that of Blalock's almost down to the last tremor, except that Turner's horse collapsed more vertically and did not break Turner's leg, as Blalock's had been broken. Turner simply found himself standing beside a dead animal in the middle of a road, stunned and wondering what to do. A man could hardly be expected to heft up a dead horse on his shoulder and move it to the side of the road as he might a wagon-crushed dog or cat.

Turner stood fretting and chin rubbing, looking down at his horse and hating it for putting him in this predicament.

He was still standing there when around the bend he'd just passed came a group of very ragged, very dirty, and very familiar women. The group of them had stopped for a break and rest in a wooded grove and had not seen Turner ride past mere minutes before his horse departed the earthly coil to enter whatever afterlife awaits the equine.

Turner gaped at the women, backed up, and tripped over an extended leg of his dead horse. He fell back hard onto his rear, landing on a sharp-pointed stone that deftly broke his tailbone and sent him into excruciating pain. He howled loudly, squeezing his eyes closed. When they opened again moments later the women were close upon him, and one of them was tugging his pistol from its holster. He realized with a start that it was Rosita.

"Who's prisoner now, you wicked, stone-hearted son of a harlot!" Rosita hissed at him, aiming the pistol at his head and thumbing back the hammer.

"No, Rosita," Emma said. "You mustn't murder him. . . . If you do, it would bring trouble to you. The law wouldn't abide it."

"The law?" Rosita replied, a look of astonishment on her face. "What law is there for a man like this one? The same law that found my father at the end . . . the law of justice, of vengeance." Rosita looked around at the faces of the former prisoners whom until today she had helped tend like so many penned animals. "Think of what this man has done to all of you! And now God has delivered him into our hands!"

"Rosita, he is not worth the cost of your life and freedom should you be accused of his murder!"

"Shoot him!" one of the other women demanded. "Put that pistol against his head and pull the trigger. Blow his brains onto this road and I will dance in them!"

Turner looked up at Rosita, a man who had brought many tears to others now about to cry himself. "Rosita, where is your father? Where is Paco?"

Rosita looked trapped for a moment; then suddenly she chuckled in a grim manner. "I wanted his advice on how to help these women escape, so I went to him and said, 'Father, may I pick your mind?' He said yes . . . so I did."

Laughter rippled through the group of women. Turner looked more hopeless by the moment. He eyed the roadside and in his mounting panic seriously considered bolting and running. He did not, being sure that Rosita, who seemed to have turned from an ally to a foe, would shoot him at once.

"What's going on here?"

The voice was Jedd Colter's, and Emma knew it the moment she heard it. Drawing in her breath and holding it reflexively, she turned and saw the man she had come close to marrying looking down at her from his horseback perch. He looked at her as if he could never tear his eyes away, a surreal feeling overwhelming him. He managed to smile. "Hello, Emma."

She felt the world swim around her and collapsed. Jedd snapped out of his own foggy sense of momentary unreality, dismounted, and went to Emma's side.

"She's just fainted," said one of the women. "She's had an . . . unusual day. We all have. Are you law?"

"I'm marshal of Scarlett's Luck. My name's Jedd Colter." He looked over at Turner, who was on his side in a very nearly fetal posture, eyes locked on the pistol in Rosita's hand. "Who is he?" Jedd asked.

"His name is Turner. A man who enslaves women so they may be sold to others worse even than he is . . . and he is the devil himself. If you are law, you should arrest him now and lock him away forever."

Emma's eyes fluttered open. "Jedd," she whispered. "Jedd."

He smiled down at her. "I'm here, Emma. I'm here. With you."

Tom Buckle got out of his saddle and walked over to Rosita. With a smile and gentle manner, he took the pistol from her. "I'll handle him now," he said to her, flicking his eyes toward Turner.

"He should hang. He has imprisoned and sold women, and even today he committed murder. He killed a crippled girl in the prison camp where he held us. Him and my own father, who is dead now."

"Your father . . . Mexican man, pickaxe through his skull?"

"I put it there. I am not ashamed to confess it."

"We didn't find the corpse of a crippled girl. . . ."

"They hid her body. There are places they have. . . . I can find her, probably."

"We'll probably call on you to do that, miss."

"I am guilty, too," Rosita said. "Over time

I have helped my father and that one there with their evils."

"Then I'm guessing you'll prove mighty handy when it's time for evidence to be spoken in court against them."

"It will be my honor to do that."

"And the same for all of us," said a woman who so far had not spoken.

Turner leaped up then, a sudden and amazingly agile move by a man who saw the evil life he'd built about to crash around him. His quick movement caught Tom Buckle by surprise, and before he knew it, Turner had wrenched the pistol from his grasp. He leveled it at Buckle's head, swore and called Buckle a "dead lawman," and was about to pull the trigger when Jedd Colter's big Dragoon boomed and put a slug through his temple. Turner was dead before he hit the ground. It was Buckle who noticed something falling from Turner's pocket as he dropped. It was, of all things, a human ear. Severed, and with a notch missing from it.

As they realized that Turner was truly dead, the women, every one of them, wept in shock combined with wild joy.

POSTSCRIPT

The divorce caused a scandal, as divorces will, but Emma survived it well. Stanley Wickham did not. When word of his offenses came out, his reputation hit the ground faster than had Rand Blalock's horse. Wickham's business suffered, a circumstance that allowed other merchants such as Wilberforce Sadler to move in to fill the void. Wilberforce's success was short-lived, though, because word leaked out that he had been prepared earlier on to go into business with the discredited Wickham. So toxic was Wickham's reputation that it poisoned Wilberforce Sadler by association, and he, too, saw his stores begin to close, one by one, until only two remained, providing him a living but not the spectacular wealth and influence he and Wickham had dreamed of. As Wilberforce's star faded, though, his brother's rose. Witherspoon Sadler launched a series of stores of his own, beginning small and avoiding the use of the Sadler name. Witherspoon Mining Supply and General Mercantile became a presence in almost every town in the mining districts, and the gentle kindliness, honesty, and excellent reputation of Witherspoon Sadler only bolstered the enterprise. Time rolled by and Witherspoon became one of California's most successful and beloved public figures. His 1852 marriage to a widow named Rachel McCall was the social event of the year, attended by people ranging from the highest state dignitaries to the most common miners and grassroots citizens whose patronage was what made his business interests thrive.

Jedd and Emma Colter were honored guests, their arrival at the wedding reception heralded so loudly that Jedd reddened in embarrassment and had to fight not to visibly shirk away from the applause.

Even though he was still serving in the humble role of town sheriff of Scarlett's Luck, Jedd was becoming a famous name not only in California but across the nation. The reason was his fictionalization in a series of cheap novels by the young writer Crozier Bellingham, who had planned to write a major, serious novel of the gold fields but instead settled for more lurid fare.

Had they been published only a few years later, the series of fast-paced adventures of *Jedd Colter: Gold Country Marshal* would have been called dime novels, and in fact, dime novel editions of the books were published throughout the 1860s. Jedd read only the first of them, and though the stories departed vastly from the facts of the real Jedd Colter's life, Jedd had to admire the clever way Bellingham incorporated the themes, if not the actual facts, from his life into his whole-cloth fiction. The most popular Jedd Colter novel, for example, was *Jedd Colter and the Diamonds of Finnegan Hall.* Bringing up second place in the roster of popularity was *Jedd Colter and the Ring of Slavers.*

Of all the Colter stories, however, none was more lurid and violent than *Jedd Colter and the Murderous Axeman.* It was also the Colter story most closely tied to fact, telling an only slightly fictionalized account of Jedd Colter's teaming up with a visiting marshal from North Carolina, named Campbell, to track down a man named Collier who had murdered an entire family over an old feud back in Carolina. Collier had left the body of the father of the family horribly mutilated. He had fled to California in a quest for gold and, he hoped, to escape from having to pay for his crime, but Campbell trailed him all the way across the country. In California, the Carolina lawman teamed up with Jedd Colter, gold country marshal, and the pair tracked down and fatally punished Collier for his brutal crime.

Life changed as well for others whose California sojourns were linked to Jedd Colter's.

When Ben Scarlett's luck in the gold fields ran out and he caught a ship around the Horn to return to Tennesee and Knoxville, the town of Scarlett's Luck began to be called, informally, simply Luck, and finally Luck-town. The Scarlett name lingered, however, in one of the secondary characters in Bellingham's Colter novels. Ben Scarlett, made-up version, was one of three deputies whose unsurpassed skill and keen wits helped their boss, Jedd Colter, deftly solve every crime that happened within the bounds of Crozier Bellingham's version of California. The fictional Ben Scarlett's fellow deputies were named Treemont Dalton and Tom Buckle.

While the fictional Jedd Colter and his three intrepid cohorts battled make-believe crimes on the pages of Bellingham's books, situations against which the real Jedd Colter had brushed up turned into authentic and important criminal cases. Working cooperatively, agents of the governments of the United States, England, France, China, Spain, and almost every other significant nation investigated and broke a human trafficking ring that enslaved and sold women all over the world, ruining life after life until at last the ring was shattered. The highly sanitized version of the "ring of slavers" presented in the pages of Bellingham's novel paled in comparison to the reality. The novel received a strong jolt of publicity, though, when Crozier Bellingham met and wed one of the young women involved in the real-life version of the "ring of slavers," a half-Mexican girl named Rosita. They made their home in Los Angeles and raised a huge and happy family.

Former collegiate president Zebulon McSwain, who mended old fences that had been broken between him and his daughter, Emma, never was called to account for the missing Finnegan ancestral diamonds. Nor was it ever learned what became of them.

It was meaningfully noted by many, however, that the home for abused and mistreated women, which was opened by Emma Colter in her oddly made former home in Bowater, had obviously received some sort of significant financial boost at the time of its founding. Few were brazen enough to speculate in the presence of Emma or her father as to what the source of that boost had been, but few doubted that they knew.

As for Emma herself, she was glad to leave her big Bowater house behind and move into humbler but far more pleasant quarters with her husband, Jedd. The family they raised was large, healthy, and happy, and the children were ever proud to tell any who would listen that their father was none other than the famous Jedd Colter, Gold Country Marshal.